Norman Russell was born in Whiston, Lancashire, but has lived most of his life in Liverpool. After graduating from Jesus College, Oxford, where he studied English, he served in the army in the Bahamas and Jamaica. He returned to Oxford to study for a Diploma in Education and later was awarded the degree of Doctor of Philosophy from the University of London. He now writes full time.

THE DARK KINGDOM

Jane Ashwood longs to see her vision of a public school for girls translated into reality, and is thrilled when the charismatic headmaster Edward Dalton becomes deeply committed to her venture. But when the prying schoolmaster Amyas Fletcher hints that Dalton's school has become a dark kingdom ruled by a veiled, intangible evil, violent death suddenly strikes and Jane finds to her horror that Edward Dalton is the prime suspect in a case of multiple murder . . .

Books by Norman Russell
Published by The House of Ulverscroft:

THE DRIED-UP MAN

NORMAN RUSSELL

THE DARK KINGDOM

Complete and Unabridged

ULVERSCROFT
Leicester

First published in Great Britain in 2000 by
Robert Hale Limited
London

First Large Print Edition
published 2001
by arrangement with
Robert Hale Limited
London

British Library CIP Data

Russell, Norman, *1945* –
The dark kingdom.—Large print ed.—
Ulverscroft large print series: mystery
1. Mass murder investigation—History
—19th century
2. Great Britain—History—Victoria, *1837 – 1901*
3. Detective and mystery stories
4. Large type books
I. Title
823.9′14 [F]

ISBN 0–7089–4452–3

Published by
F. A. Thorpe (Publishing)
Anstey, Leicestershire
Set by Words & Graphics Ltd.
Anstey, Leicestershire
Printed and bound in Great Britain by
T. J. International Ltd., Padstow, Cornwall

This book is printed on acid-free paper

Prologue

Patching's Croft, Wednesday,
31 August, 1892

Old Dr Manning sighed and steadied himself as his carriage clattered off the main road across Thornton Heath and began its journey along a winding rutted track. It was very early, and the carriage was cold. The sun had risen above the trees less than half an hour earlier.

At just before six o'clock he had been awakened by a volley of pebbles at the bedroom window. A frantic young man had shouted up to him. He had thrown up the casement and seen Noah Baker, a small-holder's son from Kingsmere Village, standing on the road.

'Doctor! Come down to Patching's, for God's sake! It's Alice . . . She's dead!'

Alice Patching, aged seventeen. It was just under a mile from New End, where Manning lived, to Kingsmere Village, but he would have to go a longer way round than that. He hoped that young Baker had heard him say that he would have to fetch a policeman.

1

Noah Baker had run off, frantic, plunging down the road as though he couldn't see his way.

Alice Patching, aged seventeen. She was young and in good health. She had no right to be dead.

The carriage rumbled into a small wooded dell where a long, low farmhouse nestled among trees. The coachman applied the brake and Dr Manning stepped down on to a stony yard, where some pigs and hens seemed to dwell together in uneasy amity. The door of the farmhouse opened, and a fair-haired woman in a black dress looked out. She was cradling a little girl in the crook of her arm.

'Dr Manning, isn't it?' she said. 'You'll be wanting my husband, I expect. I'll send him out. Herbert! It's Dr Manning.'

In less than a minute a homely-looking man with a flushed red face emerged from the house. He wore a loud check suit and a brown bowler hat, and had thrown a red woollen muffler round his neck. He was clutching what appeared to be the remains of a bacon sandwich.

'Detective Sergeant Bottomley? You'll remember me, I expect? Manning. Can you come straight away? It's a suspicious death — a seventeen-year-old girl who shouldn't be dead. I want a police officer to be present when I examine the body.'

★ ★ ★

Manning moved away from the bales of straw where the girl's body lay and stood compassionately silent for a while beside the dazed parents. They sat stiff and lost on an old bench, one of the few pieces of furniture in the ancient barn. Beside them stood Noah Baker, the strongly built young man who had roused the doctor so frantically less than an hour earlier.

Manning was a kindly, silver-haired man of seventy, who walked with a stoop, but was stronger than he looked. His voice came quiet and clear, but muted with infinite sadness.

'It is self-slaughter. She has swallowed poison.'

The parents were rural folk, whose horizons seldom strayed beyond the confines of their Warwickshire village. They seemed frozen with shock, though the father's face was twisted with bewildered grief. The young man suddenly burst into tears. He was not much more than eighteen years old. Manning knew that he had been destined as the girl's husband.

'I can't think what made her do it, sir. I'd

have looked after her, whatever she'd done. She was such a lovely girl. She'd no need to have done this to herself.'

The mother finally found her voice. Her words seemed flat and drained of emotion.

'Her bed wasn't slept in. We searched all over, and found her in here. She was carrying a child in the womb, and I never knew till Mary Wainwright told me this morning.'

Mrs Patching began to sob. She said, as though appealing for her dead girl, 'She was only seventeen, Dr Manning.'

'I know, Mrs Patching. Only seventeen. And so she couldn't cope with the disgrace. Do you know who the man was — the man who betrayed her?'

Mrs Patching, a slight, consumptive woman old before her time, dissolved into tears. Her husband found his voice.

'We don't know who it could be, Doctor. Maybe her friend Mary Wainwright will know. She's in the house now, as the wife has told you.'

Sergeant Bottomley had stood in the shadows at the back of the barn, watching Dr Manning as he made his confirmatory examination. The parents had wondered who he was, but had been too dazed to ask. He suddenly spoke, and his homely Warwickshire accent carried its own quality of healing.

4

'I'm truly sorry for you, Mr Patching, and you, missus,' he said, turning rather fine grey eyes in their direction, 'and for the young man here, too. I've daughters of my own, so I think I know how you must feel. I'd like you to go back into your house, now, while I have a look around. My name's Detective Sergeant Bottomley, from Warwick Police-Office.'

He came forward into the light, pulling off his red muffler, and stood looking down at the dead girl, who lay as though asleep, her arms thrown carelessly outwards. He looked again at the parents.

'Did you say that her friend is in the house? Mary, I think you said.'

'Yes, Mr Bottomley. Mary Wainwright. She was her special friend. Those two used to tell each other everything.'

'Then will you ask Mary to come out here, Mr Patching? Tell her there's nothing to be afraid of.'

'I'll do that,' said Mr Patching. He hesitated at the door, and then said, 'Can I at least cover the girl? Cover her with my coat?'

'Not yet, Mr Patching. I'll not be long looking round. Then you can do all that's fit and proper.'

As soon as Manning had closed the barn door behind the parents, Sergeant Bottomley conducted his own examination of the dead body of Alice Patching. He peered closely into her face, and drew his hands gently down her arms. His thick fingers felt her neck just below the jaw on both sides. He stood back from the body for a moment, and then suddenly brought his face near to Alice's once again. He seemed to inhale, holding his breath for a moment before exhaling with a sigh.

He turned to Manning, and said, 'I think that's all for the moment, Doctor. I'd like to stay here alone for a little while, if you don't mind. I need to rummage round a bit, and then I want a quiet word with this other girl, this Mary Wainwright.'

'I could have walked here from my house in fifteen minutes,' said Manning, half to himself. 'But I knew I'd need a policeman, and our local man's laid up with an ulcerated leg. So it had to be four miles out to you at Thornton Heath and four miles back.'

'You did right, sir.'

'I suppose,' said Manning, 'that I should have gone into Warwick to see Mr Jackson, your inspector. But you were nearer, and we'd worked together last year when they found that woman buried under the hearth over at the Vale. You didn't mind my calling like that at your home this morning, did you?'

Sergeant Bottomley smiled and shook his head.

'No, sir, of course I didn't mind. It certainly looks like suicide, but I'd best have a little word with this girl Mary. Perhaps you'll leave me with her for a while? I fancy I can hear her coming now.'

Bottomley looked up as a young woman in the smock and cap of a dairy maid came hesitantly through the door. She caught sight of the body, and began sobbing convulsively, her slim hands covering her face. Dr Manning left the barn, quietly closing the door behind him.

'Mary Wainwright,' said Bottomley in a low, surprisingly gentle tone, 'come over here by me. There's nothing to be afraid of, my dear. Poor Alice looks as though she'd just fallen asleep. Come over here, and sit down on the bench until I've finished looking around.'

Mary Wainwright did as she was told. She glanced once again at Alice's body and then hastily turned away. What was this man doing? He had flopped down awkwardly in the straw, and she saw him take one of the dead girl's hands in his. She shuddered, and hid her eyes in her smock. When her curiosity

7

got the better of her terror she looked up again, and saw that he had retrieved something from the straw.

'Mary,' he asked, 'have you ever seen this before?'

He looked at the frightened girl. No more than eighteen, he thought, old enough to understand the ways of the world, but too young to appreciate the danger of sharing secrets.

Mary Wainwright swallowed hard, and made an effort to compose herself. She had been frightened back in the house, in case Dr Manning had wanted to ask her questions. He was a nice man, but his gentleman's way of speaking wasn't easy to follow. This big homely man with the coaxing voice had a kind way with him, and she could understand what he was saying.

'No, master,' she replied, 'I've not seen the likes of that before.'

He had handed her a wooden cup, simple in design and beautifully polished. Pear wood, it looked like.

'Was that — '

'Yes, Mary. That's what she drank the poison from. It's still damp inside. Maybe we'll find out from that what it was she took.'

He took the cup back from her and smelt it. She saw him frown.

'Wine, Mary,' he said, though it seemed that he wasn't really speaking to her. 'Wine — Madeira, if I'm not mistaken.'

He dropped to his knees and began to rummage through the straw. In a few moments he had retrieved a dark glass bottle. She heard him give a little sigh of satisfaction. He thrust the cup and the bottle back into the straw.

'They can stay there, Mary, till I want them again,' he said, then turned to the body of Alice Patching. Mary watched while he gently placed the girl's arms at her sides. There was a commotion outside in the yard, and the noise of iron tyres ringing on cobbles as carriages were braked.

Sergeant Bottomley turned to Mary and gave her an endearing lopsided smile.

'Mary,' said Bottomley, 'let you and me go for a little walk.'

He ushered the girl out of the barn, closed the door and locked it. At that moment Dr Manning emerged from the house. Bottomley handed him the key of the barn, put an arm around Mary's shoulders and led her out through a little wicket gate into the track behind the farmhouse. They could see two carriages standing in the main road beyond a yew hedge, and a closed horse-van further along the way.

'Who'll they be?' asked Mary Wainwright.

'It'll be some gentlemen connected with the parish, I expect. Dr Manning will have sent for them while we were in the barn. I've seen that van before, though. It belongs to Mr Lascelles from Kenilworth. The undertaker, you know.'

He offered Mary Wainwright his arm, and they walked slowly away from the knot of cottages where the carriages of the doctors and dignitaries were gathered. It was a warm morning, with high white clouds and a stillness in the air.

'I never saw your friend Alice alive, Mary, but I reckon she was a very pretty girl. That's what I thought just now, looking at her in the barn. I expect she had a lot of admirers?'

'She had, master. But it was poor Noah Baker that she was going to marry. Everybody expected them to put up the banns soon. But now . . .'

They walked in silence along the dusty road. They could hear sparrows chattering and chirping in the wayside hedges.

'We'll turn back in a minute, Mary,' said Bottomley. He gave her a shrewd sideways glance, watching her struggle between grief and curiosity.

'You were her special friend, weren't you, Mary? I expect you knew about her condition

10

before ever her mother did.'

Mary began to sob again. Bottomley laid a big reassuring hand on her arm.

'Tell me about it,' he said.

'Master, she made me promise not to tell! I feel terrible, because I knew she was pregnant, but her own mother didn't know until I told her this morning! Yes, she was going to have a baby, but the gentleman had sworn that he would marry her before Christmas.'

'Marry her? He said that, did he? This gentleman?'

'Yes. All she had to do was to keep their secret until he came back. He wasn't far away — that's what she said — and he was coming to fetch her off to London where they could be married.'

Bottomley watched the girl as she spoke, and saw how her eyes left his face and glanced over the fields to the right, where a line of stately elms graced the skyline.

'A gentleman? I wonder what she could've meant by that?'

'I don't know. I begged and begged her to tell me, but she wouldn't. She wouldn't even tell me his name. 'He's coming for me secretly, Mary!' That's what she said. 'He's coming to take me away to London, so Father and Mother won't be shamed'.'

Sergeant Bottomley looked shrewdly at the girl without speaking. She bit her lip and looked away. There was a fearful tenseness about her.

'A gentleman?' Bottomley repeated the words carefully. 'I wonder what she could have meant by that?'

'I don't know, master, I don't!'

His eyes narrowed. He had followed Mary's glance earlier when she had looked across the fields at the distant trees. He watched her now, as she uttered her denial, and saw how her eyes were drawn once again to the far-off rank of proud elms. He didn't know this corner of the shire very well. Kingsmere seemed to be on the edge of things, four twisting miles beyond Kenilworth in the direction of Knowle, and close on twelve miles out from Warwick. But the doctor and he had passed those tall elms on their way into Kingsmere village. Dr Manning had told him that they bordered the grounds of Kingsmere Abbey School.

1

Warnings of the Storm

'Aconitine. It's one of the most deadly poisons known to man. You get it from monk's-hood.'

Detective Inspector Saul Jackson leaned back in his chair and looked speculatively at the lively, bearded young man with round, gold-rimmed spectacles, who had spoken these dramatic words. It was the Friday following the discovery of Alice Patching's body.

Lionel Dovercourt, a graduate in chemistry of King's College, London, was no stranger to Jackson. Earlier that year he and his father, James Dovercourt, a manufacturing chemist, had been intimately involved with Jackson in the solution of a particularly gruesome mystery.

'Monk's-hood? Do you mean that tall, purple plant you get in gardens?'

'The very same, Mr Jackson.' He added, 'When your constable arrived at Ashgate with the parcel on Wednesday night, I set to work immediately. I also determined that I would convey the results of my tests to you in person.'

It was quiet in Jackson's brown-painted office. Late afternoon sunlight filtered through the single uncurtained window from the yard, casting the shadows of the iron bars on to the scrubbed floorboards. Sergeant Bottomley sat slumped morosely on a tall chair drawn up to the table. He formed a startling contrast to Jackson, who was a burly man in his forties, with a taste for amply cut brown serge suits and lengths of gold watch-chain.

Dovercourt pointed to the table, on which stood the wine bottle and the wooden cup that Sergeant Bottomley had discovered in the straw of Mr Patching's barn.

'You did right to send those items to a manufacturing chemist,' he said. 'Father and I know all about that substance. We call it aconite in our business. We use the root to make a tincture and a special liniment.'

'And it's a deadly poison?'

'It is. People have died from eating its roots in mistake for horse-radish.'

The sergeant stirred uneasily, and his usually amiable face assumed a bleak, almost despairing expression. When he spoke his voice was thick and rather laboured, but his eyes were fully alert.

'You said you call it aconite, Mr Lionel, but just now you called it aconitine.'

'That's true, Mr Bottomley. All parts of the plant are very poisonous, but what lingered in the minute fibres of wood at the bottom of that cup was what we call the active principle, the alkaloid, which is prepared chemically from the plant. We call that alkaloid by the name aconitine.'

'And the bottle was free of poison?' asked Jackson.

'It was. We found traces of Madeira wine in the bottle, but nothing else.'

'Is aconitine a lingering poison?'

'No, Mr Jackson. It acts very quickly. It paralyses the nerve-ends and the spinal cord. Breathing stops, and death supervenes.'

His voice was loud and commanding, with all the keen assertiveness of the specialist. 'Monk's-hood,' he repeated, 'or wolf's-bane, it's called sometimes.'

'And that's what Alice Patching drank,' said Bottomley. 'She was only seventeen when breathing stopped and death supervened.'

'Sergeant,' said Jackson, 'go out into the yard and see if you can find Alf. If he's not there, try the stable.'

Sergeant Bottomley hauled himself up from his chair and walked heavily from the room. Jackson and Dovercourt could hear the

15

clatter of his boots in the gloomy passage that led from the back offices to the police-station yard.

'Is Sergeant Bottomley — ?'

'No, Mr Lionel, he's not drunk, but he's not sober either. He's upset at a suicide we've had at a village in these parts. A seventeen-year-old girl. He feels things like that very keenly. Almost personally, you might say.'

'I'm sorry he's upset,' said Lionel Dovercourt. 'People liked him in Ashgate.'

Jackson glanced towards the door. His expression held a baffled mixture of anxiety and exasperation.

'He's a great big blundering lump of a man, Mr Lionel, and he's far too fond of the bottle. But he's as cute as a cartload of monkeys. People seem to think he's a fool, but he's no fool, as many a crafty villain's found to his cost. He's been with me since 1886 — what's that? — six years.'

'Has he always been a policeman?'

'He was a soldier at first, then a small-holder. He still farms a bit, he and his wife and brother-in-law. No, I'm the one who's always been a policeman.'

'This bottle and cup — were they connected with the girl?'

'Yes.'

Lionel Dovercourt placed a brown foolscap

16

envelope on the table.

'There's my written report, Mr Jackson. It will tell you everything you need to know. I must be getting about my business. Please give Mr Bottomley my compliments. Perhaps we'll see you again some time at Ashgate.'

★ ★ ★

'So what it amounts to, sir, is this,' said Sergeant Bottomley. 'Alice Patching decides to commit suicide. So she goes to her local purveyor of alkaloids and buys two penn'orth of aconitine. After that, she visits her wine-merchant and chooses a bottle of Madeira — '

'All right, Sergeant, you can stop there for a moment. I'm beginning to share your puzzlement about this business. Alice Patching was a simple country girl. She'd never have heard of alkaloids or anything of that sort. As for Madeira . . . Did you find Alf? I told you to find him. Where is he?'

Sergeant Bottomley's hair, Jackson noted, was slicked back and shining, and there was a general air of brightness about him that had been lacking when Lionel Dovercourt was in the office. Bottomley had been holding his head under the pump in the yard.

'Alf's coming now, sir. He's been brushing

17

out the stable loft. So he says.'

Jackson smiled. Alf, the morose general factotum of Barrack Street Police-Office, was addicted to his sweeping-brush, which helped him to create a constant illusion of being busy.

Bottomley picked up the pear-wood cup and held it thoughtfully for a moment before putting it down again beside the empty Madeira bottle.

'Sir,' he said, 'whenever that poor girl, Mary Wainwright, mentioned the 'gentleman' who'd seduced her friend, her eyes looked across the fields towards those elms skirting the grounds of Kingsmere Abbey School. It must have meant something.'

Jackson's bright keen eyes rested briefly on his sergeant. They showed a waiting alertness that could be very dangerous to the unwary.

'Maybe it did, Sergeant. But then again it may have meant nothing. Perhaps she couldn't cope with your piercing glances, and preferred the rural scenery. Or maybe she just likes trees.'

'Yes, sir. But Alice Patching told Mary that the gentleman, so-called, 'wasn't far away'. What did she mean by that, sir?'

Jackson sighed. It wasn't like Bottomley to ask questions to which there were no obvious answers.

'I don't know, Sergeant. I don't know what she meant, and I wasn't there to hear her say it. Maybe she *was* thinking of that school, or maybe she was looking beyond it to the Light Infantry Barracks over at the Vale. There are plenty of gentlemen there in the officers' lines. Maybe this, maybe that . . . It's a bit too early yet to draw conclusions.'

Alf had gradually appeared while Jackson was speaking, insinuating himself gingerly and unwillingly through the door from the yard passage. Thin, silver-haired and elderly, and wearing a tight green baize apron, he brought with him an air of resigned patience.

'Did you want me, Mr Jackson?'

'Yes, Alf, I did. You're a fund of local knowledge, Alf, a mine of information to simple folk like me. So, if you wanted to buy a bottle of Madeira wine — like that one, standing on the table — where would you go to buy it, always supposing that you were living up at Kingsmere village?'

Alf leaned heavily on the brush he was holding and sighed. He had work to do. It wasn't his place to be answering questions.

'Kingsmere? That's a good step from here. A cruel hard traipse from Warwick. Why should I want to go there?'

'Let's just suppose that you do. Just to please me.'

'Kingsmere? Well, you'd have to go to the Wheatsheaf. But you'd need to order it. There's no one round there drinks fancy stuff like that. You'd have to order it from Tom Holland, the landlord.'

'Anywhere else you could go?'

'No, Inspector. Not for fancy stuff like that. There's an alehouse called the Cat on the Kenilworth road just outside Kingsmere, but they only keep mild and bitter of their own brewing, and a few bottles of spirits. But don't you go anywhere near the Cat, sir. It's all Chartists and Luddites and turned-off ostlers. Can I go now? The lane could do with a swill-down.'

Jackson nodded absently. Alf sidled out of the office before he could ask him any more questions.

'Sergeant Bottomley,' said Jackson, 'I'm going out now to Kingsmere to see this man Holland, the landlord of the local inn. I want you to tackle this den of turned-off ostlers that Alf mentioned. There was nothing sinister in the bottle, but there was poison in the cup. How did it get there? And where did poor Alice get it from? Suicide? Maybe. Or maybe it's something else.'

★ ★ ★

Inspector Jackson entered the public bar of the Wheatsheaf in Kingsmere village. A red-faced man with bright eyes looked up from a sporting newspaper that he had spread out on the bar counter between the beer pumps.

The man said nothing, but the ginger eyebrows above the bright eyes rose a little as Jackson produced an empty Madeira bottle and put it down in front of him.

'Could you get me a bottle of that, Mr Holland?'

'So you know my name, do you? I don't think we've met. What are you, a commercial traveller? I've got my own suppliers.'

Jackson smiled rather wearily. He was in no mood for wordplay.

'I knew your name, Mr Holland, because it's written over your front door as the law requires. 'Thomas Holland. Licensed to sell alcoholic beverages for consumption on or off the premises'. So let me repeat the question: could you get me a bottle of that, Mr Holland?'

'I could. But I'd have to order it.'

'From London, would that be?'

'Yes. From London. If it's any of your business.'

Jackson noted that Mr Holland had red hair to match his red face. Perhaps he was naturally pugnacious. Or maybe he was having a bad day. He produced his warrant card and placed it beside the bottle on the bar counter.

'It *is* my business, Mr Holland.'

He glanced round the room, and peered through a communicating door into a neat and tidy saloon. Pugnacious or not, Mr Holland was a good landlord. Now he could learn how to be a good citizen.

'Have you a fire certificate for these premises?'

'Why, of course, Inspector. Let me get it for you. It's in my little office somewhere. Very pleased to meet you, I'm sure.'

Mr Holland had metamorphosed into the picture of attentive respect.

'Well, never mind about that. For the moment, that is. Where would you get it from in London? The Madeira, I mean.'

'Why, sir, I'd get it from Pollards of Charing Cross.'

Jackson smiled and sat down on a bench. He glanced round the cheerful room with its sanded floor and coloured engravings of naval battles on the walls.

'Perhaps you'd draw me half a pint of mild, Mr Holland. No froth, if you can manage it.'

In a few moments a cool glass of frothless dark beer was placed in front of him. Jackson gave the landlord a sixpenny piece and waved away the change.

'It's a very nice house you keep here, Mr Holland. I expect you take orders for some of the gentry, you having connections with the London vintners and all.'

'That's true, sir. I order for a number of the titled families that favour me with their patronage, and also for the school yonder.'

'For Kingsmere Abbey School? And do you ever get Madeira for them, Mr Holland?'

'Certainly, sir. Port and sherry too, and brandy. The masters there keep a nifty cellar, so to speak. As a matter of fact I've just sent up a crate of very choice wines for their celebration on the tenth — what they call the 'Special Dessert'. I got all those from Pollard's. Mr Granger, the vice-master, who's a kind of bursar too, comes here three times a year and drinks a glass of best ale with me in the back parlour. Then he gives me his order for the term.'

'Mr Granger, you say? And he's the vice-master, is he?'

'He is, sir. Very impressive gentleman. Very lively and restless. Comes down sharp when he's so inclined.'

Jackson put his glass down on the table.

'A sad business, this affair of Alice Patching,' he said.

'Terrible, sir. They'll never know the truth of it. Girls can be very sly. Poisoned herself, so they say. Where could she get poison in a place like this?'

'You'd be surprised, Mr Holland,' said Jackson, 'where people can get things from. It's just a case of knowing where they are.'

★ ★ ★

That same evening, in a great honey-coloured Palladian mansion twelve miles distant, a man and a woman sat at dinner, their voices occasionally echoing from the painted barrel vault of a vast dining-saloon.

'Yes, Lady Jane,' said Captain Noel Valentine, 'I'm rather looking forward to this term as a master at Kingsmere Abbey School. I admit that you cunningly cajoled me into agreeing to quit Oxford for the autumn, but I confess too that I'll enjoy a change from poring over ancient texts.'

Captain Noel Valentine was a lithe and powerful man, who could make the air surrounding him alive with his presence. Even in the cavernous chambers of Herving-ton Park he gave the impression of dwarfing everything around him.

'Incidentally,' he continued, 'I've never asked you what a Lady Governor is. How did you contrive to become one? And of a boys' school, at that?'

'Every once in a blue moon, Valentine,' said Jane, 'the Governors of Kingsmere Abbey School feel obliged to appoint a woman to their Court. In fact, they've done so since Tudor times. The Ashwoods are the patrons and hereditary visitors of the school. All that corner of Warwickshire, including Kingsmere village, belongs to Sir Hugo Mostyn, but we are lords of the acres on which the school stands.'

Jane Ashwood watched her companion as she spoke. Her seemingly unconventional use of his surname was part of an elaborate banter that they had sustained since she had first seen him when she was twelve years old, and he was a dashing young officer of twenty-two. She had thought that Valentine was his Christian name, found it served as a splendid tease, and the tease had become a habit.

The Ashwoods and the Valentines were both old military families, linked not by marriage and kinship but by a tangle of regiments, battalions and campaigns. Valentine had been invited to stay for the whole day and night before he took up residence at Kingsmere Abbey. Tomorrow, Lord Herving-ton would despatch him to Kingsmere in one of his luxurious carriages.

'Sir Hugo Mostyn? Isn't he the bold, bad baronet? 'The last of the Mohawks'? I've heard rumours about him. Wild and wicked. Isn't that the man?'

'It is. He's supposedly not welcome at Court, and the doors of many of the great houses are closed against him. Or so they say. Father has his doubts about all that. Sir Hugo Mostyn has a son at the school. His elder boy was sent to Eton.'

Jane Ashwood's voice was lively but deep-toned. Valentine had once told her that her speaking reminded him of the warm tones of the viola. She would agree with that. There was nothing of the giddy violin about her.

He had always admired Jane Ashwood, and even during his long army career he had never failed to write to her, from India, West Africa, Egypt. He looked at her now, elegant in her dark claret-coloured velvet evening dress, designed to complement the beauty of her raven-black hair and the brilliance of her blue eyes, and wondered why she had never married. She was thirty-two. Why . . . ?

They rose from the table and left the dining-saloon. Coffee was always served after dinner in the Great Gallery, which was

26

considered to be one of the particular glories of the Ashwoods' family seat. Built in the early eighteenth century by the renowned architect Richard Burlington, Hervington Park, with its Ionic entrance colonnade, towering wings and elegant pavilions, was generally regarded as one of the most awesome and satisfying of the great Warwickshire country houses.

The curtains in the tall, book-lined window bays of the gallery were not yet drawn, and they could see the banks of dark cloud moving furtively over the trees of the park to close out the day. They drew chairs up to a long oak table that ran along the centre of the gallery. A silent footman had already placed the round silver tray with the coffee things there, among the terrestrial and celestial globes, sextants and astrolabes, laid out as exhibits, but once used in the earnest schoolroom of Hervington Park a century or more earlier.

Laid carefully among these exhibits, Valentine saw a number of rolled-up plans secured with coloured tape. Lady Jane, slowly sipping her coffee, watched in silence as Valentine poked one of the plans with a tentative finger. She saw the good-natured amusement enliven his dark eyes.

'Those, Valentine,' she said calmly, 'are my

designs for a school. But of course you know that already! *My* designs, note. I drew them myself, with only minimal aid from a draughtsman. A school for girls. No, don't laugh — it amuses you, I know, to think that women could be anything but the guardians of hearth and home. Nevertheless, one day, you'll see, women will assume positions of public importance. They'll become Members of Parliament — '

Valentine laughed and shook his head.

'Jane, please! Members of Parliament! Just imagine it: 'Madame Speaker, can the Honourable Lady be serious?''

There was no malice, she knew, in his amused tolerance, which was an adult refinement of his youthful teasing. No doubt he would always be dismissive of her ideas and visions, but he was a man of infinite worth — a national hero, and the idol of her brother Earl Ashwood, who was himself already a major in the Indian Army.

'Valentine,' asked Jane, 'what was it that impelled you to leave the army and become a scholar at Oxford?'

'What impelled me? Well, Jane, it was 'the lust to know'. The need to know more about the inner minds of the ancient Greek and Roman writers. When I read them, I fancy I can hear them talking, teaching, reaching out across the aeons to make us privy to their wisdom!'

'Well, you'll have ample opportunity to share that enthusiasm with some of the boys at Kingsmere this coming term,' said Jane. 'Poor Mr Gledhill, the sick chaplain, taught Classics to the senior form. Dr Dalton's rather flattered that you've agreed to this venture into teaching boys.'

The tall double doors of the Great Gallery were pushed open, and Jane's father was brought into the room by his valet, Juckes. John Ashwood, Marquess of Hervington, sat in his wheeled chair. It was Juckes who had dressed him in the suit of evening clothes that he was wearing; Juckes who had carefully combed his sparse silver hair across his high-domed head. 'Faithful', Jane mused, was quite the wrong word to describe Juckes. 'Devoted' was nearer the mark.

Jane Ashwood rose from the long table as Juckes wheeled her father into his favourite book-lined alcove. It was time, she thought, to leave the two men together. John Ashwood had been a soldier for most of his life. Among the many treasures of the great house, his Victoria Cross, won at Balaclava, took pride of place. He and Captain Valentine had much in common.

'Father,' she said, 'I'll leave you alone to

gossip with Valentine about Egypt and the Crimea. Valentine, I'll not see you before you set out for Kingsmere tomorrow. All success to your venture into teaching boys. I'll stay here at home, thinking about my school in the air!'

She had talked lightly of 'gossip', but very few people could understand her father's slurred speech. Two years earlier, in 1890, he had been confined to bed and chair following a stroke. Valentine and Juckes were among the few people who could interpret what her father said. Juckes . . . At once devoted and punctilious, he could be subtly impertinent, an infuriating enigma. He had been in the family since she had been a small girl, and Valentine a dashing young man.

As she gathered up her precious plans from the table and walked towards the door, she caught her father's questioning glance. She knew what it meant. She saw it every time the three of them came together. Had Valentine said anything? And the unspoken answer was always the same. No, he had said nothing. Perhaps there was nothing to say.

★ ★ ★

The growl of voices in the low-beamed smoky bar of the Cat reminded Sergeant

Bottomley of the resentful menace of caged dogs on some remote farm when strangers approached. Everyone seemed to be complaining about the government, or the landlords, or the price of everything.

Bottomley sat in a dark corner of the candle-lit room and asked for a measure of gin. The bearded barman brought him the measure, and he told him to leave the bottle on the table.

'Is there anything else you'd like?'

The man's gruff voice sounded as though it were uttering a threat rather than asking a question. Bottomley tossed back his gin, poured himself another measure and looked steadily at the bearded figure, who was rocking slightly on his feet as though contemplating a sudden lunge.

'I'm waiting for a man called John Shearer. He's doing a job for me.'

'Shearer? The farrier with the game leg? He's not much use to anyone. Limps around like an old man in the almshouse.'

'He's of use to *me*,' said Bottomley, treating the man to a vague, rather menacing smile. 'He sees things. Finds things that others don't notice. He don't need his legs to do that.'

At half past eleven the door of the Cat opened and lame John Shearer, the farrier,

31

came in. He was a journeyman who worked for a wage in smithies and forges for miles about. He had done jobs for Bottomley before. Bottomley had sought him out and enlisted his help late that afternoon.

The sergeant motioned to him to sit down, and pushed his empty glass and the gin bottle towards him. He watched while the man sipped his gin, and could see the light of success in the farrier's eyes.

'You'd better come out in the moonlight, mister,' said John Shearer. 'I'll show you what I found, and if you'll walk with me through the fields, I'll show you where I found it.'

There was steady moonlight that night, and the swaying trees were tipped with silver. They came out on to the road through a gap in the hedge, and Shearer produced something from a bulky poacher's pocket sewn into his loose greatcoat. He put it into Bottomley's hands.

It was a plain wooden drinking-cup. Even in the moonlight Bottomley could see that it was the fellow of the one that had fallen from the dead hand of Alice Patching.

'Show me where you found it, John,' said Bottomley.

They walked in silence along the winding road from the village through the fields. The moon raced on ahead of them through the racks of cloud. Where the road suddenly straightened itself out in obedience to some ancient Roman track-way the limping farrier stopped, and pointed to a tangled blackthorn hedge on the left of the road.

'It was in there, mister. I scoured the hedge on either side, and the bit of field behind the hedges, as you said. And I found it here, thrust in among the branches.'

'Thrust in? It couldn't have been just thrown in? Tossed away by a running man?'

'No, mister. It was shoved tight in among the branches, so no one could see it. Hidden away. What will you do with that cup?'

'I'll tell you what I'll do, John Shearer. I'll buy it off you. Once it's mine, then it's my business what I do with it.'

He felt deep in his trousers pocket and jingled the money there. He brought out a shilling and two silver threepenny pieces.

'Here's one and six, John. When next I need you, I'll know where to find you. Good night.'

Herbert Bottomley stood in thought near the blackthorn hedge, holding the wooden cup in his hands. He placed it to his nose, and inhaled deeply, holding his breath for some critical seconds before exhaling. His release of breath sounded like a sigh of despair.

Two cups. That was what he'd thought from the start. Two cups, and one bottle of Madeira. And perhaps some crude sleight of hand. Mr Lionel would look at this newly found cup, but he'd find nothing there but the lees of wine.

Bottomley lifted his eyes from the straight road and looked across the moonlit fields at the cluster of school buildings beyond the elm trees where some lights still burned.

Two cups . . . .What had Alice Patching been doing on the night she died? Had she been drinking a toast in the barn with the 'gentleman' she'd told Mary Wainwright about, a toast to their approaching happy runaway life in London? Perhaps. And perhaps the 'gentleman' had sat there with his unpoisoned pear-wood cup in his hands, waiting for her to die.

2

The Tragic Cast Assembled

Two strong men stood talking on the steps of Kingsmere Abbey, the ancient Warwickshire public school a few miles from Kenilworth.

'So, Granger,' said one of the two strong men, 'I leave it as your special charge to receive Captain Noel Valentine when he comes this afternoon. I shall be away all day, but will most certainly be back early on Sunday morning.'

His voice was high and commanding, in keeping with his determined chin and firm, resolute mouth. Although he stood quite motionless while he spoke, his brown eyes betrayed a kind of restless energy.

'We're very lucky to be getting him, Headmaster,' said Granger. 'It's not every Oxford don who could be enticed away from the 'dreaming spires' for a term to the grim realities of a boys' school.'

Granger was very formally dressed in a black suit and frock coat. He was well over six feet tall, and when he spoke his tones were clear and confident. A stranger, at first glance, may have wondered for a moment which of the two men was the head of the school.

'Well, Granger, we can thank Lady Jane Ashwood for that. It was particularly kind of her to persuade him. Very kind indeed. But, of course, they have been fast friends for many years. Let him feel that his gesture is appreciated. It means we can start the term next Wednesday with a full complement of masters. Good day to you.'

The headmaster turned towards a light carriage that was waiting for him, but Granger had evidently something further to say.

'May I ask where you are going, Dr Dalton? In case of urgent necessity, you understand.'

The headmaster stopped in his tracks, and turned to look at the man called Granger with scarcely concealed vexation.

'I should have thought any such necessities could be dealt with very ably by yourself. But since you ask, I am going to Oxford.'

'Oh, indeed, sir? Which college are you visiting?'

The headmaster's expression turned from vexed surprise to outraged anger. He had come to detest the perpetual hint of mockery behind his deputy's polite but increasingly intrusive enquiries. They had become too frequent of late for comfort.

'I'm going to Corpus Christi.'

As he said this, he dropped his eyes, as though unwilling to meet the other's steady gaze. Without another word, he hurried down the steps and got into the carriage, which immediately moved off.

Granger remained on the steps, looking thoughtfully along the drive, where the headmaster's carriage was still in view as it made for the Kingsmere road. He turned his head as another figure emerged from the shade of the entrance, a self-effacing kind of man of about forty, slightly stooping and rather pale, with thinning hair changing from an indeterminate sandiness into grey. His forehead was marred by extensive puckered scarring, which drew his right eyelid down at the corner, partly closing the eye.

Granger's rather forbidding face broke into a smile.

'Ah, Sandford! A lovely day, don't you think? A perfect sky, a first-rate school, and a splendid headmaster. Leastways, I suppose we are a first-rate school. A little old-fashioned perhaps, a little antiquated, so to speak, but what of that? What has Rugby or Clifton to offer that we cannot supply, hey?'

Sandford made no reply, but an embarrassed flush began to suffuse his face. He seemed to have forgotten his purpose in coming out of the school, for he walked slowly back up the steps. Granger turned to follow him.

Yes, thought Granger, a splendid headmaster, a splendid fraud, a splendid liar!

★　★　★

'I expect you'll find school-teaching rather tame after Egypt and all that.'

Theodore Granger had stopped with his hand on the handle of a white-painted door in one of the panelled walls of Kingsmere School's entrance hall, as though the thought had suddenly struck him.

Captain Noel Valentine laughed.

'Tame? I doubt it, Granger! Soldier I may have been, but teaching Greek and Latin is meat and drink to me. It always has been.'

Granger smiled and pushed open the white door, revealing a carpeted hallway, illuminated by a skylight three floors above.

'This, Valentine, is what we call Staff House. I'll take you up to your quarters.'

They ascended to the second floor, where Granger threw open the door of a room directly facing the head of the stairs. It proved to be a light, airy sitting-room, with two long sash windows affording a view over parkland quietly basking in the afternoon sun.

'This is poor Gledhill's set,' said Granger. 'I think you'll find it to your liking. We serve tea in the Combination Room on the floor below at four, though there aren't many masters around at the moment to eat it.'

'I'd have thought the troops would have returned to their posts by now?'

'Oh, no, not yet. The next three days will see most of them back, but at the moment there are only a few of the staff here. You'll meet them later, I expect. The headmaster's away today, and won't be back until tomorrow. Poor Gledhill, of course, is in Cannes — the right place to be while convalescing from typhoid. He left a note for you before he went. It's over there, on the mantelpiece. I'll come to fetch you down to tea at four o'clock.'

The energetic vice-master had gone before Valentine could say anything in reply. He examined his set. There were two doors to the right of the sitting-room, one of which opened into a bedroom, and the other into a small service pantry, in which he found his luggage standing ready for unpacking.

Egypt and all that . . . Fancy Granger dragging that business up! His mind flew back to the year 1882, when he and his men had fought and won the bloody battle at Tel-el-Kebir. So much loss, and yet so much gain . . . By mid-September, the whole of Egypt and the Sudan were occupied. Ten years ago! It didn't seem that long.

He threw up the sitting-room window. Glancing downwards he saw to his surprise the ivy-covered façade of a neat mid-eighteenth-century house, in the third storey of which he was evidently standing. Far below he could see a well-kept lawn, and beyond this a carriage-drive disappearing to right and left. Directly ahead lay a well-wooded belt of parkland, and in the distance a bright line of silver showed the presence of a stretch of water. To his left he could just see the corner of what appeared to be a miniature two-storey Renaissance palace.

Valentine turned away from the window and took Gledhill's letter from the mantel-piece, where it had been propped up against a vase. He tore open the envelope and extracted a small sheet of note-paper.

Capt Valentine (it ran)
So good of you to take my place. There's not much to tell you — Granger will show you my classroom and store of texts. Watch out for young Gerald

40

Mostyn. I've no doubt that he will make himself known to you.
Ambrose Gledhill.

Gerald Mostyn? Where had he heard the name Mostyn recently? Ah, yes — the Bad Baronet, Sir Hugo. This Gerald was probably his son. Really, Gledhill could have been a little more explicit! Still, poor man, he'd had much to do, no doubt, to write at all.

Exactly on the hour of four the vice-master came to collect him. On the landing beneath, Granger paused for a moment, and pointed to what appeared to be the outer door of a house, complete with a brass knocker.

'That door, Valentine,' said Granger, 'leads into the headmaster's house, so whenever you are summoned to his presence, that's the way to go, not all the way downstairs and through the grounds to the front of his house — which, by the way, is at the back of the school!'

The last words were said with a smile, but for Valentine the expression 'summoned to his presence' had held something of the carefully concealed impudence of a sergeant-major talking about a commissioned officer of doubtful abilities. It would be interesting to know what lay behind it.

They entered the Combination Room, a

very large, comfortably furnished place, quite evidently a room in which people lived and relaxed. Tea had been provided on a table in the centre of the room. Two men were sitting there.

'Sheffield,' said Granger, 'this is Captain Noel Valentine, who's standing in for poor Gledhill until Christmas. Valentine, this is Mr Sheffield. This other gentleman is Mr Sandford. Help yourself to some tea, Valentine, and sit down somewhere.'

Valentine settled himself with tea and sandwiches in a bruised but comfortable chair near the window. Granger perched himself on an upright chair near the table. He had the air of a man who had no intention ever of relaxing too obviously.

'I'd better give you a brief indication of how we arrange things at Kingsmere,' he said. 'We don't have houses here, Valentine. The boys are grouped by age, and we take them as young as eleven. Those little fellows we call the Children, and they have dormitories. The middle years are the Scholars, each of whom has a room of his own. They live in a big three-storeyed building behind the hall. And the senior boys are the Gentlemen. They share with us the privilege of each having his own 'set' — bedroom and study, that is.'

'I take it that someone supervises these three groups?'

'Yes, indeed. As Vice-master, I also look after the Gentlemen. Sheffield there is Master of the Scholars.'

'For my sins!' Sheffield chuckled. He was a dark-complexioned, worldly-looking man of about fifty, with an ample black beard.

'And the Children?'

'They, Valentine, are shepherded in their own little kingdom by a man called Fletcher. Incidentally, I've not seen Fletcher all day. Sandford, do you know what's become of him? I wanted a word with him.'

'I believe he's gone down to Lower School, to potter around among his papers in that monstrous desk of his,' Sandford replied.

'Well, it may be just possible that he's decided to tidy it up after fifty years. If he starts to reflect over every note and ancient imposition, he'll be there till doomsday!'

'It's an interesting thought, Vice-master,' said Sandford. Then, turning in his chair, he said to Valentine, 'Mr Fletcher, who is Master of the Children, is by way of being the oldest inhabitant here, and I should say that he's the most highly regarded of us all among the boys.'

'Except, of course, for the headmaster,' said Granger, in a tone of voice that it was almost impossible to interpret. His face retained its solemnity, but surely, thought Valentine, he had meant this for a joke? Sheffield permitted himself a guarded smile. Sandford, he noted, looked away, and became almost incoherent, faltering out 'Oh, yes, by all means . . . '

There was something here that Valentine could not fathom, something that impelled Sheffield to change the subject with no attempt at a subtle transition.

'You know, Valentine, this whole place will be utterly transformed within a week. Our delightful boys, vast hordes of them, will take the venerable pile by storm, and fill up every nook and cranny with activity, noise, riot, and so forth. I don't envy poor old Flodders his dubious privilege of shepherding the very young of our brood down there in the undercroft.'

'I take it,' said Valentine, 'that 'Flodders' is a nickname?'

'Well,' said Sheffield, doubtfully, 'that's certainly true, but it's now become virtually an alternative name for Fletcher — why, he even uses it himself!'

The vice-master put down his cup with a clatter. Whoever Fletcher is, thought Valentine, this restless man soon gets tired of hearing about him.

'Fletcher,' said the vice-master, 'is content

to live in a world of his own making. The rest of us have to live in one made for us by others. So come, gentlemen! Let us seize the moment! There's work to be done!'

★ ★ ★

Sunday dawned bright and clear. Valentine rose soon after eight. When he went down to the dining-room he found it deserted, with the remains of several meals still lying on the long central table. Schoolmasters, he thought, must be inordinately early risers.

There were plenty of heated dishes still on the sideboard. Valentine helped himself to bacon and eggs, and was just pouring out a cup of tea when the door was opened with some vigour, and a strong old voice exclaimed, 'Ah! so here you are, Valentine! Making away with all the bacon, no doubt, hey?'

The speaker was a man of seventy or more, with the stoop of old age in his shoulders, but with a lively animated face wrinkled with humour, and with bright shrewd eyes looking over pince-nez. An ample halo of thick white hair crowned his head, and formed a contrast to the rusty black in which he was dressed.

Without waiting for an answer, he darted to the sideboard, and rummaged among the dishes, returning to the table with a heaped-up plate.

'Yes,' he said, 'Valentine, hey? Tutor in Classics at Oxford, a soldier turned scholar, till called away to lower service in a school for a term. The only man to refuse an honour from Queen Victoria, saying he'd done nothing more than his duty. A knighthood, no less!'

The old man glanced at Valentine with a mischievous twinkle, and then became rapidly absorbed with sausages and bacon.

'How the devil did you know that? Who are you, anyway?'

' *'Fama nihil est celerius'*,' said the old man, smiling.

Noel Valentine laughed. ' 'Nothing's swifter than rumour'! Not many people dare to quote Livy at me in that fashion! Tell me, are you Fletcher, the Guardian of the Infants, or whatever ancient title is borne by the man who looks after the little boys?'

'That's right. Master of the Children. I'm Amyas Fletcher, or Flodders, as they call me, and you'll soon hear from various quarters that Flodders pokes and pries! That's how I knew what you said to Queen Victoria — by poking and prying. After you'd walked out backwards, she said: 'There goes a very loyal man, or a very silly one'. Now then, coffee.'

46

Back at the table, the old man sipped his coffee for a while. His impish expression gave way to something more grave and sober. He gave a slight sigh, put his cup down gently on the saucer, and spoke again.

'Tell me, Valentine, are you familiar at all with the two cultures?'

'The two cultures? Well, I suppose there's Science and Art — '

'No, Valentine, I'm thinking of the state of things where large numbers of boys are to be found. You see, in every school there are two cultures, existing and flourishing *in tandem*. There's the one that we, the masters, belong to, the culture of learning for its own sake, and for the refinement of the mind and the moral sense; the culture of playing the game, of helping the weak, of — you know, all that sort of thing.'

As he spoke, the vestiges of his earlier rather eccentric manner seemed to fade, and an intense seriousness took its place.

'And then there's the other culture, *their* culture. Of course, the boys, in their relation to us, pay lip-service to *our* culture, and do their sums, and conjugate their verbs, and go into obedient raptures over Virgil or Homer. But underneath, Valentine, is the dark kingdom of which all boys are subjects, a kingdom ruled by the morality of the jungle!

Cruelty . . . Mental torment, too. Some boys are trapped in that horrible underworld for years, and there's no way out. And that's why I poke and pry.'

Valentine sipped his tea for a while. He knew what Fletcher was talking about. The army had not been free of that kind of inimical tradition.

'Don't misunderstand me about the two cultures,' Fletcher added. 'Boys can't help being like that, and I'm not judging them. They can be very agreeable when they want to be, and they have the ability to keep an old man young. I've taught here for fifty years, Valentine, and I still can't wait for the rogues to return!'

'I imagine I saw a few boys, or young men, walking in the meadows as I came down here this morning.'

'Yes, there are two or three of the Gentlemen — they're the Upper School fellows, you know — who have been here all through the vacation, their parents being abroad and so forth. But that's not the same as this great mausoleum being filled with three hundred lively boys, and brought back to life again!'

The old man rose from his chair, sweeping crumbs off his coat on to the carpet.

'Now, Valentine, I expect you have some

time on your hands, so let me show you some of the choicer delights of Kingsmere!'

They left Staff House, skirted a fine Jacobean staircase, and entered the gloomy, oak-panelled main corridor of the school. Valentine looked politely into a number of battered and forlorn classrooms, full of desks deeply defaced with carved initials, and stale with the smell of old ink and chalk. Of greater interest was School Hall, with its lofty, hammer-beamed roof and high table.

'We've some good portraits here,' said Fletcher. 'King Henry there over the High Table is supposed to be by Holbein.'

Valentine looked with interest at a more recent portrait of an aged, balding man in academic robes. It was a very fine portrait of a very faded sort of man.

'G.F.Watts painted that,' said Fletcher. 'It's very fine and powerful, don't you think? That's old Pierce-Littledale, who was head-master before Dr Dalton. He was eighty when he retired in '81. Granger had been headmaster in all but name for five years before that. Everybody thought he'd be offered the headship, including Granger himself. It was a great shock when the Court of Governors brought in Dr Dalton from Plymouth to take Pierce-Littledale's place.'

'Mr Granger strikes me as being a very

capable man indeed.'

'Oh, he is. He's got a good brain — a sharp mind, you know. He's a mathematician by training, though he's not done much teaching for the past few years. Too busy!'

Fletcher ushered Valentine out of the hall and through a side door into a bright sunlit garden, across which reared up, in full view at last, the Renaissance palace which he had glimpsed from his window. Splendid in red brick, nude of ivy or other excrescence, it was Victorian to its foundations.

The garden in front of it contained a hot-house, and was divided into various beds of what Valentine took to be herbs of some kind.

'That,' said Fletcher, waving vaguely towards the palace, 'is what we call 'Foliott's Building'. It was put up in '82, just after Dr Dalton came here, and it's his celebrated scientific laboratory. I went in there once, years ago, but it's all too bewildering for an old man to take in. Bottles, you know, and flasks, and chemicals. Very dangerous, I should think. Let's go back into the school.'

They returned to the main corridor, and soon the dark Tudor panelling ended as they came into what appeared to be the undercroft of a cathedral. This was the oldest part of the school, the remains of the Benedictine abbey that had once occupied the site. Various ancient stone chambers had been adapted centuries ago as schoolrooms, with now-battered Tudor fireplaces let into the walls. Wide lattice windows made the area brighter and more cheerful than the shadowy, dark-panelled central core of the school.

Fletcher led Valentine into an old vaulted classroom. Behind the master's dais was a fixed blackboard, and beside this a low doorway crowned with a truly magnificent poppy-head ornament. Fletcher opened the door.

'Watch out as you come in here!' he said. 'These medieval arches are unconscionably low. Either the old monks were very small, or they regarded banging their heads as a reasonable penance!'

They entered a tiny room, lit by a single narrow window, near to which was a door, leading presumably into the grounds. The room contained two armchairs, a small table, and a tiny fireplace with a glowing coal fire, upon which Fletcher placed a kettle ready filled for a coming brew. Against the wall behind the door was a small writing-desk, groaning under the weight of heaps of books and dusty papers.

Valentine flung himself gratefully into one of the chairs. Old Fletcher's mind was

51

evidently still on the subject of Dr Dalton.

'Yes,' he said, as he began to brew some tea, 'we all expected poor Granger to succeed to the headship, but Edward Dalton had created quite a stir by establishing the teaching of natural science at Nelson College, in Plymouth. The chairman of our Court of Governors, Sir Walter Foliott, was very impressed, and pulled a few strings in order to get Dalton here as head. That was in 1881. Granger, I might add, was not best pleased!'

Fletcher placed the tea things on the small table, and sank into the other armchair with a little sigh. He glanced round the small, quiet room.

'This is my little den,' he said. 'I spend a good deal of time down here in term. I often take my lunch here, and sometimes an abbreviated dinner, too. I did that yesterday, which is why I didn't see you until this morning. Did you dine in Staff House?'

'I did. Very pleasant it was, too. Mr Sheffield was there, and a quiet, scarred man — Sandford.'

'Sheffield and Sandford date from the previous regime, when Pierce-Littledale dozed away quietly in his house, and Granger ran the whole show. Poor old Sandford's a specialist teacher of English. He was the last appointment Granger made to the staff before Dalton came.'

The thick walls of the ancient monastic buildings seemed to hoard a welcome quietness. Valentine suddenly felt that this old schoolmaster with his twinkling eyes and shock of white hair was a positively benign influence in the school.

'You know, Fletcher,' he said, 'I find your part of the school the most attractive by far. For some reason I feel a sense of unease in the rest of the school. Perhaps it's the general air of shady gloom. All that dark panelling, you know, right up to the sooty ceiling.'

'Perhaps, perhaps,' said Fletcher, holding his cup with both hands, and looking steadily at Valentine. 'Perhaps that's what it is. Or perhaps it's because back there you're picking up the moods and tensions of others — hey? Feelings, you know, and things people say . . .'

Old Fletcher put his cup down on the table. He treated Valentine to an impish smile.

'Well, now, I'll tell you how I knew what you'd said to the Queen. When the headmaster mentioned that he'd succeeded in getting you here from Oxford, I wrote to a man called Abercrombie, an ancient friend of mine at Hampton Court, who knew most of the lords in waiting whose vocation it is to hover around the Sovereign. He remembered all about you, and your audience, what you said, and what *she* said. And that's all there was to it.'

Fletcher cocked his head on one side, letting his pince-nez fall off into his lap.

'You don't mind, do you?' he asked.

Valentine laughed. 'No, Fletcher, I don't mind a bit.'

'Good. I've been very pleased to have you down here, Valentine,' said Fletcher. 'But — dear me! It's nearly ten o'clock. I expect we've both got work to do before lunch.'

It was a kindly dismissal. Valentine retraced his steps out of the ancient undercroft and along the great corridor. What had he just heard that awakened a vague anxiety in his mind, a feeling that he had missed an urgent command to be on his guard? Something that Fletcher had just said . . . no, it had gone.

But the indefinable sense of unease remained to tease his mind.

3

The Nurture of Youth

Just before two o'clock that afternoon Valentine opened the inner door to the headmaster's house and made his way down a steep flight of stairs to a cramped, rather musty little passage on the ground floor. A door immediately facing him carried a sign reading 'Headmaster. Please Knock and Walk In'.

Dr Dalton, who was seated at a large, ornate desk in the centre of the room, rose to greet him. He motioned to a tapestry-covered upright chair placed in front of his desk, and Valentine sat down.

'It's really very good of you to come to us like this,' said Dalton. 'It's been very sad about poor Gledhill. Our local parish of Kingsmere is vacant at the moment, and various clergy have been taking the Sunday services. Gledhill, naturally enough, was happy to help out, and presided at matins there one Sunday morning.'

Dalton pursed his lips in something like disapproval, and turned the pages of a diary on his desk.

'Yes, it was the fourteenth of August. Well, you know, Valentine, he was very late returning that day, and when he did arrive it was clear to see that he was unwell. He was pale and agitated, and he retired immediately to his bed. Dr Manning — our local physician — was sent for, and from him we learned that it was typhoid.'

Valentine listened to the finely modulated tones of the headmaster, at the same time noting with a surge of pleasure that a copy of his own school text-book, *Advanced Latin Verse Composition*, lay on Dalton's desk.

'I gather that Gledhill's now well on the way to recovery? He left a brief note for me before he went away, so I assume that the worst is over.'

'Oh, yes, indeed, but he was quite gravely ill for a fortnight — delirious, in fact. Frankly, I had doubts of his ability to pull through. However, he did so, and Manning in effect ordered him to convalesce abroad for some months. He'll be back before Christmas, I expect. He'll recover in Cannes. He's taken a chest of medicines with him, but it will be the climate out there that will do it.'

Dalton pointed a well-manicured finger at Valentine's textbook and smiled.

'Your own fame, Captain Valentine, has

preceded you, as you see. You'll find copies of your book in Gledhill's classroom.'

'I'm very pleased to see my humble offering there on your desk, Dr Dalton. Let me return the compliment by asking you to tell me something about your philosophy of education. I've heard bits of it from some of your staff, but don't yet see the whole picture.'

Dalton stirred in his chair, and leaned forward, elbows resting on the desk, and his hands clasped together as though in prayer. His eyes became animated with the light of excitement as he looked steadily at Valentine without speaking for a few moments. Then he began to outline the principal tenets of his synthesis of Science and Art. It was all articulated with such enthusiasm and conviction that Valentine found himself spellbound by Dalton's delivery.

This man, surely, was unfolding not a theory but a vision. It was a system for the future, in which man would be fully ennobled by the banishment of ignorance and vice, and by the final triumph over pain and disease.

Dalton was in full flood until nearly three o'clock, and when at last he rose to go, Valentine realized that he had been listening, totally absorbed, for almost half an hour.

* ★ ★ ★

Valentine left Dalton's study through a
second door, which led into the front hallway
of the house. With time to spare, he strolled
in the grounds behind the main school
buildings, lost in thought. He wondered
whether Jane Ashwood was aware of this
man's total commitment to education. He
would ask her views about Dalton next time
he called at Hervington Park.

Suddenly the unmistakable ringing sound
of swordplay came to Valentine's ears.
Emerging from a dense shrubbery he came
out on to a stretch of rough grass, where
three youths of seventeen or eighteen were
pretending to conduct a duel. All three had
discarded their striped blazers and caps,
which had been thrown carelessly in a heap
near to where Valentine was standing.

One boy, who had been half reclining on
the grass watching the other two, stood up
when he saw Valentine, who made a sign for
them to continue. The boys were using
harmless practice foils, though the clash of
steel and the exhibition of skills was
impressive enough.

Of the two boys who were fencing, one was
heavily built but very agile. His opponent was
a tall, slight youth, and although he fenced

58

well, he was clearly no match for the heavier boy. Valentine watched them. The heavier boy, he thought, would make a good soldier. He fought well, but without any dangerous vanity, and his face was fixed in a good-humoured half smile.

The tall lad fought with great concentration and with a kind of effortless grace, but Valentine could see how he bit his lip in anxiety. Come on, lad, he thought, lunge at him, parry his attack . . . Couldn't the boy see that he was failing to get under his opponent's guard?

A discarded practice foil lay on the grass. With a sudden resolve Valentine picked it up. He moved swiftly behind the lad and said curtly, 'Move aside, boy! Watch me. Watch my attack.'

The lad immediately obeyed and threw down his foil. Valentine engaged the heavier boy, who smiled with delight. This was more fun than sloshing away at a classmate. He would write home that very night to tell his parents that he'd fenced with Captain Noel Valentine, the Victor of Tel-el-Kebir . . .

Valentine held his left arm behind his back, effortlessly parrying his opponent's strokes. He kept the game going for a minute or two, and then, with a series of lightning manoeuvres which bewildered the heavy boy, he passed effortlessly under his guard and sent his foil flying through the air.

Valentine's opponent ran nimbly across the grass, retrieved his sword, and solemnly returned, carrying it across his hands like an offering.

'Sir,' he said, 'I surrender my sword. The better man won!'

Valentine laughed. He accepted the sword, and then with equal solemnity handed it back, hilt first.

'What's your name, young man?'

'Lovell, sir.'

'Well, Lovell, I return your sword with honour. You did very well against a former professional soldier!'

Lovell blushed with pleasure, and the other two boys broke into spontaneous clapping. They gathered up their things, and Lovell collected the foils. He and the boy who had been a mere spectator moved off in the direction of the school buildings. The boy whom Valentine had helped lingered behind.

'May I have a word with you, sir?' he said. 'My name is Gerald Mostyn.'

There was a faintly autocratic tone in the boy's voice, but it was his eyes, rather than his voice, that particularly caught Valentine's attention. They were of an intense, almost luminous blue, and they gazed frankly into

Valentine's with an almost mesmeric power. He was as fair complexioned as his friend Lovell was dark.

'I'm particularly pleased to meet you, Mostyn,' said Valentine. 'You're the only pupil whose name was known to me before I strolled down here. Mr Gledhill left me a note mentioning you by name. 'Watch out for Mostyn', he said. Unfortunately, he didn't exactly say *why*!'

Mostyn smiled, and Valentine saw how a slight tenseness in the boy's stance disappeared. He suddenly seemed more relaxed.

'Mr Gledhill's like that, sir. He writes very brief comments on your work, and at times it's impossible to know what they mean. Mr Sandford says that it's his 'laconic style', which may well be true.'

'So would you care, Mostyn, to make up the bits that the laconic Mr Gledhill left out?'

'Well, the fact is, sir, I had mentioned to Mr Gledhill that I was thinking of reading for Orders, and he had promised to lend me some Greek and Latin Biblical texts. I'm very good at Latin and Greek. I know that Mr Gledhill will be back by Christmas, but I'd rather not waste a whole term, and that's why I asked him just before he left to mention me to you. I was hoping — '

The boy stopped short in some embarrassment, but Valentine quickly replied, 'That I
would do some extra Greek and Latin with
you? Naturally, I shall be delighted to do so.
The question of your vocation, of course, is
for others to examine.'

A sudden shadow crossed Mostyn's brow,
and he bit his lip, as though some
unsought-for burden had been placed upon
him. When he spoke, there was a slight
tremor in his voice.

'I feel it's only fair to tell you, sir, that my
father is Sir Hugo Mostyn.'

Valentine looked gravely at the boy, but
made no immediate reply. His memory had
stirred at mention of that name. Jane
Ashwood had told him that Sir Hugo
Mostyn, the Bad Baronet, owned the village
at the school gates.

It was time to make some comment.

'I see. And is your father, also, see'.ing to
take Holy Orders?'

'Why, no, sir, but — '

'In that case, Mostyn, we need not chatter
about him. Let's concentrate instead on
equipping you with the necessary quantities
of New Testament Greek!'

★ ★ ★

'Mr Amlett came round this morning, Saul. Grinding knives and shears on that great wheel of his. He was in Kingsmere on Saturday.'

Saul Jackson sat in his old cane-backed chair near the fire. His neighbour, Sarah Brown, was seated opposite him, hemming a pair of sheets. He watched her busy fingers as she worked.

'Mr Amlett? That man never stops talking! I suppose he brought all the village gossip about poor Alice Patching?'

Sarah Brown threw him an appraising glance, and he saw that she understood his sensitivity about this particular case.

'He told me that the girl's mother is sickening for something. She was never strong, he said, and losing her daughter's been a mortal blow.'

'Did he say anything about the father? Mr Patching?'

'Apparently he's just gone very quiet about it. He went out again to his fields the day after, and that lad who was to marry her went with him for company. He told me his name, but I've forgotten.'

'Baker. Noah Baker.'

'Yes, that was the name. Mr Patching was banking on him coming into the family and working the fields. That's what Mr Amlett told me. I suppose Mr Patching was hoping to do less with the lad helping him.'

Jackson scraped the bowl of his briar pipe with a penknife and tapped it out on the hearth. He sighed. It took little imagination to see the havoc that Alice Patching's death had wrought.

'I wonder what Noah Baker will do now?' asked Jackson.

Sarah pursed her lips and shook her head. Jackson watched her as she gazed though the latticed window across the darkening orchard to the winking lights of her own cottage beyond the apple trees. Presently she spoke.

'I expect Noah Baker will keep company with another girl when the time's ripe, Saul. He's got his own life to live. He can't live poor Mr Patching's life for him.'

'Did Mr Amlett say anything about that other girl? Mary Wainwright?'

'Yes, Saul. Her father's packed her off to his married sister in Northumberland. A holiday, it's supposed to be.'

Sarah Brown caught his eye in the gloom. It was one of those moments when he knew from her expression exactly what she was thinking before she spoke. It was a formality to ask her what she meant, but he did.

'Well, Saul, her father wants her out of the way, to make sure she doesn't go the same way as Alice Patching. According to Mr Amlett, the folk in Kingsmere are saying she was done away with.'

The folk in Kingsmere, Jackson thought grimly, are right. But it wouldn't do to say anything openly. Not yet, at least. Sarah Brown smiled and shook her head as she stood up.

'No, Saul,' she said, 'I'm not fishing for information, and I don't want you to tell me anything. But that's what folk are saying. Those sheets are done now. I'd best be going.'

It was a way she had to slip unobtrusively through doorways, so that you hardly knew she'd come or gone. Mr Amlett! Mr Amlett says this, Mr Amlett says that. Perhaps Mr Amlett should confine his activities to knife-grinding, and leave detection to others. What did Mr Amlett know about it?

Jackson rose and lit the candles on the mantelpiece. The old beamed living-room of his cottage seemed to leap towards the light. The vignetted photograph of his dead wife looked searchingly at him from its place of honour above the mantelpiece. He could never look at it without seeing a wall of raging flame, and hearing the wicked crackle of burning timbers.

Charlotte Anne Jackson,
aged twenty-nine.
Also Rebecca, daughter of the above,
aged two years and three months.

He thought of them both, lying at rest since 1877 in Coldeaton Churchyard. Then he thought of Alice Patching, aged seventeen, who was to be buried on the following day, Tuesday, in the ancient burial-ground at Kingsmere.

A throaty cough from the darkened garden told him that Sergeant Bottomley had walked up from Warwick to see him before he struck out home across Thornton Heath. He had worked late in the Police-Office on matters of his own, long after Jackson had climbed the steep road to his cottage in Meadowcroft Lane, high above the town.

Sergeant Bottomley gathered the skirts of his mustard-coloured greatcoat around him, and sat down at the fire, carefully placing his bowler hat like a flanged basin on the floor beside his chair. Jackson went into his small kitchen and returned in a few moments with a tankard of ale.

'There you are, Sergeant,' he said. 'I've nothing stronger, I'm afraid.'

Bottomley smiled rather absently and sipped the dark ale. On other occasions he would have risen to Jackson's bait about his fondness for strong drink, but not that night. He turned his shrewd grey eyes on to the inspector.

'Sir, do you agree with me now? About Alice Patching, I mean?'

'Yes, Sergeant,' said Jackson, 'I *do* agree with you. It was murder! And that's why you and I will attend her funeral tomorrow. You'd better read this letter I received from Mr Lionel Dovercourt. He sent a man over from Ashgate to deliver it, rather than use the post. It's in answer to a question that I telegraphed to him on Saturday.'

He handed Bottomley an envelope, from which the sergeant extracted a single sheet of paper. He spread it out on his knee, leaning forward to read it by the fitful light of the fire.

'*What you suggest, Mr Jackson,*' he read, '*is quite possible, though I am aghast at the possibility of such heartless villainy. The thing could be done very effectively by preparing a strong solution of the hydrochloride of aconitine in water. The vessel would be filled with the deadly liquid, covered with a lid, and left overnight. Next day, it could be emptied out, rotating the while, and then put aside to dry out naturally. Any crystals of the alkaloid left adhering to the sides of the cup would be dissolved by the fresh wine poured into it. It would be easy to provide a fatal quantity of the poison in the way I have described. One-and-a-half grains would do it.'*

Bottomley handed the letter back.

'So that's the way of it, sir. The innocent bottle and the poisoned cup. And so the breathing stopped, and death supervened . . . And then our villain sneaked away on foot, thrust his own harmless cup into a blackthorn hedge, and made his way to — Where could he be going, on foot, creeping away through the night? Not to the Vale, sir, it's too far off. Not to the Light Infantry Barracks. No, it was to that school, sir, the school beyond the elms.'

★   ★   ★

An elderly black man with close-cropped white hair stood at the end of the garden terrace of Hervington Park, his hands clasped behind his back. He was dressed in a black suit with knee-breeches and white stockings, with a white scarf tied loosely at his throat. He was watching Captain Noel Valentine approaching on horseback across the acre field skirting the main road. It was too late to slip back into the house. He would stand where he was.

Valentine swung down lightly from his horse as a groom ran forward to take the bridle. The black man bowed slightly, and then resumed his rather statuesque stance.

'Good evening, Juckes,' Valentine said. 'I've called to see Lady Jane. I rather think that she's expecting me.'

There was a strangely familiar aromatic perfume in the air that Valentine could not quite identify.

'Lady Jane is in the Great Gallery, sir. And she is certainly expecting you. 'Juckes', she said to me, 'you go out there and stand on the terrace until Captain Valentine arrives, then bring him straight to me'. Yes, sir, that's what she said.'

There was something soothing about the West Indian valet's lilting speech that had always appealed to Valentine — that, and his humorous directness. He treated Valentine to a wide, rather impish smile.

'And how is Lord Hervington today?' asked Valentine.

'My Lord is as ever, sir, patient under his afflictions. The hand of a dark angel touched him, and struck him all but dumb. These things will be, sir.'

Juckes turned away and entered the house. The mention of Lord Hervington had caused the smile to fade from his lips. He looked abstracted, as though his mind was elsewhere. There were tears in his eyes.

'My Lord will never get better, sir. He knows, and I know, that his days are numbered. His son and heir, Earl Ashwood, will succeed here. Earl Ashwood has written to tell me that I am to stay here. And so I will serve him, and also Lady Jane, who will continue to live here in My Lord's house.'

Valentine regarded the valet with puzzlement.

'What you say about Lord Hervington, Juckes, may well be true, alas! But as regards Lady Jane — are you so sure about her future? I should imagine that Lady Jane will marry in due time.'

Juckes stiffened slightly, and dropped his eyes. When he spoke, his voice was almost a whisper.

'Lady Jane, sir, has been chosen for other things. Unless, of course, some valiant gentleman overwhelms her and carries her where he will! But I do not think that will happen. So Lady Jane will live here in her father's house. Or go where it has been ordained.'

They ascended the steeply curving stairs and reached the first-floor landing. Valentine experienced a feeling of deep disquiet. He had never thought of Jane as a dedicated spinster, which was what Juckes had implied. Perhaps he had come at the right time. And why did the man speak of a 'valiant gentleman' as a suitor? Valiant . . . Had Juckes set himself up as a matchmaker?

Jukes opened the doors into the Great Gallery.

'Captain Valentine has arrived, My Lady,' he said, and closed the tall double doors silently behind him.

★ ★ ★

'Are you staying for dinner, Valentine? You seem to have chosen an awkward hour for visiting. Too late for tea, too early for anything more adventurous. Why have you come? It's only Monday. Didn't you like it at Kingsmere?'

Jane Ashwood's flippancy met with no similar response. Valentine frowned and bit his lip. He glanced covertly at Jane's plans, which still lay on the long gallery table.

'I'll not stay for dinner. As a matter of fact, it wasn't terribly convenient to ride over like this today. I've things to do, and I want to be back at the school before sunset.'

'Well, Valentine, you can hardly blame *me* for inconveniencing you. After all, it was you who desired to visit *me*!'

Valentine seemed not to hear her. He looked undecided and ill-at-ease, as though what he had come to say was becoming increasingly difficult.

'It was very kind of you to send Juckes on to the terrace to watch out for me,' he said. 'Very civil of him to stand there like a statue, waiting for me!'

Lady Jane laughed.

'Did he tell you that? You know as well as I do that he makes up these wild stories. He's done so ever since Father brought him back from the West Indies. He's an incorrigible fibber. When I was little he used to tell me how he'd been captured by pirates, sold into slavery, discovered buried treasure . . . If you found him standing on the terrace, then he'd gone out there to smoke a surreptitious cigar.'

A cigar . . . So that accounted for the exotic perfume!

Valentine looked once more at Jane's set of plans. He prodded the stiff pale-blue sheets of paper with a finger, as though something dangerous was lurking among them. Jane watched him curiously, but said nothing. When he suddenly spoke, what he said was so unexpected that she jumped with alarm.

'Have you shown these plans to Dalton?'

'What?' she faltered.

72

There had been an almost comic belligerence in his voice, as though he were accusing her of something not quite nice.

'What do you mean?'

'Have you ever let Dalton look at these plans of yours?'

'No, of course I haven't. Dr Dalton and I share very similar views about the nurture of youth, but 'youth' in that context means boys. He would not be interested in my peculiar fancies.'

'How do you know that he wouldn't be interested? Have you ever mentioned your idea to him? About a public school for girls, I mean?'

'No.'

Valentine stood up. He crossed to one of the tall windows and looked out across the manicured lawns of the Home Garden. After a few moments he swung round, and fixed her with one of his fierce glances.

'Has this projected school of yours any substance beyond those pretty plans there? Do you know anything about schools?'

She had been educated by governesses, as he well knew. He, of course, had been to public school. To Charterhouse. Why should he seem to be so brutally dismissive? She suddenly realized that he was steeling himself to renounce his old, settled attitude of tolerant amusement, and that he was not finding it easy.

'I know what I would like a school to be,' she replied, 'and I've written down my own views in very great detail. Not just how to conduct such a place, but the necessary theory underlying it. What should be taught to girls. What needs to be taught to girls. The purpose behind the whole project.'

She opened a drawer in the table and took from it a leather-bound note-book.

'All that I have thought and planned about my school is in this book,' she said.

She handed it to him, and watched him flick through the initial pages. Then he sat down at the table, half turning towards the windows to catch the dying sun. He read several more pages attentively, but without betraying any noticeable reaction. Finally he closed the book and, stood up.

'This afternoon,' he said, 'Dalton told me his philosophy of education. I sat there enthralled, listening to a visionary. I thought about that meeting for an hour afterwards and then sent a groom the twelve miles here on horseback with a message.'

'You said you wanted to see me — '

'Yes, and now I'm telling you *why*. Let me show Dalton those plans. And — yes, let me show him that book! Then go to Kingsmere yourself, and *talk* to him. Tell him what you envision, and be bold about it. You may be surprised at his reaction.'

★　★　★

Inspector Jackson and Sergeant Bottomley walked through the village of Kingsmere, which nestled on either side of a wide earth road known as Kenilworth Street. They watched some of the people walking in the same direction along the road. One or two, wearing crepe arm-bands or other signs of mourning, glanced incuriously at them, and then continued to walk in silence up the rutted street.

'So here we are, Sergeant,' said Jackson, 'going to attend Alice Patching's funeral service. And why are we doing this? Because we know she was lured into a poisonous love-tryst with some smooth-talking devil who might just turn up to smirk a little at his handiwork. So keep your wits about you.'

At one end of the street, where the village petered out into the road to Kingsmere School, stood the ancient church of St John, squatting low in its churchyard, almost directly opposite the Wheatsheaf. A single bell was tolling mournfully. Various conveyances were drawn up outside the church. Among them was a handsome carriage, its doors bearing a crest, and with a liveried groom tending the black horse between the shafts.

'Do you recognize that coat-of-arms, Sergeant Bottomley?' asked Jackson. 'A boar's head in a sort of lozenge, and some fancy Latin words in a little scroll. An old friend of ours — though he wouldn't thank me for being so familiar.'

Sergeant Bottomley made a sound halfway between a laugh and a stifled cough.

'So *he's* come, has he?' he muttered as they entered the gloom of the old church. 'Very gracious and thoughtful of him. Very condescending, sir.'

The two detectives sought out an obscure pew in the dark rear of the church. Jackson looked around him. Yes, there was that poor consumptive woman and her husband in the front pew with the lad Noah Baker, and there was poor young Alice Patching coffined in solemn state in the chancel. He saw an elderly clergyman in a black preaching gown hovering near the vestry door, and recognized him as Parson Price, over from Kingston Lucy to take the service.

Jackson turned round to look at the rear of the church, where a very florid carved screen enclosed an old chantry chapel. He smiled.

So that was where His High and Mightiness had hidden himself! Sitting alone away from the common herd.

The service began, and Jackson became attentive. In some twenty minutes' time the solemn words and measured cadences of the rite came to an end, and the congregation followed the mournful procession out into the churchyard.

The committal at the graveside was briefly performed, and then the remains of the young girl were lowered into the earth. The little knot of people who had accompanied the parents to the graveside began to move away. Some spoke briefly to the stricken parents, including the man who had sat apart in the chapel. Jackson saw him remove his silk hat, and stoop a little to speak to the grieving mother.

Mrs Patching curtsied, and her husband said, 'The wife and me are much comforted by seeing you here at our girl's funeral, sir. Thank you most kindly.'

The man whom he had addressed was tall and commanding, dressed very fashionably although in mourning, and it would have been difficult to know who to compliment, his tailor or himself, for the seemingly effortless grace and elegance of his appearance. He was a very handsome man, although his face, through long habit, had been moulded into an expression of extreme hauteur. In his general bearing, he left no one in doubt that he was an aristocrat, and a man accustomed to be obeyed.

As the grieving parents were led away by friends, the gentleman turned on the path, and caught sight of Jackson and Bottomley. His eyebrows rose in an expression of supercilious surprise. Bottomley immediately removed his battered bowler, and treated the haughty man to a sweeping, if slightly unsteady bow. Jackson raised his hat in greeting.

'Sir Hugo Mostyn, sir. I don't suppose you remember me?'

'Why the devil shouldn't I remember you? You did me the favour of rounding up that thieving scum of poachers and plunderers on my land at Shenstone last year. Inspector Jackson from Warwick. Your official position, as you know, precluded my rewarding you, but you had — and have — my thanks.'

Sir Hugo lifted his hat slightly, turned his back on them and walked haughtily out of the churchyard. He was assisted into his elegant carriage by his coachman, and driven away along the village street.

'I never quite knew what to make of that man,' said Jackson. 'He's supposed to be as proud as Lucifer, but he treated the two of us well enough.'

Sergeant Bottomley's eyes narrowed as his gaze followed the carriage.

'Proud he may be, sir, and more than that, if all the stories you hear about him are true. But he was able to spare some of his precious time to come out here today and comfort a couple of humble folk in their grief. It's a long drag out here from Shenstone Old Place. A man of his rank who'll do that, sir, isn't as black as he's painted. Not by a long chalk.'

4

The Night of the Special Dessert

By mid-morning on Wednesday, 7 September, the somnolent rooms and corridors of Kingsmere Abbey School were resounding to the thunderous clamour of many boys assembling for the new school year.

Noel Valentine had gone down to the study after breakfast, and presented Dr Dalton with Jane Ashwood's book and plans. The moment, he recalled wryly, had not been particularly auspicious. He had found Dalton adjusting the red silk hood of his academic dress prior to making a sortie into the school.

'Indeed? For girls, you say? Well, by all means leave them with me, Valentine. I shall be pleased to see what Lady Jane has devised.' There had been a polite but dismissive little smile on his face. So much, then, for poor Jane's vision. At least, it had been worth a try.

Valentine had parted from the headmaster and braved the bustling press in the main corridor. Old Amyas Fletcher appeared from the direction of the entrance hall, seemingly borne along by a shrill-voiced phalanx of younger boys, one of whom was making an involved excuse for some misdeed or other. 'Oh, Wilkin, you rogue!' cried Flodders in a theatrically fierce tone, before disappearing with his clamouring escort of Children into the old Benedictine undercroft from which he ruled his kingdom.

'A noisy business, don't you think?' said a voice near at hand. 'It'll be quite different tomorrow, when teaching-term begins.'

Valentine had been briefly introduced to the speaker on the previous evening. Adrian Fielding-Stenhouse was the head of sciences, a thin, spare man, untidy as an urchin, who had been Dr Dalton's first appointment to the staff. He was clutching a bottle of some liquid or other that seemed to Valentine to have a lethal look to it. He greeted Valentine with a friendly, if rather bemused, smile.

'Come out to my place for a while,' said Fielding-Stenhouse. 'It's quiet there for the moment. Perhaps you'd carry this bottle for me. It's quite safe, you know! It's only sulphuric acid.'

Valentine took the bottle, and cradled it in his arm. His mind was for the moment elsewhere. Was he alone, he wondered, in sensing that Kingsmere Abbey was an institution treading water? There were certainly pockets of activity about the place, but in general there was a feeling of laxity, a lack of focus. He had known battalions like that, quietly falling apart through lack of the right kind of leadership.

Fielding-Stenhouse motioned vaguely to the garden fronting Foliott's Building. 'This, Valentine, is a rather special herb-garden,' he said. 'I'm very interested in the vegetable alkaloids, and in preparing pure samples of them from the plant specimens growing here. I started to take an interest in these 'poisons', as most people would call them, in London, when I attended Bartlam's lectures at King's, and it's gone on from there!'

Leaving the ground floor of Foliott's Building unvisited — it appeared to house a small library and some storerooms — they went upstairs, where there was a good-sized laboratory, with proper benches containing sinks with curved taps above them.

'Just put that bottle of acid down somewhere, Valentine. Anywhere will do.'

Order, Valentine thought, that principle of scientific method, was not much in evidence. The benches were littered with flasks and bottles, some stoppered, some not, all vying for space with open books and sheaves of papers. There were several crates on the floor, disgorging wood-shavings in bulbous growths. Beside one of them Valentine saw an invoice, bearing the imprint of a boot.

Against one wall Valentine noticed a large glazed cupboard, the shelves of which were filled with neatly labelled bottles and phials. These, presumably, contained the fruits of Fielding-Stenhouse's research. It seemed typical of the place that a large card containing printed symbols had been crammed against the cupboard shelves at an unseemly angle, and secured in place by the doors being hastily closed upon it.

'You get a good view from up here,' said the head of science, moving across to a window. 'You see that water over there? That's the Mere, where the boys keep boats. Very popular, as you may imagine.'

'It must be difficult to keep an eye on them — the boys, that is,' said Valentine. 'There seem to be a number of wooded islands there. I should think that boys and boats, unsupervised, could be a hazard.'

'Yes, you're right.'

Fielding-Stenhouse's good-humoured face suddenly turned grave. Without turning round from the window, he said, 'You know, we lost a boy out there in the Mere. About four years ago.'

'Lost him?'

'Yes. Stephen Dacre, his name was. Poor young fellow. He was only thirteen.'

'What happened?'

'Their boat upset, you know. I remember it was young Mostyn — he's one of the Gentlemen now — who made a very valiant effort to save him, and was almost drowned himself. We've been very careful indeed ever since.'

* * *

Valentine took his leave of the head of sciences, and left the school buildings by a side gate which gave on to the pasture land bordering the Mere. He suddenly felt ill at ease. Laxity . . . They had 'lost' a boy, had they? The word suggested that Stephen Dacre was one of a number of chattels. You could lose your hat, or stick, lose a book . . . You could lose any number of things among the chaotic lumber of Fielding-Stenhouse's laboratory.

Why did he feel such foreboding disquiet? It was difficult to pinpoint what was wrong with Kingsmere Abbey. The boys were not consciously neglected, that at least was obvious. 'Neglected' was not the right word; 'disregarded' was perhaps nearer the truth.

Valentine walked along one of several

well-defined tracks leading across the uneven pasture towards the Mere, and came upon the young boy called Wilkin standing in the grass. He was holding a sinuous black cat, which glanced rather balefully at Valentine as he approached. Wilkin, a fair-haired, round-faced young lad, smiled rather nervously at Valentine.

'You're Wilkin, aren't you? I saw you talking to Mr Fletcher earlier on. That's a fine cat you have there! What's his name?'

'Sir, she's a lady cat. She's called Minerva Felicity Augusta.' The young boy added, 'She's Mr Gledhill's cat.'

That explains it, thought Valentine. Only a Classical scholar could have dreamed up such names.

Young Wilkin put Gledhill's cat down on the grass, where she immediately slid away in pursuit of a bird.

'She had a brother, you know,' Wilkin said. 'His name was Augustus.'

'What happened to him?'

'He was a lovely cat, sir. Very charming, he was. He tried to jump across from the hall parapet to the chapel roof. He nearly made it, but not quite.'

'Nemesis,' Valentine said softly.

'No, sir, *Augustus*,' said Wilkin. He explained kindly: 'He was a Roman emperor.'

★ ★ ★

The teaching-term started the next morning with a brief assembly in the School Hall. There was little formality about the occasion. Dr Dalton wished the boys a happy and industrious term, gave them news of Gledhill's convalescence, and briefly introduced Valentine to them. Then the boys dispersed.

The Children and Scholars left the hall first, and then the Gentlemen followed. Valentine watched them progressing in very orderly fashion to the various classes for that day. He saw Fletcher and Mostyn walking side by side, absorbed in earnest conversation. It was a more placidly reassuring scene than that of the previous day.

Just after eleven o'clock he made his first foray into teaching some Greek to Ambrose Gledhill's class of seventeen-year-olds. It very soon became apparent to Valentine that Gerald Mostyn was already an outstanding Greek scholar. The other boys were quick and clever, but they all betrayed a good-humoured resignation to the fact that they would never be in Mostyn's league. It was an auspicious beginning to what Valentine hoped was going to prove a very rewarding experience.

At ten o'clock that night Dr Dalton sat down at his desk, and spread Jane Ashwood's plans out in front of him. He pushed aside some of his own books and papers to make room for them. At his right hand stood a decanter of port and a glass. He had come down to the study mid-morning, intending to spend a dutiful half-hour or so glancing through the Lady Governor's plans and jottings. He had read no more than a few pages when he had found himself held fascinated by what she had written. Now, with the school day finished, he could give his whole attention to Jane Ashwood's note-book.

Why, he wondered, had she never even mentioned this topic to him? She had created a vision of what the future could hold for the education of girls in Warwickshire. She had planned meticulously a great sister school to Kingsmere, to be built on land belonging to her family just a few miles away.

At half past ten he lit the shaded oil-lamp on his desk to assist the dim light of the candles on the mantelpiece, and poured out a glass of wine. He looked once again at the blueprints. There, clearly drawn, were the hall, the chapel, the teaching blocks, the high-walled playing-fields . . . He turned the pages of the notebook, and read further.

Money . . . For her vision to be made reality there would be need of a lot of money. But then, the Ashwoods were rich even by aristocratic standards. She would need advice, a partner equally committed to the enterprise. Who better than himself? For he understood her vision. The idea of it coming to fruition stirred a strange excitement within him, something which he had not felt for years.

He began to make notes, writing rapidly in pencil as ideas of his own tumbled out. He read and worked far into the night, listening to the little clock on the mantelpiece as it struck the passing hours.

Tucked into the back of Jane's note-book he found a letter, with the heading Sandringham House. The Princess of Wales had read with great interest Lady Jane Ashwood's letter. In the event of such a school being established, she would be pleased for it to take the name: The Royal Alexandra School for Girls.

At two o'clock he sighed and stretched himself. He drank his glass of port and got to his feet. Why had she not shared this magnificent dream with him before this? He would get to work at once, but he would have to be very careful and very subtle. Such things could not be achieved without great care and caution.

He walked to the window of his study and looked out at the dim night. Suddenly he made a little sound of annoyance. A naked candle! Did the fool want to burn them all to death? The vision would have to fade for a while. Something urgent needed to be done. He would do it himself.

* * *

Valentine found it impossible to sleep that night. He dozed fitfully until jerked into wakefulness by a sudden noise from the floors beneath him. From somewhere inside Head-master's House the sound of ascending footsteps came to him. Slow and measured, they came upward, and stopped. A door opened, and the stately march continued on its way through the passages of Staff House. Even in his state of sleepy confusion Valentine recognized the inimitable gait of the head-master.

Reaching out in the dark, he took up his watch, and pressed the repeater spring. Three rapid clicks told him that it was between half past two and three o'clock in the morning. What could Dalton be doing at this hour?

He lay in darkness for about ten minutes,

and then rose, crossed to the window, and drew back the curtain. His eye was immediately drawn to a light in Foliott's Building, over to his left. In the upper room which he now knew to be Fielding-Stenhouse's laboratory, a candle was burning, its little light exaggerated into a great glow by pupils opened wide in darkness.

A shifting shadow played around the light as someone passed in front of it. Presently it was extinguished, and the world outside Valentine's windows was plunged into darkness. He lay back on his tumbled bed, blinking at the dull green square of window which still lay on his eyes, and after a few minutes had passed he heard again the majestic tread of the headmaster as he returned from his errand. Again there came a pause at the inner door, and then the sound slowly descended to the lower floors of Headmaster's House.

★　★　★

'Mostyn? Which do you mean, the father or the son?'

'I meant the son, Caswell,' said Valentine. 'He's the only pupil I know well enough to be curious about. He told me that he was good at Latin and Greek. That was an understatement, if ever I heard one: he's quite brilliant!'

Harry Caswell, the school's games master, was in his early thirties, wiry and athletic, but with a deliberately cultivated air of languor that seemed to add to his charm. His face was adorned with luxurious side-whiskers. Valentine had liked him immediately, and the two men had quickly become friends. Caswell had been the last member of the staff to return from the summer vacation. He had only just re-established himself in his set, which was next to that of old Amyas Fletcher.

'Brilliant? So I believe. He's one of Fielding-Stenhouse's sorcerer's apprentices, you know, pottering about in that laboratory of his. Poor old Stenners! He's in trouble this morning.'

'Why, what's he done?'

'He left a candle burning upstairs in Foliott's Building. Dalton found out, and gave him a dressing-down this morning. Stenners denies it, but I don't know . . . He's addle-pated enough for anything!'

The seemingly languid master launched himself from his chair, and fetched a box of cigars. For a moment there was a flurry of matches, and a companionable silence followed.

'So Mostyn wants to read for Orders, you

91

tell me? Well, why not? He's a personable enough young fellow. Tries hard, and all that. Plays a good game of cricket. Not that there's much in that line here. He's not very good in the ring, though. Tends to drop his guard too soon.'

'He does that in fencing, too. I joined in a little practice bout with him before term started. He leaves himself too exposed. But tell me about the father, Caswell. Sir Hugo Mostyn, I mean. I've heard that he has a sinister reputation. Gerald Mostyn seemed rather embarrassed when he spoke of him.'

Caswell smiled. He was sitting well back in an old sagging armchair, nursing a wire fencing-mask in his lap. Two foils lay at the side of his chair.

'It so happens, Valentine, that I know Sir Hugo Mostyn quite well. He's a patron of the boxing fraternity in these parts, and I'm quite a well-known amateur of the ring. I have an immense liking for him. He's trying to live up to a reputation that I suspect others have manufactured for him. That supercilious attitude he assumes cuts no ice with me. He's simply hiding behind a mask.'

'A mask . . . ' Valentine seemed struck by Caswell's choice of word.

'Yes. Sir Hugo's a true aristocrat of the old school. Some people don't like him, but that's because they can't read him. But *I* can. I can't read his son Gerald, though. Deep waters there, if you ask me.'

'Gerald has a brother, I'm told?'

'He's got an elder brother at Eton. Another Hugo. Now he's a nice, big, blundering sort of lad. I've met him at boxing bouts. He occasionally boxes for one of the Eton clubs.'

Valentine looked round his host's crowded room. What odd things people collected! In a glazed cabinet near the fireplace were arrayed a set of white ivory dice, and a pack of well-thumbed linen-backed playing cards tied with string. There were also a number of Indian brasses and a set of wooden cups of simple design. Beside these sat demurely an ebony inlaid figure of what Valentine took to be a Hindu deity.

'That's Vishnu,' said Caswell, following Valentine's gaze. 'The preserver of men and women. He's a good omen, and that's a very rare image. Those cups are Indian loving-cups from Bengal. Very simply carved but highly polished. Pear wood, they are.'

'You have connections with India?'

'I was born there. In Hyderabad. My father was in the service of the Nizam.'

Valentine suddenly remembered the events of his restless night.

'I heard him, you know,' Valentine said.

'Dalton I mean. It was in the small hours, around three o'clock. I looked out of the window, and saw what must have been his shadow moving about. Then the candle went out. So there *was* a candle lit, you see.'

'Well then,' said Caswell, flinging his cigar butt in the fire and standing up, 'maybe Fielding-Stenhouse's memory is defective. Or maybe Dalton's seeing things — spots before the eyes, you know!'

It was a dismissive answer, thought Valentine, but it wasn't true. There *had* been a candle burning, and Dalton had extinguished it. Perhaps Fielding-Stenhouse had reasons of his own for protesting his innocence.

⋆ ⋆ ⋆

During term time the staff of Kingsmere Abbey School dined with the boys in the School Hall. However, on the evening of the first Saturday after the start of each term a celebratory dinner was held in the private dining-room of Staff House. A traditional feature of these dinners was the 'Special Dessert', a generous selection of various kinds of fresh and candied fruit, and a festive array of different ports and brandies laid ready in the Combination Room, and the adjoining drawing-room, which was tacitly reserved for senior members of the staff.

By nine o'clock on the evening of 10 September the occupants of the drawing-room were conscious of an air of general well-being. Mr Holland's consignment of port and brandy had been found to be excellent, and showed no signs of giving out. The shaded oil-lamps shed their mellow light upon the room, and all was well.

The vice-master was there, and old Fletcher, who waved a hand cheerily at Valentine before depositing himself in what was evidently a favourite chair. Fielding-Stenhouse seemed to have recovered his composure and was talking animatedly to Sheffield about the respective merits of Greek and Botany. The general conversation was half bantering, half serious. Valentine was content to watch and listen.

'Now, Fletcher, dear old chap,' said Caswell, who was lying rather than sitting in his chair, and holding up a glass of port to the lamp near him, 'with respect to this port, do you think the Duke of Cambridge would have approved?'

'Ah! Dear old Adolphus Frederick,' sighed Flodders, 'rest his soul! We'll not see his like again! No, Caswell, His Royal Highness would *not* have approved, because although

95

very good to us now, this port would have been raw and youthful then. The duke was a connoisseur of everything, including men. He would very soon have seen through *you*, Harry!'

There was a murmur of laughter, in which both Fletcher and Caswell joined, and the latter inclined himself towards Valentine, who was sitting near him, and said, still in his bantering tone, 'Flodders, you know, Valentine, is a left-over from the Regency, and bases his social behaviour on that of His late Royal Highness the Duke of Cambridge. It was he who advised him to crown his dinner with good port, but always, on retiring, to drink down a glass of whisky and tomato sauce.'

'You fool, Harry,' the old man chuckled, pulling himself upright in his chair, and peering at the younger man through his pince-nez.

'Valentine, this, as I think you know, is Harry Caswell, an insolent puppy. Beware of him. He instructs the boys in the manly arts of boxing, and single-stick, and fencing, and such-like. It was not the duke, but a former physician to the Prince Regent who advised me to take, every night, a glass of gin and bitters, and I have done so from that day to this.'

'Why gin and bitters in particular?' asked Sheffield.

'Both ingredients banish the noxious fumes of fortified wines, settle the stomach, and steel the nerves for the next day's doings. At this very moment a glass of that elixir stands upon my bedside table, and in an hour's time I shall 'knock it back', as the saying is nowadays.'

' 'Knock it back?' ' said Fielding-Stenhouse vaguely. 'Extraordinary!'

'That's why you've lasted so long, Fletcher,' said the vice-master. 'That gin of yours acts as a lingering pickle!'

Again there was a ripple of laughter, and a general movement towards the decanters. Fletcher remained in his chair near the fireplace, but Caswell came across and deposited a glass of port at his elbow. Valentine noticed the look of grave affection that the 'insolent puppy' gave to the old man as he did so.

'I wonder whether this year the headmaster will look in on us before we end the proceedings?' said Sheffield.

Granger laughed, and it was not a pleasant sound.

'The headmaster? Oh, dear me, no, no . . . There's a sort of alcoholic levity about this gathering that would hardly appeal to Dr

Dalton's sense of rectitude and decorum.'

There was a sudden silence. Most of those present had never before heard the vice-master offer a public criticism of the head, and certainly not one that bordered so nearly on ridicule. Fortunately the silence did not last long, as it was broken by Fletcher, who seemed not to have noticed the effect of Granger's sarcasm.

'Rectitude?' he grumbled. 'Oh, bother rectitude. Bother decorum too, for that matter. You know, Valentine, there's far too much rectitude about, these days. No one cares a hang for the inner man as long as the outer man conforms to the rules. It was different in my young days. We were coarser, I expect, but we were honest, too. It's not like that now.'

He turned in his chair and looked speculatively at Valentine.

'Valentine, dear fellow, watch out for rectitude! Years and years ago we had a man here called Boyden. Now, *he* was full of rectitude! Well, do you know, he had not one, but two — er, ladies, in different parts of the country, each suckling a little indiscretion. I found that out by poking and prying. Oh, dear! Beware of too much rectitude, my dear Valentine, it can lead one down strange paths.'

'I told you he was a Regency buck!' cried Caswell.

'Be quiet, Harry,' said the old man, and there was something in his tone that caused the younger man to look curiously at him. Valentine caught the tone too, and listened to Fletcher with renewed care. He was already wondering why Fletcher had chosen him in particular as his audience.

'Now, Valentine, you saw me having a verbal tussle with little Wilkin the other day. That child has led me a rare dance since he came to Kingsmere. He and I are locked in a deadly battle of wits, the old man and the young sprig — I don't know who'll win, I'm sure.'

'But you like him, don't you?' said Caswell.

'Of course I like him. He's as straight as a die, is my Wilkin. No false rectitude for him! I used to teach in Upper School many years ago, Valentine, but I found the sophistication, the growing awareness of deceit — oh, you know what these young fellows grow to be . . . or, at least, I hope you do. Boyden, now: no doubt he went in for rectitude as a youth, and ended up with two ladies! I'm quite sure there are some budding Boydens in Upper School. No, let me alone with my naughty sprigs. There's no guile in them.'

'What happened to Boyden?' asked Caswell.

'Happened to him? Nothing happened to him. He moved from here to a school in the north somewhere, and eventually became its headmaster, so I hear. I never said anything!'

The old man chuckled, and looked quizzically at Caswell.

''Pon my word,' replied the young man, in the easy drawl that he affected, 'it would seem that the way to get ahead in this profession is to have some ladies. Do you realize that at the present time not a single member of the staff here is married? What's to become of us?'

Flodders began to lever himself out of his chair. 'You're right, Harry, you're right. We're a lot of old maids! At least — Well, it's nearly eleven o'clock, and time for me to seek repose. Good night to you all!'

At the words 'at least' Valentine saw Granger give Flodders a sudden startled look. Whatever those words meant, they had special significance for him.

Valentine was intrigued. He saw that as Fletcher moved towards the door, Granger leapt up to open it for him, then slipped out before him into the passage. From where he sat, Valentine knew that he could not help but hear what the two men were saying to each other out in the corridor.

'Come, now, Fletcher,' said Granger in a low but intense voice, 'what do you know about this?'

Valentine saw how old Fletcher stiffened and drew in his breath with vexation. Almost immediately, though, he gave his familiar impish chuckle.

'Oh, dear! *In vino veritas*. I said just a little more than was wise tonight, and I shall give my gin and bitters a miss when I retire.'

He took Granger by the sleeve and drew him further away along the passage. Valentine could just hear his parting words.

'I'll tell you this, Granger: I know as much as you evidently do, and probably more. It's a delicate matter, to say the least. This recent business has made it more beastly than I thought.'

'Do you intend to do anything?'

'I'm not sure . . . I've told him that the game's up, you know, but that's all I've done. I should do more, because I think it's a damnable thing. Maybe advanced years are turning me soft . . . Look here, I'll make you a promise: when I decide to act, I'll tell you first. But I'm not yet quite sure what to do. Good night.'

Valentine walked slowly from the drawing-room and upstairs to his set. Beneath the seemingly smooth running of the school there was an uneasy undercurrent flowing. There was something gravely amiss that both Granger and Fletcher knew about, but which some undefined code of silence had turned into a secret. Perhaps it was no business of his. But whatever that secret was, Valentine mused, Amyas Fletcher had told someone that the game was up.

* * *

After half an hour, quiet descended upon Staff House, but not all in the school were at rest. In the headmaster's study Dr Dalton sat behind his desk, some scattered papers lying unread in front of him. His face was suffused with an angry flush, and he had clasped his hands so tightly that the knuckles showed white. Suddenly he spoke aloud, and his tone was low and menacing.

'No, it was not possible that I should endure it. After all I have done for education in this country, am I to be destroyed by this pestilence walking in the darkness? No! This very night will see the end of it!'

* * *

Noel Valentine slept soundly and dreamlessly that night. He was awoken by someone shaking his shoulder, and calling urgently, 'Valentine, Valentine! Wake up!'

He sprang up in his bed and saw the white face of Sandford bending over him.

'What is it, man? What's happened?'

'It's Fletcher. I've just found him . . . Whenever there's been a festivity like last night's Special Dessert either myself or Caswell looks in to wake Fletcher up. Caswell and I are early risers.'

A spasm of pain crossed Sandford's face.

'I went in this morning, and saw him lying with his face buried in the pillow. Valentine, he's dead!'

5

A Lesson in Logic

Valentine accompanied Sandford as though he were in a dream. Valentine had liked the impish Master of the Children. He felt cheated and affronted by his death.

They entered the sitting-room of Flodders' set, which was further along the passage from the Combination Room. It was quite elegantly furnished with old-fashioned Georgian furniture. The bedroom curtains were still drawn, so that the light was very dim, but Valentine could see the contorted, still figure lying face downward on the bed. Only the shock of white hair was visible above the crumpled bedding. He did not venture in, but instead turned to Sandford and said, 'You are quite sure that he is dead?'

'Oh, yes. I felt his hand. It was as cold as ice. Valentine, it's unbelievable! In one sense Flodders *was* Kingsmere School. I can't envisage the place without him.'

Valentine turned to look at the ashen-faced Sandford. It was time, he thought, to make this diffident man *do* something.

'What do you propose to do now?' Valentine asked.

'I'm going to find Granger. I've already sent for Dr Manning. Granger, not I, must inform the headmaster. I woke you up because I wanted someone to remain on guard here. In case . . . In case anyone just wanders in, you know. It doesn't seem right to leave poor Fletcher alone.'

Sandford hurriedly left the room. Valentine mused wryly on his preoccupation with the hierarchies of school life. Somehow, it seemed a stifling parody of military rank and precedence.

He glanced once more into the bedroom, and noticed the gleam of gold reflected from the old man's pince-nez and watch on the bedside table. He saw that it was just after seven o'clock. How loudly Fletcher's watch ticked! It was the only sign of life in that darkened room.

Hushed voices on the landing signalled the return of Sandford with the vice-master. Granger looked profoundly shocked, and like the other two he merely glanced at the inert figure in the inner room.

'This is a terrible business, gentlemen,' he said, 'terrible! Poor old Fletcher. What a sad termination to a career of fifty years! His heart, I expect. I'll fetch Dr Dalton immediately.'

Sandford felt for a chair and sat down near the door of the bedroom. Valentine looked at an array of oval portraits in faded gilt frames fixed above the fireplace. Perhaps they had been relatives of Fletcher's, painted in the days before photography. Below them, on the mantelpiece, were two delicate blue glass candle-sticks with opened letters stuck behind them in bundles. An enamel trinket-box with a mirrored lid held a number of gold dress studs. Yesterday, all these things had had an owner . . .

'You're used to death, aren't you Valentine?' Sandford's quiet voice summoned him back to the present situation.

'What? Yes, Sandford, I am. But deaths in battle are not quite like this. The man your sabre cuts down has no known history to you. But here — in this room — we can glimpse something of a man who was our intimate friend. Fletcher was part of our own lives, in a way.'

' 'Any man's death diminishes me',' said Sandford half to himself, ' 'because I am involved in Mankind. And therefore never send to know for whom the bell tolls; it tolls for thee'.'

Before Valentine could ask the source of

Sandford's quotation, Granger returned with Dr Dalton. The headmaster looked pale and tired. There were black shadows beneath his eyes, as though he had not slept. His face was grave, but he was clearly in full command of himself. When he spoke, his voice had a quiet, calming effect.

'This is a sad business, gentlemen. Kingsmere will not be the same without Fletcher. And yet, perhaps, it is what he would have preferred: to die in the midst of work at so great an age.'

He passed into the bedroom, and they saw him stoop over the inert figure and gently move the head . . .

The cry that Dalton uttered was so unexpected that the three men staggered with the shock. Valentine, though no stranger to terrible sights and sounds, felt the hairs on the back of his neck bristle. Ashen-faced and trembling, Dr Dalton all but staggered from the bedroom, clutching at the door-posts to save himself from collapse.

'Gentlemen,' he gasped, 'I have had a most terrible shock. I did not think . . . Granger . . . You must — '

Dalton, now beyond words, and ashen grey, groped his way blindly towards the door. Sandford quite suddenly regained a sense of purpose. Effectively ignoring

Granger and the niceties of rank, he placed a supporting arm around the trembling headmaster's shoulders and led him gently from the room.

* * *

'So poor Amyas Fletcher has died,' said Dr Manning. 'Well, well! I've known him for more years than I care to remember. Gentlemen, would you care to show me where he is?'

Some time had elapsed since the stricken Dalton had been led from the room. Sandford had returned, but had seemed subdued, and disinclined to talk about the headmaster. An unbearable silence had been broken for the three men by the arrival of old Dr Manning from the village.

Manning passed in to the bedroom. Valentine watched him through the open door. The doctor went through the formal procedures of establishing that the man lying before him was indeed dead. But then he suddenly stiffened and paused, before leaning forward and peering intently into the dead man's face.

Eventually Manning stood upright, and began to look about him. He was searching for something. He went down carefully on his knees and felt under the bed. Slowly he stood erect, holding in his right hand an empty brandy glass.

When he came back into the sitting-room, he brought with him a palpable change of attitude, an almost physical emanation of wary suspicion.

'Gentlemen,' he said, 'I'm not satisfied. This is not a natural death. I shall make arrangements to take away the body for examination, and until I have returned, the door of this set must be locked, and the key retained by someone who is not present at this moment.'

'Not natural?' Granger's voice was suddenly sharp, and held an edge of imperiousness. 'What do you mean?'

'He was poisoned. I shall take this glass with me. It will be subjected to forensic inspection. The coroner, too, will have to be informed.'

Sandford, who had been repeating the word 'poisoned' to himself as though to determine its meaning, suddenly put into words the dreaded thought that was in the minds of his companions.

'Do you mean to say that he was murdered?'

'Well, Mr Sandford, since you use the word, yes: he was murdered. I find the situation quite remarkable. I know you all so well, at least, you and Mr Granger here. And Captain Valentine there is a national figure. But I can't fathom what you are all up to. What is this devil's game that you are playing?'

'Game?' exclaimed Granger, springing up from his chair. 'What do you mean? Are you accusing us of murdering him? Accusing Mr Sandford, and me, and Captain Noel Valentine, the Victor of Tel-el-Kebir?'

'I accuse nobody, Mr Granger. But what am I to think when you send me into a darkened room to examine a dead body, hoping that I'll be sufficiently senile at seventy not to notice who I'm examining?'

The old doctor blushed with anger.

'Did you think for one moment that I would not be suspicious? In that half light I *was* deceived for a time, and you almost got away with it! Now tell me, tell me: *who is that poor man in there?*'

★ ★ ★

Theodore Granger threw back the heavy curtains from the window, so that the rising light of morning fell clear upon the corpse. It was easy to see now that it was not Fletcher. There was the same shock of white hair, but

110

the man was younger by at least ten years. The hands were coarse, with cracked, discoloured fingernails. The features, bloated and swollen-veined, were those of a chronic drunkard.

The man lay in Fletcher's bed, undressed and clad in a nightgown, with Fletcher's watch and pince-nez beside him on the table. His body showed no signs of violence, but even to the layman the contorted figure, and the frozen, agonized face, spoke of death by poison.

Granger's calm, authoritative voice broke the silence.

'Dr Manning,' he said, 'I agree that the matter seems very odd and suspicious. But I can assure you that none of us thought for one moment that it was not Fletcher who had died. We none of us saw the . . . the man's face. This is Fletcher's bedroom. We naturally assumed that the body was poor Fletcher's.'

The old doctor sighed and nodded his agreement. His moment of baffled anger had passed. Of course they'd assume it was Fletcher. What else could they have thought? It was not his trade to solve mysteries.

'You're right, Granger, and you have my apologies, for what they're worth. This is the second unnatural death I've been called to within the week. I think the Angel of Death must be passing over Kingsmere.'

'What was the other unnatural death?' Sandford whispered.

'A girl who committed suicide. A peasant girl.'

'It may well be so about the angel,' said Granger, 'but it's not our business to speculate about that. Now, this man is dead, and there is nothing that we can do for him. My concern as vice-master must be with the living. What has happened to Fletcher? Where is he?'

'A mystery indeed, Granger, and one which you must solve without my help! I must go to Warwick immediately, and inform the coroner and the police. I should think it very likely that Inspector Jackson will come later this morning to ask some questions. Meanwhile, I'll make immediate arrangements for the body to be removed. Someone other than yourselves, gentlemen, as I have told you, must lock this room and secure the key. There is nothing personal in that: it is the necessary protocol.'

★ ★ ★

Harry Caswell came out of Fletcher's set and slowly turned the key in the lock of the outer door. When he had done so he placed the key in one of the pockets of his coat.

'There you are, Vice-master,' he said. 'The key stays with me until Dr Manning or a policeman asks for it.'

Granger had waited until the doctor had gone downstairs with Sandford and Valentine before telling Caswell to secure Fletcher's set. The young games master had appeared in the corridor as Manning was leaving, and Granger had briefly explained matters to him.

'Vice-master,' he said, 'if you will give me your permission, I'll start an immediate search of the school to see if Fletcher is on the premises. I can't imagine what has happened to him, and time is of the essence.'

'An excellent idea, Caswell. Take a few of the others with you and spend all day on the search if necessary. It's nearly half past eight. Sunday chapel is at ten. Between now and then I'll concoct some kind of plausible tale to satisfy the boys' curiosity. Well done, Caswell. Start your search at once.'

★ ★ ★

The school chapel, a massive, airy building designed in the seventeenth century with some idea of imitating a Roman temple, rose behind the ruins of the Benedictine abbey which formed Fletcher's kingdom.

The chapel bell began to summon the school to Sunday service at a quarter to ten. Throngs of boys appeared from all directions, the younger ones led by masters in full academic dress. An ear attuned to boys' whispered conversations would have heard the words: 'Something's happened!' going from group to group.

Once inside the building, the staff assembled in their special stalls at the east end of the chapel. The pupils took their seats in tall box-pews, both on the ground floor and in three large galleries that stood on slender iron pillars. It took a thunderous few minutes for the boys to reach their appointed places and settle down into silence. Then Granger left his stall and stood on the marble steps in front of the sanctuary. The action itself was so unusual that the boys stirred a little before giving the proceedings, for once, their undivided attention.

'Gentlemen, Scholars and Children,' said Granger, 'before I ask our visiting clergyman to begin today's service there are some things that I wish you to know. Last night, a gentleman who was staying in Staff House very sadly died.'

He paused until the stir and murmur had subsided, and then continued.

'During the course of this morning they

114

will come to take away the body of this unfortunate gentleman, and as it is not quite clear how he died, a member of the detective police will visit the school.'

Another excited murmur greeted this remark, and once again Granger waited without comment until it subsided.

'I need hardly say that the headmaster will be fully occupied with this matter for the whole of today, and possibly for part of the coming week. On no account, therefore, is he to be disturbed.

'One further item,' Granger concluded. 'Mr Fletcher is indisposed, and I should think he will be confined to Staff House for the rest of the week. For the duration of his absence, the Children will be supervised by the Deputy Master, Mr Parry Davies. I will now ask the Reverend Mr Palfrey to begin the morning service.'

Granger returned calmly to his stall, and the service began. Prayer, and psalm, lesson and canticle, the timeless Office of the Church of England unfolded its peculiar glories, but on this Sunday it was a maimed offering. Hardly a mind was intent on what was said or sung, and words were mouthed as minds dwelt elsewhere. Many were puzzled and anxious, some were awed by the solemn thought of death in their midst. One mind

115

and soul was dangerously consumed with the terror of guilt.

* * *

While the school was listening to Granger's address, Mr Lascelles, the local undertaker from Kenilworth, accompanied by his assistant, arrived at the school in their closed van to remove the body. Another draft vehicle arrived at the same time to collect a trunk. Thus the grim errand of the men in the closed van was shielded to some extent by the presence of the second vehicle.

Harry Caswell had been deputed by Granger to receive Mr Lascelles and his man in the entrance hall. They had brought a coffin with them, which they manoeuvred skilfully up the stairs to the first floor of Staff House, where Caswell unlocked the door of Fletcher's set. Presently the men emerged, carrying their burden, which they had decorously swathed with a pall. Caswell carefully locked the outer door, and conducted the two men down again through the deserted staff quarters. They hurried out to their van, placed the coffin inside, and moved slowly away down the drive. Not a word had been spoken.

By midday, Harry Caswell and the three

members of staff who had offered to assist him had finished their search for Fletcher. They had entered every room in the school, looked into every large cupboard and chest, explored the attics, and ranged with lighted lamps through the vast cellarage. Their labours had been fruitless. As far as was humanly possible to ascertain, Fletcher, alive or dead, was not in the school buildings.

★ ★ ★

Inspector Jackson slackened the reins for a moment to allow the two black horses pulling the olive-green police van to pass between the tall brick gate pillars. The heavy, iron-tyred vehicle rumbled over a rattling cattle-grid and on to the entrance drive of Kingsmere Abbey School.

'It's long years, sir,' said Bottomley, who was sitting beside him on the box, 'since I crossed the threshold of a school. I never liked these places. I was glad to get out of mine.'

The iron gates, Jackson thought, could do with a lick of fresh paint. The blackthorn hedges needed to be cut back. There were damp, rutted depressions in the shale path. It needed to be raked.

'I expect they were glad to see the back of

117

you, too,' Jackson replied. 'You've been a sore trial to me these many years, Sergeant, as you know. You must have been a little demon when you were at school.'

Jackson thought wryly of his own school-days at the parish school, and of Mr Jardine, the master, with his ugly face and beautiful copperplate writing. He wasn't all that keen on schools himself.

In a few minutes they rounded a small coppice and came in view of the school buildings, which provided them with intriguing glimpses of towers and turrets, and of other buildings just out of sight. There was a curious stillness and expectancy in the air.

Jackson brought the horses to a halt and applied the creaking brake of the heavy van. He glanced briefly at the school lawns. To a countryman's eyes they seemed on the verge of reverting to pasture.

The two detectives climbed down from the roof of the van. At the same time, the rear door was opened, and two young men in plain clothes stepped out on to the drive. One of them handed Bottomley a canvas bag with a leather handle. They were both in their late twenties, one clean-shaven, the other sporting the beginnings of a close black beard.

'Now, you both know what I want you to do,' said Jackson, 'so go and do it. If anyone asks you questions, be polite, but don't answer. Show your warrants, if you have to. That'll guarantee that no one will try to obstruct you. Off you go.'

Bottomley suddenly cleared his throat and touched Jackson's arm. Two men had emerged from the front entrance of the school to receive them.

'Watch out, sir,' Bottomley whispered. 'Here's a couple of the gaffers coming down the steps.'

Jackson looked at the two men who stood stiffly in front of the entrance. One was a commanding figure, over six feet tall, and dressed in a smart frock coat. He looked as though he was relishing the chance to be in charge. His companion was a faded kind of man with a scarred brow, the type of man, thought Jackson, designed by nature to be led rather than to lead. Even from where he stood Jackson could read the almost angry disapproval of the situation in the man's face.

'Detective Inspector Jackson?' said the powerful man. 'This is an unfortunate business. My name is Granger: I'm the vice-master of Kingsmere. This gentleman beside me is Mr Percy Sandford, my . . . my valued colleague. The headmaster is a little unwell as a result of this affair, but will join us later. Come into the school.'

Braving Granger's barrage of words they followed him up the steps into the spacious entrance-hall. Jackson's glance took in a wide, uncarpeted Jacobean staircase, to the right of which was a range of glazed cupboards containing various trophies. In front of them stood a long mahogany table. From the ceiling was suspended a rather forbidding iron corona holding a ring of oil lamps, each with its own polished metal reflector.

Granger was still speaking.

'Naturally, Inspector, you'll want to see the room where . . . where it happened. If you are ready, I'll take you along there straight away. The keys of the room are being held by a colleague, Mr Caswell — '

Jackson raised a hand as though to ward off any further suggestions. He smiled, in spite of himself. This, presumably, was the Mr Granger who was not above drinking a glass of best ale in Mr Holland's back parlour at the Wheatsheaf three times a year.

'Mr Granger,' said Jackson, 'let me make my intended course of action clear to you. It will save unnecessary words if I'm allowed to ask the questions — which I'll do when the time comes. For the moment, I'd like your Mr Caswell to surrender to me the keys of the room where the deceased person was found. Then, if possible, I'd like you to provide me with a little room somewhere, where I and my sergeant here — Detective Sergeant Bottomley — can confer. A bolt-hole, so to speak. Any little room will do.'

Granger, he noted, had become suitably subdued. He was, as Jackson had quickly appreciated, a man who understood the nature of authority, and when it was to be exercised.

'Well, Mr Jackson, I can offer you a kind of store-room here behind the stairs. It's not very commodious, but it should suit your purposes. I'll bring you the key.'

'That will do admirably, Mr Granger. Now, at two o'clock this afternoon I'd like to see those gentlemen who were present at the discovery of the body. Dr Manning told me their names: yourself, Mr Sandford here, Captain Noel Valentine, and the headmaster. It would be as well if Mr Caswell were to be present also. Can that be done?'

'Certainly, Inspector. And will I find you here at two o'clock?'

Jackson smiled. He had not realized that clever men could show such naïvety.

'No, indeed, sir. I may be anywhere — once I've been given those keys, that is. But when I need to consult you, sir, you may rest assured that I'll find you!'

'Well, now, gentlemen,' said Inspector Jackson, 'it seems that you have presented me with two mysteries here, a suspicious death, and a mysterious disappearance. It may be that the two are related, but then again it may be that they are not.'

He looked round at the group of masters who had assembled in the study of the headmaster's house just after two o'clock. To his right he sensed, rather than saw, the figure of Dr Dalton, who, when Jackson had shaken hands with him, had looked to him fearfully ill and hollow-eyed, but fully in command of himself. He sat in a big winged armchair near the fireplace, having surrendered his desk to Jackson.

'Now, I have asked you here today because you are all, in one way or another, witnesses, with first-hand knowledge of what occurred this morning. Later in the day, and maybe on other occasions too, I shall want to ask you each some questions in private.'

He stopped and smiled at them. Sandford, the man with the scarred forehead who had seemed personally affronted by the whole business, smiled back. He probably didn't realize why he was doing so.

Jackson fished in his coat pocket for a fat

note-book tied up with tape, which he carefully opened, and laid on the desk.

'To start with, though, gentlemen, I'd like to ask you some general questions, so that you can all hear each other's answers, in a manner of speaking. First, now, did any of you gentlemen recognize the man you found dead in bed?'

There was a murmur of noes, and Jackson wrote something in his book. He pushed it across the table towards Sergeant Bottomley, who sat upright on a chair at the desk, and the assembled masters saw the red-faced sergeant smile and shake his head.

'I see. And now for my second question: who do you think he might have been?'

'Oh, but see here, Jackson,' said Granger rather testily, 'we have just said that we did not recognize him, so how can we say who he was?'

That, thought Jackson, was probably a typical outburst from Mr Theodore Granger, Vice-master. Evidently he was regaining his sense of command.

'Very good, Mr Granger, sir!' Jackson replied good-humouredly. 'Very good. Well, sir, perhaps if I said *what* do you think he was?'

'A vagrant, I think, a tramp, or someone of that sort?'

'Or a burglar,' offered Sandford.

Sergeant Bottomley uttered a kind of strangled hoot of mirth which he turned into a respectable imitation of a cough. Jackson saw Captain Noel Valentine, the Victor of Tel-el-Kebir, look up sharply. The captain's lips silently formed the words: 'Good God!' What, thought Jackson, did *that* mean? Valentine had evidently been overcome with a sudden revelation.

'Yes, I see,' Jackson continued. 'A tramp or a burglar. There are difficulties there, though, gentlemen, as I'm sure you'll see, presently. Dr Manning tells me that your tramp or burglar was poisoned. Maybe he did it himself, maybe someone else did it to him. Do tramps and burglars break in to schools to put on night-gowns and poison themselves? Well, I shouldn't think so, you know.'

Were they taking him seriously now? Yes. Their attention to his words seemed to be total. He continued.

'But if there *are* some tramps and burglars who break in to schools to poison themselves, they'd have to bring their own poison with them.'

'I don't see why,' drawled Caswell. 'There are plenty of poisons here in the school.'

'Oh yes, indeed, sir,' said Jackson, beaming at Caswell, 'I know there are poisons here,

124

and I shall have quite a lot to say to a lot of people about that later on. But you see, your suicidal tramp wouldn't know that there were any poisons here, would he, sir? So your tramp was almost certainly poisoned by someone else. Or murdered, as they say.'

He sat back in Dr Dalton's chair, and surveyed his audience with what he hoped looked like genuine benevolence. He watched the grim shadow of the word 'murder' fall across their faces.

'And then again, that suggests that whoever did it — poisoned the man I mean — *did* know that there were poisons to be had here, and how to get at them. And so, we come back to the puzzling question.'

He stopped, and began to write a note in his book.

'What puzzling question is that?' asked Granger.

'Hey? Oh! Well, the question is, who wants to poison a tramp? Very often people tackle burglars and vagrants and so on, but usually with a weapon, or fists, you know. They never poison them. Imagine it!'

He would leave them to digest that idea. Whoever the man was, he must have been known to somebody in the school, and that 'somebody' had murdered him . . .

'And now, gentlemen, we come to the

second mystery, the disappearance of Mr Fletcher. And here's my last question for you all: where is he?'

This time, Jackson noted, nobody ventured an easy reply. He could sense their growing respect for his abilities. They were apprehensive about what he might say next.

'Well, it would seem that Mr Fletcher has gone away. Why should he do that? Some people, you know, go away from places because they have committed a crime. A murderer usually flees the scene of his crime.'

Suddenly Dr Dalton spoke. His voice was strained and weary, but still firm.

'Oh, come, now, Inspector, that is plainly ridiculous. I admire your ingenious logic, but the very idea of old Mr Fletcher murdering this unknown man and then fleeing into the night, is merely grotesque.'

'Of course, sir, of course it is!' Jackson replied. 'We'll leave that idea for the moment. I was very pleased to hear that some of you had searched the building thoroughly in an attempt to find Mr Fletcher. Very commendable, if I may say so.'

He suddenly smiled, and it was a secret smile to himself.

'Now, I have brought two bloodhounds with me — '

'Bloodhounds?'

'Yes, Mr Granger. Not dogs, you know, but the human variety. It was they who were able to inform me that there are potentially lethal poisons on the premises. In a beautiful red-brick building in the garden, so they told me.'

'Foliott's Building,' said Granger. 'It's a chemical laboratory, duly registered with the authorities.'

Jackson smiled. He thought of Mr Holland of the Wheatsheaf and his fire certificate.

'Indeed, sir? Those two officers of mine are also very good at searching, and that's what they're doing now. It's easier for them, you see: they don't waste time looking for everything, they just go looking for what they know they'll find.'

Jackson closed his note-book and stood up. He could sense the relief from his audience as he did so.

'Thank you, gentlemen,' he said, 'for all your patience. I shall be with you for a week, I expect, or longer, if things turn out more complex than I've anticipated, and various other police officers may appear from time to time. I shall have a great number of questions to ask. It will smooth all our paths if I'm given true and honest answers.'

6

Fruits of the Borgia Garden

'Bottomley! You scoundrel! I *thought* it was you! When I heard that strangled cough of yours just now I was quite certain!'

Jackson and Bottomley had just regained the entrance-hall of the school when they were stopped in their tracks by the hearty tones of Captain Valentine. They turned round to see the renowned soldier-scholar blushing in embarrassment.

'It is you, isn't it, Bottomley?' he asked, in quieter tones. 'I'm sorry to have greeted you so roughly. Even as I did so I remembered that time passes, and people progress to different spheres. But it's not every day that I see an old comrade-in-arms from Egyptian days.'

Sergeant Bottomley attempted to stand to attention, thought better of it, and offered Valentine a clumsy bow. So that was why Valentine had reacted as he did in the headmaster's study! He and Bottomley had served in the wars together. Jackson noted that his sergeant was secretly delighted to have been recognized.

'Captain Valentine,' said Jackson, 'I recognized you, sir, because, of course, your engraving was often in the public prints. But I didn't realize that you knew my sergeant.'

They had reached the dim passage behind the Jacobean staircase, where a glass-panelled door opened into the small room Granger had given them as a sanctum. It smelt musty and dry, and what light there was filtered through a narrow slit of a window high on one wall. Most of the tank-like place was occupied by a plain scrubbed table, upon which was heaped what appeared to Valentine to be a bundle of old clothes.

'So this is your company office, is it?' said Valentine, looking in. 'I'm sorry, Mr Jackson, if I appear to have inflicted myself upon you in this way. But when I saw Sergeant Bottomley, as large as life after all these years, I simply had to renew our acquaintance.'

Jackson looked thoughtfully at Captain Valentine, and liked what he saw. His eyes twinkled, and he motioned the famous soldier to enter the little room.

'And he was a scoundrel, sir, was he? In Egypt, I mean,' he asked he closed the door.

Valentine blushed again, and then laughed.

'Well, let us say that in dire and dangerous situations, Bottomley could procure the unprocurable. He could produce anything — food, drink, tea (which I don't class as drink), kettles . . . Couldn't you, Sergeant?'

Bottomley smiled and mumbled something not very distinct. He began to unbuckle the straps of the canvas bag which he had brought with him that morning. Jackson wondered whether Valentine would realize that Bottomley's simple action was a signal that further reminiscences in front of his present superior officer would be unwelcome.

'Captain Valentine,' said Jackson, 'now that we've established a sort of link, if I may put it like that, I think, sir, that you could be of positive help to me.'

'In what way, Inspector?'

'Well, sir, I know for a fact that you have only very recently arrived at Kingsmere School. You're an outsider, here, if I may put it like that, which means that you've not had time to forge close links with long-standing members of the staff. So I'm going to ask you to come with me to Mr Fletcher's room and answer some specific questions there.'

While he was talking, Bottomley had opened the canvas bag, and had taken from it the empty Madeira bottle and the pear-wood cup. He had placed them almost ritually upon the table. Jackson looked keenly in his direction. What was Bottomley up to?

Whatever it was, it had clearly interested Valentine. Jackson had heard the soldier draw in his breath sharply.

'That cup, Sergeant — does it have any bearing on this case?'

Bottomley answered his question with another.

'Why, sir, have you seen that cup before?'

'I've seen similar ones, Sergeant, here in the school. Mr Caswell has some among a collection of Indian curios. Loving-cups from Bengal, he said. Made out of polished pear wood.'

Bottomley reached into the bag and brought out a second cup, which he placed beside the first.

'Why, you have two of them! They're identical. Perhaps they're all part of a set.'

Bottomley glanced keenly at Jackson, who nodded very slightly. He knew now what his sergeant was doing.

'No, Captain Valentine,' said Bottomley, 'they're not identical. That one on the left, sir, contains traces of a deadly poison.'

'And the one on the right?'

Sergeant Bottomley frowned, and there was something rather frightening about the face that he turned upon his old superior officer.

'That cup, sir, was found thrust into a blackthorn hedge. Whoever put it there hoped that it would be hidden for ever from the sight of men.'

'And does it, too, contain traces of poison?'

'Oh, no, sir. It contains something far worse: traces of Madeira wine.'

★　★　★

Noel Valentine glanced briefly around Fletcher's sitting-room, then turned to face Jackson, who had just asked him a question.

'Where were we positioned in the room? Well, Inspector, Mr Sandford stood over there near the window. I was over there, beside the fireplace. Mr Granger merely glanced into the bedroom, and then went off to bring the headmaster. He returned with him very quickly. Dr Dalton said a few words about Fletcher, and then went into the bedroom. Suddenly he uttered a terrible cry — '

'A cry, sir? Do you mean that Dr Dalton shouted aloud?'

'He . . . It was a kind of shriek. I really can't think of a more appropriate word. As Virgil put it, 'horresco referens' — 'I shudder to relate it'. My hair stood on end to hear it. It seemed to contain its own tale of ruin . . . Then he staggered out into this room and said that he'd had a terrible shock.'

Inspector Jackson pulled a chair out from the wall and sat down. His round face was expressionless. He seemed to be utterly absorbed by what Valentine had told him. Presently he stirred as though from a reverie.

'What happened after Dr Manning came?'

'Well, Inspector, as you know, Manning found out that the dead man wasn't Fletcher at all. He said that murder had been committed, and that we must all leave the room. Later, so I've been told, the task of locking the room behind us was entrusted to Mr Caswell.'

Valentine saw in his mind's eye the two wooden cups that his old orderly Bottomley had produced. They were, he realized, instruments of death. And Harry Caswell had a collection of them in the dim cupboard beside his fireplace.

'Mr Harry Caswell,' said Jackson, thoughtfully. 'Mr Harry Caswell's set is next door to this one. So somewhere on the other side of that wall there should be a collection of loving-cups from Bengal, made out of polished pear wood.'

He seemed to be savouring the words, and Valentine wondered whether he was being invited to ask a question about the grim vessels that Bottomley had produced from his bag.

Jackson suddenly appeared to change the subject.

'How were you all dressed?'

'What? Well, Sandford was fully dressed, and so was Caswell. Apparently they're early risers. I was clad in a dressing-gown. Dr Dalton — '

He stopped, and Jackson saw a frown of concentration gather on his brow.

'Dr Dalton was also fully dressed, but he looked crumpled and worn. He had shaved, but I rather think he had slept in his clothes.'

Jackson thought for a while, and then suddenly asked, 'Do you think Mr Caswell would ever have harmed Mr Fletcher?'

'What? No, Inspector! Decidedly not. I've seen the way he looks at old Fletcher. He's devoted to him. There's a bond, a link . . . No, the idea of Caswell harming Fletcher had never even occurred to me.'

Jackson's next question was equally unexpected.

'Do you like Mr Caswell, sir?'

'Yes, Inspector. He's an easy man to get on with. Easy for someone like me, at any rate. He's good in an emergency, too. For a man who's obviously attached to old Fletcher, he's taken his disappearance very calmly.'

'And is Mr Sandford easy to get on with?'

'Sandford? He's a diffident man. Some

people would find him stand-offish, but that's only modesty, I think. The more I see of Sandford the more I like him.'

Valentine frowned. Talking about Fletcher and Caswell was reminding him of something, something that also involved Granger, the vice-master . . .

'Ah! Got it! Inspector, I've just remembered something that happened at the Special Dessert. Fletcher dropped some kind of hint about the state of things in this school, and Granger evidently knew what he was talking about. Granger had a whispered conversation with Fletcher out in the corridor.'

As well as he could remember, Valentine gave a careful account of what he had overheard.

'Something 'damnable',' said Jackson, 'and by the next morning he had disappeared. You know, sir, I don't much care for the feel of this case, and that's the truth. I think it's much deeper than it looks, and I'm very uneasy about it.'

'Uneasy?'

'Yes, Captain Valentine. There's something wrong about the way we're seeing it — or the way we're being shown it, if I may put it like that. My sergeant hasn't said so in so many words, but I know he feels the same way.'

Jackson was disinclined to pursue the

135

matter any further. He went into the small bedroom of Fletcher's set and motioned Valentine to follow him. He moved across to the bed, and invited Valentine to stoop down near the wall. The varnished oak floorboards near the skirting were spattered with three or four dark splashes of blood.

'Intriguing,' murmured Valentine. 'That blood is the result of a very unpleasant injury, Mr Jackson. But I wouldn't have thought it indicated any threat to life.'

'I'm inclined to agree with you, sir. Nevertheless, it's blood, and not quite dry yet. What was that word you used, sir? 'Intriguing'. Intriguing, but also damnable. Yes, it suggests all kinds of things to me. There's a picture coming into focus, but it's not clear yet . . . I feel that when it becomes sharper, I'm not going to like it very much.'

Valentine glanced around the room. He had an eye for detail, and something had disturbed him. Something was missing that had been there while he had been waiting for Sandford to return with Granger that morning.

'Ah!' he exclaimed with satisfaction. 'I notice, Inspector, that you've removed Fletcher's watch and pince-nez — '

'What? Oh, no, sir, no, We haven't taken them. There were no such objects in the room when we arrived. Are you quite certain that you saw them?'

'Quite certain, Inspector. I particularly noticed them. Gold pince-nez on a black ribbon, and a gold full hunter watch.'

'Well, well. Now, that means that — unless . . . '

Jackson suddenly smiled very genially at Captain Valentine.

'I must bid you good day, Captain Valentine,' he said. 'I've work to do downstairs, and Sergeant Bottomley's loose in the school. Making a sortie, you know. But before you leave, here are two simple questions I'd like you to answer. First, what would you want a pair of gold pince-nez on a black ribbon for?'

'To see with.'

'And a gold full hunter watch?'

'To tell the time with!'

Valentine looked at the wall dividing the two sets and then at Jackson. He could glimpse the beginning of an idea.

'You don't think — ?'

Jackson held up his hand as though to ward off further words.

'Let's just wait and see, sir. It's early days yet.'

★ ★ ★

137

'Mr Sandford, sir!'

Sergeant Bottomley detached himself from the shadows behind the Jacobean staircase and greeted Sandford with a hoarse whisper, which he thought suited for use in schools. As he watched the startled, rather haughty master turn to face him, he said to himself, The time's come, Mister Percy Prim, for you and me to have a cosy word together.

'Sergeant Bottomley? How can I help you? Perhaps we'd better go somewhere a little less exposed. It's Sunday, you know, and the boys are not taught.'

Sandford turned on his heel and led Bottomley into the Great Corridor, where a number of young boys gazed at the sergeant with unsubtle curiosity.

'Mr Bottomley,' Sandford said, 'is what you have to ask me confidential? If so, we'll go somewhere a little more remote.'

'Well, sir, I'm agreeable to be taken anywhere you like, as long as it's private.'

Sandford pushed open a rather battered glazed mahogany door and led Bottomley across a small grassed court shadowed by tall surrounding walls. Facing them was a heavy classical portico of early eighteenth-century design.

'This little court is what we call Abbot's

138

Garth,' said Sandford. 'It leads into the Middle School.'

Bottomley noted that the grass was better kept here, though a scattered patch of pigeon feathers suggested unpleasant possibilities. He glanced upward. A demure black cat sat perfectly motionless on a stone parapet. Above the parapet rose a clock turret, its head in the sun. A golden dial told him that it was twenty to three. An inscription under the dial in clear Roman lettering declared:

I mark the passage of thine idle hours.
AD 1678

'I expect you've been at the school for many years, sir?'

Sandford treated Bottomley to a sardonic, half-humorous smile.

'Long enough, Sergeant. Long enough. But come: let me take you through to the Middle School.'

They passed under a Classical portico and into a long unfurnished stone gallery giving access to a line of empty and silent classrooms. The place had a curious familiarity for Bottomley, a smell of damp masonry, and a suggestion of mildew. Of course! Cells. That's what it was like.

They entered one of the stone classrooms

139

and sat down, each in an ink-stained desk. A lazy light filtered into the room, casting shadows of the window bars across a long blackboard fixed to the wall. Bottomley felt that he had been ushered into a neglected maze by an incurious guide.

'And now, Sergeant Bottomley, how can I help you?'

'Mr Sandford, sir, you may have heard about the young girl down in the village who died from drinking poison? She was buried this Monday gone. Alice Patching, her name was, and she was seventeen years old.'

Sandford's face showed his scarcely concealed distaste for the subject.

'What happened to the girl? Dr Manning mentioned her, but I know nothing of the matter.'

'She'd been seduced and betrayed, sir, but she believed that the man who did that to her would come and marry her.'

The light suddenly went out of the sun, and the room darkened. Sandford seemed not to notice the shifting shadows. His polite, indifferent expression never changed. Bottomley continued his story.

'Alice Patching believed that the man who'd betrayed her would come and fetch her away to London. She wouldn't reveal who the man was, but she said two things about him, first that he was a 'gentleman', and secondly that he 'wasn't far away'.'

Bottomley's shrewd glance caught Sandford's uneasy eyes. The schoolmaster's voice faltered as he replied.

'I . . . I see the drift of your remarks, Mr Bottomley. You're thinking that this school is a fine store-house of gentlemen conveniently near to Kingsmere village, and that maybe one of us . . . one of my colleagues . . . But why are you pursuing this line of investigation? What has a village tragedy got to do with this wretched business of the dead intruder?'

Bottomley smiled, and Sandford felt uneasily like a rather petulant child who was being indulged by a kindly and patient adult.

'Well, you see, sir, the girl in the village died of poison, and so did the intruder upstairs. You'll remember Mr Caswell saying that there were plenty of poisons here in the school. That's a very interesting point, you see, because poisons are not as easy to come by as people seem to think. At least, not fancy poisons like the one that killed Alice Patching. So maybe the poison that killed her came from here.'

Sandford got to his feet and stood near an empty fireplace set in a dull wooden surround in which generations of boys had carved their initials. He unconsciously began to tidy up a

141

row of dog-eared books on the mantelpiece with quick, nervous movements of his hands. He looked personally affronted and humiliated.

This teacher resents what he sees as a slur on his precious school, Bottomley thought. That's why he's brought me down here into this half-hidden building, to keep me out of the public way.

'I take your point, Sergeant,' Sandford said at last. 'Nevertheless, I feel bound to say that our school is not the only local source of 'gentlemen'. There are at least a dozen seats of noble and gentle families in the district, each with various young male offspring — '

'I know, sir. Everybody keeps telling me that, and about the officers' lines at the Light Infantry Barracks over at the Vale. We'll look into those places if we have to, sir, never fear. But in the meantime, I'd ask you to look at everyone here at Kingsmere through a different pair of spectacles.'

Bottomley levered himself out of the very small desk into which he had wedged himself. He looked steadily at Sandford with his probing grey eyes, and said, 'But perhaps you've already donned those new spectacles, sir? Perhaps you already sense that there's something badly wrong here in your school?'

The shot went home. Sandford blushed,

and found himself unable to meet Bottom-ley's steady gaze. The sense of being a gently rebuked child became stronger. He suddenly wondered whether he and his colleagues were effectively cocooned from most people's lives. Don a different pair of spectacles . . . It was an image worth considering. He remembered the words of the poet John Donne that he had quoted to Valentine in Fletcher's room: 'Any man's death diminishes me, because I am involved in Mankind'.

Sandford opened the classroom door and then stopped for a moment on the threshold.

'I take your words seriously, Sergeant Bottomley, and will act accordingly. Never-theless, I urge you not to insist too much on a connection between that village tragedy and the people in this school. I don't want you to think that I'm unsympathetic. I'm truly sorry for that girl and her family, but one man's idea of a gentleman is another's idea of a scoundrel. I expect people of that sort — peasant folk, I mean — could easily be misled by claims of gentility.'

As they crossed the grassy court called Abbot's Garth the clock in the turret struck the hour. Bottomley glanced up at the inscription under the dial.

' 'I mark the passage of thine idle hours',' he quoted. 'That reminds me, Mr Sandford,

143

of the old adage: 'The Devil finds work for idle hands to do'.'

★ ★ ★

Harry Caswell passed under the wide arch into Lower School, and walked into Fletcher's empty classroom. He stood for a moment at the back of the vaulted chamber. The dim light had a quality of greyness, imparted by the steady drizzle of rain outside.

Something dropped to the floor in Flodders' den. Caswell exclaimed in surprise. He heard a noise of hurried footsteps, followed by the dull thud of the outer door closing. Opening the narrow door under the poppy-headed arch, he entered the little room. A heavy dictionary lay on the floor, where it had evidently been dislodged by someone who had been searching through the papers in Fletcher's desk.

Caswell threw open the outer door and glanced into the tangled garden that surrounded that part of the old building. The rain was falling mournfully on the leaves, and had formed muddy pools on the path. The ground was too sodden to have left the print of feet. Caswell shut the door and turned to Fletcher's desk.

He saw immediately that the unknown

searcher had been partly successful. Hurried hands had scooped their way through the dusty and untidy clutter of old papers and dog-eared exercise sheets, and had found a packet of documents, carefully folded in a cover of thick waxed paper. The packet had been opened, and it seemed that one document at least had been removed, but the noise of Caswell's approach had evidently panicked the searcher, and he had fled.

Caswell had just taken up the opened packet of papers when he was conscious of eyes looking at him. He spun round from the desk, and saw Sergeant Bottomley standing utterly motionless in the doorway. So still was he that for a moment Caswell thought it was an illusion of the dim light.

Bottomley smiled lopsidedly, and made a sort of inclination in Caswell's direction that may have been meant as a bow. There was a faint aroma of gin in the air.

'Mr Caswell, sir! So we've had intruders, by the sound of things.'

'Yes, Sergeant. Somebody had come in here from the garden, and was rooting through Mr Fletcher's desk. It looks as though whoever it was got away with something. Look here.'

Sergeant Bottomley sidled into the room, and as he did so his shadow fell across the flagged pavement. He pointed down, and grinned apologetically.

'When following a person, sir,' he said, 'never let your shadow fall across their path. If you do that, you give yourself away.'

'Well, well,' drawled Caswell, 'thank you for that little lesson in sleuthing. Do those words by any chance hint that you've been following me?'

Bottomley shook his head, at the same time holding out his hand for the packet of documents. Caswell surrendered them. In this situation, he mused, 'finders keepers' did not apply.

'Not following you particularly, sir. But I've been down here quite some time. I saw you arrive, and I heard the unknown intruder come in from the garden. Had you not come down here, sir, I'd have got him. It's a sort of an axiom, sir, that if *I'm* on the watch, you'll never see me.'

He peered into the untidy desk, and then glanced at the fallen dictionary. He shook his head sadly. Caswell saw him mouth the word 'amateurs'. Bottomley made as if to walk out of the little room, but stopped on the threshold and said, 'Do you own some little wooden drinking-cups from Bengal, sir?'

'Why, yes, I do. You'll find them in my set

146

upstairs in Staff House. Why do you wish to know?'

'I just wonder whether you've still got the whole collection of them, Mr Caswell. Perhaps you'd make sure when you have a minute. I'm fairly certain, sir, that two of those cups were used to plot and carry out a particularly vile murder.'

7

Letters from a Dark Past

When Bottomley entered the little room behind the stairs, he found Inspector Jackson sitting at the bare wooden table, examining what Valentine, earlier, had assumed to be a bundle of old clothes. Bottomley told him about his encounter with Sandford, and what had happened later in Fletcher's den.

'Well, well, Sergeant,' said Jackson, 'it looks as though I was wise to take precautions about our Mr Caswell. He has friends, you know, and those friends have a horse and cart.' Jackson looked at the packet of papers in Bottomley's hand.

'I see you've brought me a present, Sergeant, from Mr Fletcher's classroom. We'll look at that in a minute. But first, I want you to see what the two bloodhounds turned up before I sent them back to Warwick.'

Jackson pointed to the crumpled heap of clothing on the table.

'Here, Sergeant, we have the fruits of their search: the trousers and jacket of a man's suit. No waistcoat. They'd been tied into a bundle with sisal string and thrust deep into the school midden near the entrance to the stables.'

'Did they find nothing else, sir? Shirt, underclothing?'

'They didn't, which is very interesting indeed, as you obviously appreciate. All they found was this suit. I knew they'd find it somewhere, or as good as knew, as they say. It's stained, as you can see — and smell — with cold porridge and beef gravy. That's from the midden.'

Jackson gingerly unfolded the jacket on the table and peered closely at it.

'Quite good black serge, but torn and worn. No tailor's labels. Nothing in the pockets. No handkerchief, money, keys, papers. One inside pocket — empty. One small inside ticket pocket, also empty — hello! Well, well, Sergeant, fancy that, now!' Jackson had extracted what proved to be the return half of a train ticket.

'The picture becomes clearer, Sergeant Bottomley. Our unknown man was of middle age, white-haired, wearing a black serge suit, and had travelled up here on a third-class ticket from Plymouth via the Great Western Railway.'

Bottomley gave a kind of gentle chuckle.

'You sound like that detective in the

magazine stories, sir. He says things like that to his doctor.'

'That detective, Sergeant,' said Jackson sternly, 'has the advantage of an unseen author who solves all his clues for him. We're different. So what do you think of that ticket?'

'It's a return ticket, sir. So he was here on a visit with a purpose, to see someone in particular. Not exactly the same as Mr Sandford's burglar.'

'No. Or Mr Granger's tramp or vagrant, for that matter. Now, what have you got for me there?'

Bottomley removed the waxed paper wrapper from what proved to be a collection of six letters. They arranged them open on the table, anchoring them at top and bottom with a motley assortment of bottles, note-books and tobacco tins.

Jackson lit a curly briar pipe, and puffed away at it while he read.

'At first sight, Sergeant,' observed Jackson after a minute or two, 'these letters don't seem to have any bearing either on the murder of our unknown man, or upon the disappearance of Mr Fletcher.'

'No, sir,' said Bottomley, 'but that's what Mr Harry Caswell was down there to find. He hadn't just gone down to root around aimlessly. He'd gone there with a purpose.'

'Maybe he was looking for *this* one?'

Jackson pointed to a yellowing piece of note-paper, on which was written in very tall, spidery handwriting:

17 April, 1887

Received from Mr A. Fletcher the sum of four hundred pounds, to terminate the account of Mr H. Caswell.
                    (signed) C.P. McKerrow.

'You know what that is, don't you, Sergeant?'

'Yes, sir. It's a receipt for paying off a shark. Five years ago. It explains a lot, that note.'

'It does. And when the time's ripe, one or the other of us had better find out who C.P. McKerrow is, and pay him a little visit.'

Jackson put his pipe down in a tin lid that was serving as an ash tray.

'All the other letters, Sergeant, seem to be one side of a wide correspondence centring on some kind of investigation, and — presto! Like a conjuror's rabbit out of a hat, the first letter out of the waxed wrapper is from Plymouth!'

Hudson's Hotel,
Plymouth
4 October, 1883

Dear Mr Fletcher,

I am pleased to inform you that, at the time to which you refer, two ladies and one gentleman were resident in the hotel. The ladies were Miss Lucy Eynesham, daughter of the late Capt Eynesham of this town, and Mrs Danecourt, a lady of advanced years, who has since died. The gentleman was Mr Bolt, a surveyor, and your friend saw a lot of him, and also of Miss Eynesham, who seemed much taken with him.

I was very happy to hear from you, and to oblige you in this matter and I thank you yet again for the help you gave to my son in securing for him a placing in his trade at Epsom.

I am, Sir,
Your obedient servant,
John Hudson.

'That letter's our way in to this case, Sergeant, even though it seems to have been written nine years ago. You'd better cast a critical eye over the others.'

The bleak severity of the next letter was in

marked contrast to the genial tones of John Hudson.

> 7 Exeter Place,
> London
> 11 November, 1883

Sir,

I have to hand your letter concerning my cousin. The whole affair is still offensively painful to my husband and myself, and we have long ago banished it from our thoughts. I regret that I can be of no further assistance in this matter.

> *Amelia Bell-Forest.*

'Amelia sounds a sour piece of goods, sir. Now this next one's short and to the point. I wonder who Tommy is? He doesn't say much, does he?'

> *Corpus Christi College,*
> *Oxford*
> *5 September, 1892*

Dear Fletcher,
    No, he hasn't, and no, he didn't.
> *Tommy Baxter*

'Note the date of that letter, Sergeant. It's just a few days ago. That should be significant.'

Bottomley read the two remaining letters. The missing Mr Fletcher, he mused, seemed to have had a wide range of friends in useful places.

The Reform Club
2 March, 1890

Dear Fletcher,
What are you up to, you ancient villain? Are you contemplating matrimony? Whatever it is, I have made some enquiries in the district, and am able to satisfy your curiosity to some extent, at least.

Mrs Dolling is a widow, with, I believe, a grown son, Eric. She is a lady of the highest respectability, independent and comfortable, though not, I should think, wealthy. She lives at Draycot St Peter, in Oxfordshire. It is some two miles to the south-east of Abingdon. Why do you want to know all this? She is too young for you!

Ever yours
Owen Melchester

'And finally, sir, a letter from a doctor living in Lincoln's Inn. I wonder how old Mr Fletcher came to know him?'

Welman's Court,
Lincoln's Inn
18 March, 1890

Dear Fletcher,

What an extraordinary man you are! What odd things you want to know! There are a number of Grangers of about that age who are doctors, and I have covered myself in grime slogging through dusty ledgers in Surgeons' Hall to oblige you.

Yours would seem to be D.K. Granger, MD, one of those Grangers who are related to the Palmerstons, and he practises in Oxfordshire at a place called Draycot.

Thank you for the case of Madeira — what a long memory you have!

Yours sincerely,
Simon Ellis, MD.

While Bottomley read the letters, Jackson's lead pencil moved swiftly over the pages of his note-book. Then he swept the letters together and put them into a cardboard folder.

'Five letters, Sergeant, spanning nine years, and a lot of names that we'll have to flesh out into people. John Hudson of Plymouth, a hotelier, who mentions a Miss Lucy

Eynesham, and a Mr Bolt. Why did our Mr Fletcher want to know about them? Then there's a lady in London, Amelia Bell-Forest, who apparently had painful memories of her cousin, (whoever *she* was), and a retiring widow from Oxfordshire, living in Draycot St Peter. According to another of these letters Draycot's also the native place of someone called D.K. Granger, MD. Does the name ring a bell, Sergeant?'

'It rings a school bell, sir. I expect old nosy Fletcher was checking up on the vice-master's family. The man who wrote that letter telling him about D.K. Granger also mentioned that Fletcher had sent him a case of Madeira.'

Madeira . . .

Jackson closed his note-book and looked round the bare little room. It suddenly felt stifling. He stood up, and began to walk around restlessly.

'Madeira! You were right all along, Sergeant. Alice Patching's death was murder, and the trail leads right back here to this school. But the folk here would rather not know about such unpleasant matters. They prefer to see it as purely a haven of learning, and ignore the homicidal fiend who's on the prowl. And he is, you know! There's a devil lurking round this cluster of courts and classrooms.'

Every year, soon after the beginning of term, Sir Walter Foliott gave a dinner for the Court of Governors at his opulent home, an eighteenth-century mansion called Lockwood House. That year the dinner took place on the fourteenth of the month, the Wednesday following the mysterious death at Kingsmere School.

Jane Ashwood stole a glance along the polished dining-table. Mellow light glanced off the silver appointments and the costly crystal, and created a ruby glow in the decanters of old port. That would go round later, when Jane and the other ladies had left. At the moment, though, they had just finished the sorbet and were waiting for the pheasant.

At the head of the table sat their host, Sir Walter Foliott, a short, elderly man with white locks and a patrician air. She found it curiously startling that a man well over seventy should have such youthful eyes. This elegant house looked like an ancestral home, but the Foliotts, she knew, were from Staffordshire originally. It had been canals, not land, that had turned them into notables.

Jane had been enormously relieved to find that no one had even mentioned the business of the dead intruder, though there had been an obvious constraint at the meal which showed that everybody knew what had occurred.

'We were just saying, Dalton,' observed Sir Walter Foliott in his loud and confident tones, 'that Kingsmere is like a close and trusting family, with you as the father. Not many schools can boast of that. They're getting too large these days.'

'You are very kind, Sir Walter,' Dalton murmured. 'I may venture to add that not every school can boast such a generous benefactor as yourself.'

The words, Jane knew, were not idle flattery but a grateful statement of fact. There was a murmur of assent from along the table. The pheasant arrived, and for a while there was a movement of liveried footmen with silver dishes.

At intervals down the centre of the table tall white candles rose in groups of three. Jane shifted slightly in her chair so that she could look through the barrier of wax at Dr Dalton, who had been placed opposite to her.

Dalton, she thought, looked drawn and tired, almost haunted. He seemed intent on ignoring her completely. She had been foolish to listen to Valentine. Her school in the air should have stayed where it belonged — in her private imaginative world.

Suddenly she realized that Dalton's bright eyes were focused on her. He was leaning slightly to his left, listening to Sir Walter Foliott's cousin, Miss Pringle, a little, bird-like woman in a black gown relieved at cuffs and collar with cream Brussels lace. What was he seeing? Jane was wearing an impeccably cut dress of green satin, which showed off to best effect the magnificent diamond necklace that had been for many years an heirloom in her family. The candle-light threw out a million stars from the five encrusted pendants of the necklace.

That's what he's looking at, she thought wryly. It's the diamonds, not the Weaver of Dreams, that's holding his attention. She could guess what Mary Pringle had whispered to Dalton. 'The Versailles Cascade ... It once belonged to Marie-Antoinette.' Miss Pringle would then have lowered her voice conspiratorially, and added, 'I'm told it's worth half a million.'

Dalton's eyes returned to his plate. Jane allowed him to fall out of focus behind the glowing barrier of candles.

Suddenly the strident tones of Mrs Bradshaw, the wife of one of the governors, rose from near the top of the table. A heavy, domineering but fair-minded woman devoted to Good Works, she was noted for her lack of tact. Jane saw Dalton wince.

'Don't you think, Dr Dalton,' asked Mrs Bradshaw, 'that a headmaster should be married? Sir Walter talks about a head being the father of a family. Surely it would set a wholesome precedent to youth if their chief mentor had a wife and children of his own?'

The gentle murmur of talk along the table died away, and all faces turned to look at him. For a brief moment words failed him, and he seemed to turn pale. Jane looked up now, and caught his eye. Whatever he saw in her expression, it seemed to bring him back to life. He looked suddenly excited and exhilarated.

'My dear Mrs Bradshaw,' he said, 'there's a lot of sense in what you say, as always! But there *are* unmarried headmasters, you know, and no one seems to think the worse of them. The Roman Catholic public schools have monks for headmasters, and they're very well regarded. No one's suggested yet that *they* should be married!'

There was a ripple of laughter, in which Mrs Bradshaw herself joined. Dalton had answered her in humorous tones at which she could not possibly take offence.

Across the table, on her side of the candles, Lady Jane Ashwood noted that Dalton's answer had made no statement about his own marital status. He lived alone in Headmaster's House, and had always done so. A widower? Perhaps. He had never mentioned a wife. She wondered what he had seen in her face that had restored his animation after the assault of Cecilia Bradshaw's tactless enquiry. Perhaps, she mused, he had detected something more personal than mere embarrassed concern.

The dinner drew to its close, and the ladies left the men to their port. Jane felt strangely disturbed, and after exchanging a few pleasantries with the other women of the party, who had settled themselves in the drawing-room of Sir Walter's hospitable house, she made her way to a quiet conservatory overlooking the rear lawns.

She had sat in thought for only a few minutes when a shadow fell across the tessellated floor. She started in surprise. It was Dr Dalton. He stood with a glass of port still in his hand, as though he had hurriedly left his companions in the dining-room. Dalton's face was transformed from its usual calm, slightly supercilious expression of world weariness. His eyes blazed with an avid, all-consuming light.

'Lady Jane, I've been waiting to see you alone all evening. We must talk, you and I.

Why did you not show me those plans before? Why did you keep them to yourself? This — this vision that you have, this dream — you must flesh out those airy palaces with deeds as well as words.'

She felt the blood rushing to her head and throbbing in her temples. There was a thrilling, mesmerizing quality in Dalton's voice that she found overwhelming. His eyes shone with an almost hypnotic intensity. His powerful words made her realize for the first time that her ideas were not the idle dreams of a leisured woman.

She suddenly felt compelled to speak to him about his own professional worries. She told herself that as a governor of the school she had a right to do so.

'Dr Dalton, you cannot know how happy your words have made me. Now, I beg you, let me share at least some of your present anxiety. Everyone here tonight has pretended that the affair never happened. I mean the business of the poisoned vagrant.'

She saw the headmaster's spasm of shock as she spoke. For a moment she wondered whether she had spoken out of turn. Dalton very slowly sat down near her, and shaded his eyes with his hand. She heard him sigh, and the sound was more like a groan.

'Lady Jane,' he said quietly, 'it was the

worst moment of my life. I thought I was being shown the lifeless body of an aged colleague, dear old Amyas Fletcher. Instead, I saw the hideous corpse of a drunken, bloated ruffian, clad in Fletcher's nightgown. I was profoundly shocked, as indeed were Captain Valentine and Mr Caswell, who were present.'

'And none of you knew who the dead man was?' she asked gently.

'No. I am convinced it was some drunken intruder. Whoever he was, he seems to have died through drinking poison.'

Dalton removed his hand from his eyes and sat upright in his chair. His dark eyes still gleamed with firmness and resolution.

'Lady Jane, I am determined that this shocking affair will not interfere with your plan for a sister school to Kingsmere. Are you prepared to accept my assistance in the matter?'

Dalton gave her no time to form a reply. Ignoring convention he seized her by the arm and led her out of the conservatory on to a garden terrace.

'Lady Jane,' he said, in a low but vibrant voice, 'you cannot realize this affair alone! This school must be built! You must put me at your command, and tell me the ways in which I can serve you!'

She was conscious of the rapid beating of

her heart. She felt elated, liberated at last from the amused tolerance of male patronage. This man was not like Valentine. He was enraptured by her vision.

They found a small summer-house on the border of the lawn, and sat there, talking of the great institution that she had envisioned. It would rise on a fair tract of land to the north of Kingsmere. She mentioned a leading architect who designed vast buildings in the Gothic style.

'No, Lady Jane, this is a new creation, not an imitation of the past! Have you seen Norman Shaw's work? He's like the best of the Georgians, but spare and subtle; he understands tradition, but he respects function and craftsmanship . . . '

She listened enraptured while Dalton carefully and sensitively began to anchor her dream in the reality of bricks and mortar. He spoke to her of costing, of special firms of builders, about clerks of the works . . . In the end, she found herself overwhelmed by the dynamic man beside her. Together they would give substance to her airy fancies. Together . . . He continued to talk, but she no longer heard what he said. Her eyes never left his face.

He stopped speaking, and she saw him smile at her. There was something wistful, almost boyish, about the way he looked at her, an expression that she had never seen in him before.

'Shall we do this great thing together?' he asked softly. 'Shall we?'

Once again she felt her heart beating so strongly that she was alarmed in case Dalton heard it. In a moment, she knew, he would draw closer to her, take her hand, perhaps . . . and she would not withdraw it.

'The carriages have arrived, My Lady.'

Juckes was at the door of the summer-house, where he stood as still as a man of stone. Jane wondered with a start how long he had been there. Dr Dalton stood up and bowed, and the moment of magic was lost. But Jane Ashwood knew without any shadow of doubt that there would be other such moments. A link had been forged between her and Dalton that nothing would be able to sever.

*   *   *

The derisive, uncontrolled baying of rebellious youths came from one of the classrooms in the Great Corridor. Even from the depths of his study below, Dr Dalton recognized the voice of the man begging for calm as that of Percy Sandford.

Within moments the headmaster had erupted through the inner door into Staff House, and hurried down the stairs. On the ground floor he was joined by Granger.

'Shall I deal with it?' asked Granger curtly. 'It's Sandford. He was unwell this morning with that feverish lethargy he gets. If we don't move soon to stop that row, other colleagues will throw etiquette to the winds and rescue him.'

Dalton was half out in the corridor as he replied, 'We'll see to this vile outrage together!'

Dalton flung open the door of the classroom. Immediately the noise ceased, and fourteen young men stood rigid at their desks, arms thrust down at their sides. At the front of the room a chair lay near Sandford where it had been flung, and the master, pale and shaking, stood against the wall.

He was bitterly humiliated by what had happened, but his measure of wretchedness was complete now that he had to stand before both Dalton and Granger as witnesses of his failure.

The headmaster stood in silence for over a minute before he spoke. Some of the boys, he noticed, were actually panting from the exertion of their misbehaviour. Tired he may have been, but there was no doubting his total command of this particular situation. His voice was quiet, but its effect on the boys was electric. They were a group of Gentlemen, eighteen years old.

'Mr Sandford,' said Dalton, 'I am sorry that your lesson should have been marred by the presence of louts and hooligans. Perhaps you would care to return to Staff House for the rest of this session?'

Sandford could not raise his eyes or even speak. He bowed to the head, and left the room.

'Now, Gentlemen,' said Dalton, eloquently investing the word with heavy sarcasm, 'I should be grateful if the perpetrator of this outrage will step forward.'

He looked at the chair lying on the floor. No one moved.

'I will thrash every boy here if necessary, but I will not be defied. Now is the last chance for the boy who did this to own up.'

A large, heavy-featured boy sullenly stepped forward from his desk. He brought with him a reek of spirits. This was Forman, a youth who was greatly feared by the younger boys. He was one of the ogres of the Other Culture.

'So, Forman, you have decided to disgrace the school by acting as a lout. Such behaviour will not, of course, be sustained for one

167

moment. Go to the porter's lodge.'

There was a stir among the other boys, who still stood to attention in their desks. This was the ultimate loss of face for a Gentleman. To be thrashed by the headmaster, even though it was done in the privacy of the lodge rather than publicly in Hall, was to lose all credibility with the younger pupils. Forman's star was about to set.

The head left the room while Granger added his biting sarcasm to what had already been said. He was successful in getting the whole story of the incident from the boys. As he suspected, it arose from a combination of Sandford's illness and Forman's drunken loutishness. The headmaster had dealt with the matter superbly, thought Granger. He felt a sudden pang of doubt and puzzlement. Had he been wrong about Dalton?

In the school lodge, the porter stood ready. Forman had already removed his tail coat, and, as the headmaster appeared, he took up his position behind the porter with his arms over the man's shoulders. With a slight grunt of exertion the porter seized the youth's arms and bent forward, so that the headmaster was presented with a clear target.

Dalton's arm rose nine times, and nine times the stinging cane descended. Then the porter stood up. The head left the lodge, the porter resumed his seat, the youth put on his tail coat and haughtily walked out. None of the three said a word.

Forman had quit the lodge with his head held high, preserving a kind of ruined dignity in his haughty silence. But once he had stumbled into his set in Upper School and fallen into a chair, he began to cry with pain and humiliation. There was a murderous expression on his face, as he hissed through his tears, 'I don't blame old Sandford, but I'll get even with Dalton for this, the swine! I'll get my revenge on him!'

8

The Bachelor's Wife

John Hudson was a big man with broad shoulders. He was completely bald, but sported a very fine white spade beard. He filled the little round swivel chair placed before his business desk in his private office on the first floor of Hudson's Hotel, holding the letter that he had written to the missing school-master nine years earlier.

With its back nestling against a wooded slope and its elegant frontage commanding fine views of the estuary of five rivers, Hudson's Hotel dominated the little cove that constituted part of the fretted coastline at Plymouth.

'We're just a little bit away from our great seaport here, Mr Jackson,' said John Hudson, 'and we've always been regarded as a holiday house for genteel folks. Quite like the seaside, really — that's what most people say, who've stayed here.'

Jackson had instantly admired Hudson's Hotel, a square, four-storey building of smooth granite, graced by green-painted cast-iron balconies with slender iron columns, and an attractively florid public bar entered discreetly from the side of the house near the trees. It was at the entrance to the public bar that he and Sergeant Bottomley had parted company.

'So Mr Amyas Fletcher has disappeared? Well, dear me, Mr Jackson, I am sorry! I shall never forget him, you know, though it's years now since he came here. I was quite a boy then, of course, and my father was still alive. Goodness, it's nigh on fifty years ago that I first saw Mr Fletcher.'

Mr Hudson swung round in his swivel chair to face the splendid view of the estuary. He crossed one leg over the other, clasped his hands together for a moment, then launched into speech.

'Mr Fletcher was a young fellow in his twenties when he first came here. Very pleasant, and very good with children. Always a cheery word! He'd come down from Epsom two or three times a year with his cousin, and they'd stay for a week or two. The cousin was what I'd call a narky sort of man, very clever and all that, but a bit eccentric. Nice enough though, if you don't mind grumblers. Mr Baxter, his name was. He and Mr Fletcher used to go sailing in the estuary and riding round about, and they'd go to the Assembly

171

Rooms for the dances and receptions they used to have in those days.'

'So Mr Fletcher had a cousin called Baxter? Did you ever hear the cousin addressed as Tommy?'

'Why, yes, fancy you knowing that! Thomas, I suppose it was, really. Thomas Baxter. A quirky sort of man. I expect he's dead, now. He went to be a tutor at Oxford or Cambridge, I forget which.'

'You said in that letter, Mr Hudson, that Mr Fletcher had been of some use to your son?'

'Yes. Another John, he is. He's head groom now to Mr Orlando Cooper, who has the big racing stables just outside Epsom. It was Mr Fletcher, bless him, who got my John in there when he was seventeen. Years ago now, of course, like everything else. Just excuse me for a moment, Inspector. It's very nice chatting to you like this. I'll get us some refreshment.'

Hudson levered himself out of his chair, opened the door of the little office, and began to lumber downstairs. Jackson heard the hotelier's genial voice calling, 'Henrietta! Bring up tea for two, will you?'

While he was alone, Jackson took a thick manila envelope from an inside pocket. He slid out two photographs, which showed the dead face of the Man in the Night-gown. Strange, Jackson thought, to be presented with the peaceful, composed features of a murderous ruffian. For that, he supposed, was what the man had been.

Late on Monday night, Mr Angel at the mortuary had sent him a preliminary report. The unknown man had been poisoned with aconitine, administered in the glass found by Dr Manning near the body. Mr Angel had also enclosed the two macabre photographs.

Mr Hudson returned, panting a little, and fitted himself back into his chair. Jackson slipped the envelope and its contents back into his pocket.

'What's happened to your sergeant, Inspector?' asked Hudson. 'I saw you both arrive from the window over there, but your sergeant never materialized!'

'Sergeant Bottomley's partial to a drop of gin, Mr Hudson, so he's gone to pay a visit to your public bar. Very fine it looked, too. I must say, Mr Hudson, that you've got a very nice place here. Very nice indeed. And so you remember Miss Lucy Eynesham?'

'Indeed yes. Lucy Eynesham. She was a very fetching young lady, very pretty, you know. Some folk said she was too clinging, by which they meant, Mr Jackson, that she was easily dominated. Easily swayed. I remember her father saying to *my* father once: 'Hudson, that little girl of mine bends too much with the wind'. He was right, too, to my way of thinking. But she was very pretty, you know. Very charming, really.'

The door opened to admit a young woman in the frilled cap and apron of a waitress. She treated Jackson to a cheerful smile, which he returned. She carried a large square tray laden with tea things. Not for the first time Jackson wondered how these slight girls could carry such heavy loads.

'Her father, I note, was a Captain Eynesham? A seafaring man, perhaps?'

Mr Hudson did not answer directly. Instead, he concentrated on the rituals of the tea tray. He handed Jackson a cup of tea, and then crossed to the window.

'If you look out there across the creek, Mr Jackson, you'll see a tall brick house with a flag mast in front of it. Do you see it? The house with the slate roof-tiles. Well, that was where Lucy's father, Captain Robert Eynesham, lived. But no, he wasn't a sea-going man. In fact he was a retired army officer, and a very wealthy man.'

'Wealthy?'

'Oh, yes.'

Jackson could sense that Mr Hudson was beginning to enjoy himself. His grey eyes twinkled, and his bald head shone with what seemed like extra polish. It wasn't often, Jackson supposed, that the cheerful hotelier could gossip and talk scandal with his guests.

'Captain Robert Eynesham, Inspector, inherited a fortune from a relative who had been a sugar planter in the West Indies. I couldn't tell you the details, Mr Jackson, but it was a very substantial fortune. Very substantial indeed.'

'You amaze me, Mr Hudson! The things you know! And then, nine years ago, Mr Fletcher wrote you that letter?'

'He did. He did, Inspector. I wondered at the time why he wanted to know who was staying in the house on the date he mentioned . . . I'm trying to recall what year it was he asked me to check upon. Yes! It was 1875 or 6. Quite a long time ago, really.'

'Tell me, Mr Hudson, why was Miss Lucy Eynesham staying here? You've just pointed out her house to me, across the water there.'

Mr Hudson stroked his fine grey beard, and sipped his tea with calculated slowness. He put down his cup on his saucer with a tinkle of china.

'Well you see, Inspector, at that time her father, Captain Robert Eynesham, had fallen ill with what they called in those days a bloody flux. Miss Lucy came over here to stay for a month while her father was in the infirmary. That's why she was here. Quite a sanatorium we were, as I remember. Old Mrs Danecourt was here, too, as I faithfully told Mr Fletcher in this letter. She died later that same year of a dropsy. Sometimes I think the doctors invent these names for diseases in order to frighten us to death!'

'And then there was a Mr Bolt?'

'Yes. Mr Bolt is still happily with us. He's retired now, and lives in a little house in Barbican. As a matter of fact I have one of his calling-cards here.'

He reached into an open roll-top desk and took a card from one of many stuffed into a pigeon hole.

'There you are, Inspector. Very highly regarded, is Mr Bolt. He's troubled with his legs these days — laid up, you know. But he's a mine of information on all things to do with Plymouth. He did a lot of work at Nelson College, the school for gentlemen's sons here at Plymouth. They were building what they call laboratories at the school, and it was convenient for Mr Bolt to stay here for a week or so. Mr Bolt in those days lived at a place called Okehampton, right up beyond Dart-moor.'

'And now, Mr Hudson, let me touch on the romantic theme if I may. It seems that a friend of Mr Fletcher's was staying here, wasn't he? That's what your letter suggests, at any rate. And Miss Eynesham was very much taken with him. With this friend of Mr Fletcher's, I mean.'

'Quite right, Inspector. I don't know whether anything ever came of it, though. It was just about that time that Captain Robert Eynesham succumbed to the bloody flux. Miss Lucy Eynesham was very secretive after that melancholy event, and left the area very soon afterwards. She was only twenty-four, you know, and probably wanted to make a fresh start elsewhere.'

'So the Eyneshams don't live in Plymouth any more?'

'No, Inspector. The house on the cliff yonder was bought by a Mr Padgett. He's lived there with his family for years, now. He's in the livestock business, but in a quiet way. Quite genteel, I suppose.'

'This friend of Mr Fletcher's,' said Jackson. 'Can you by any chance remember his name? Or perhaps look it up in your register?'

'The friend? Well, in fact, Mr Jackson, it was the man who's now headmaster of Mr Fletcher's school in your part of the country. Dalton, his name was. Dr Edward Dalton.'

★ ★ ★

'These books are very old, sir, and bound as you see in what they call vellum. Sheepskin is what it is, really.'

The parish clerk at the tiny village of Walton-by-Plymouth would have called himself stout. He was, in fact, fat, with huge legs and arms but delicate white hands. His great body filled the fur-tipped gown that he wore, and his face was globular and suet-like.

The clerk's voice, though, was high-pitched and mincing. He addressed all his remarks to Jackson, ignoring the hunched figure of Sergeant Bottomley, who had wedged himself between the window and the table in a minute chair.

The fat man held the spine of the great book to his lips and blew a stream of black dust across the little vestry. He reverently placed the book on the desk, and opened the pages flat. Jackson looked down at the columns of neat entries in faded brown ink. The clerk hovered delicately at his shoulder.

'And how is Mr Bolt, sir? It's a little while since I saw him last.'

'Mr Bolt is very well, Mr Pickavance. He seems to be enjoying retirement, by all accounts. Very fond of gossip, is your friend Mr Bolt. He told me to visit Nelson College, and gave me a little written introduction to the bursar there. That was a very, very

178

interesting visit, I don't mind telling you, Mr Pickavance.'

Mr Pickavance smirked and gave a kind of sidelong bow, which Jackson thought was like a hundred weight sack of sugar being dumped on a dank pavement.

'And then he told me to come out here and talk to you. He said you'd know about Miss Lucy Eynesham and her doings.'

Mr Pickavance smiled, revealing a good many white teeth. He looked at the page open in front of Jackson on the vestry table of the little church.

'Not to your liking, sir? Let me turn the page.'

The thick parchment leaf crackled as it turned. Almost immediately Jackson saw what he was seeking. The entry this time was in a darker black ink.

'Look Sergeant! 'Edward Alberic Dalton, bachelor ... Lucy Eynesham, spinster'.' Married here on October the eighteenth, 1876. Sixteen years ago. Yet Dalton lives alone in that house of his at the school. A widower, perhaps. And underneath this entry someone's added: 'By Special Licence of His Grace the Archbishop of Canterbury'.'

Jackson turned to the parish clerk and treated him to a genial smile.

'Now that's an interesting little point, Mr

Pickavance. A Special Licence. I think they're granted for unusual reasons?'

The clerk's little eyes glittered for a moment behind the folds of well-nourished flesh. He sat down on a tall stool and folded his delicate white hands on his lap.

'You'll understand, Mr Jackson, that the particular wedding you've singled out there in the register took place sixteen years ago. That was in the Reverend Arthur Sturgess's time. Mr Sturgess is now in Glory, and buried outside in the churchyard. You get these licences from Doctors' Commons in London, and they enable you to be married without putting up the banns. In this particular case . . . '

The smooth tones of the parish clerk faltered with a clearly-assumed modesty.

'In this particular case, Inspector Jackson, discretion was of the essence. The lady in the case, as they say, was well known in these parts, but in the matter of her relationship with this Dr Dalton, she had rashly anticipated the tying of the conjugal knot. It was, I believe, becoming obvious that she was no longer enjoying the status of a maiden.'

The big meaty face of Mr Pickavance broke into a becomingly modest blush as he betrayed the secret of the woman who had come all those years earlier to this remote village to marry the man who was now headmaster of Kingsmere Abbey School.

'And did you ever hear,' asked Jackson, 'whether the lady in question ultimately became a mother?'

'She did, Inspector. Within seven months of her marriage — ahem! — she gave birth to a son. She called him Eric.'

★　★　★

'Mr Holland,' said Jackson, putting down his empty tankard, 'come and sit down here with me, if you'll be so kind. I want a word with you.'

The red-haired landlord of the Wheatsheaf had warmed to Jackson since their first meeting. He had remembered the inspector's dislike of froth on his beer, and had drawn him a particularly impeccable glass of mild ale.

'Yes, sir. What can I do for you?'

'I've a feeling, Mr Holland, that my sergeant and I are going to need a base here in Kingsmere. It's a long drag back each night to Warwick, with this village not being on the railway. Perhaps you and I can come to some kind of arrangement?'

Mr Holland concentrated his attention on

business. He smiled and rubbed his hands together.

'I can let you have rooms here by the day or by the week, Mr Jackson. Very modest terms, including coal and candles. Meals can be provided at most times for a modest extra cost. Or, sir, you can have use of the cottage in the grounds to yourselves for fivepence extra per day.'

'Also including coals and candles?'

'Most assuredly, sir. Of course, you can stay in the house itself, but I think you'll like the cottage. Let me show it to you. If you'll take it by the week, we can agree a special price for two.'

Half hidden among trees at the rear of the Wheatsheaf, a small stone cottage stood in an overgrown patch of weedy garden. Mr Holland had brought a large key with him, which he turned in the lock of the front door. It yielded with a groan of protest, and a pall of stale air descended on them from the closed building.

'As you can see, Mr Jackson, it's dry and spacious: a little sitting-room, a little kitchen — not that you'll need that, with meals taken in the hotel. Two little bedrooms. I'll have fresh linen in, and everything aired. It'll be a pleasure to have you on the premises, Inspector.'

'I'll need the key, Mr Holland, at all times.'

'You shall have the key, sir. You'll like it out here in the grounds. We usually open this cottage three or four times a year when contractors and such like come down to do work at the school. It's nicely self-contained, and very private.'

'Then it's a bargain, Mr Holland.'

They left the cottage, and returned to the garden of the inn. Jackson seemed disinclined to go back into the bar. He looked down the dusty road leading away from the village, where a horse-drawn cart stood under the shade of an ancient oak. A man in his mid-sixties, with grizzled hair and a face heavily tanned by long years of work out-of-doors, sat in the cart, thoughtfully smoking a clay pipe.

'Now here's a question for you that you might like to answer, Mr Holland,' said Jackson, his eyes riveted on the road. 'I've visited the school, as you'll know, and so has my sergeant. Very impressive it is, too. And it stands in spacious grounds, complete with a lake.'

'The Mere, sir. That's what they call it. In all there's two hundred acres of grounds and pasture at Kingsmere School.'

'Well, Mr Holland, here's my question: if I wanted to know something about those grounds, about how to get out of them and how to get into them, or about who might come or who might go — where could I find out things like that?'

Jackson was still watching the road. He saw Harry Caswell appear from the direction of St John's church, accompanied by a powerfully built young man in his twenties. Caswell climbed nimbly into the cart. The young man untied the reins, and presently the vehicle rumbled off down the village street away from the inn.

'Mr Jackson,' said the innkeeper, 'if you want to know about that sort of thing comings and goings at the school, and so forth — you'll need to talk to a man called Joseph Hodge. Joe Hodge. He's what they call the groundsman these days, but years ago he was called the pasture-keeper. He'll tell you what you want to know, and a good deal more besides.'

At a point where the road began to curve away gently towards the little suburb of New End there was a lane, from which Jackson saw a light open carriage emerge. He noted with approval how the carriage regulated its speed to keep a couple of hundred yards behind the tanner's cart. Presently both carriage and cart disappeared from sight.

Inspector Jackson smiled. He was now able

to give Mr Holland his full attention.

'And this Joseph Hodge. Where can I find him?'

'He comes in here most evenings, Inspector, but he lives on the school premises in a cottage near the headmaster's house. You talk to him, Mr Jackson. There's nothing much escapes Joe Hodge.'

★   ★   ★

'I expect there's plenty of places that are out of bounds to these boys, Mr Hodge,' said Sergeant Bottomley. He was sprawled in ungainly comfort on a bench placed against the front wall of the groundsman's cottage on the edge of the pasture. Beside him sat Hodge himself, a lean, heavily sun-bronzed man in his mid-fifties, smoking a clay pipe.

Bottomley thoughtfully scanned the vast range of buildings stretching from the headmaster's house on his left to the towering bulk of the school chapel far to the right.

'All sorts of places are out of bounds, Mr Bottomley. But there's no stopping a boy from doing something once he's set his mind to it.'

Joe Hodge laid his pipe aside on the bench beside him. His body suggested that he was about to doze off, but Bottomley saw how his

185

bright eyes remained alert and open. Bottomley slipped a manila envelope from his pocket, and took out a photograph, which he handed to the pasture-keeper.

'Have you ever seen *him* before, Joe?'

Hodge's eyebrows rose a little. He stared for what seemed a full minute at the photograph before handing it back to Bottomley. He looked across the pasture at the headmaster's house and sighed.

'Yes, Mr Bottomley, I've seen him before.'

'And when was that, Joe? When did you see him?'

Sergeant Bottomley took a very small note-book and a stub of pencil from his coat pocket. He turned over a few dog-eared pages until he found a clean leaf.

'Tell me about it, Joe,' he said.

⋆ ⋆ ⋆

'Already! The sinking ship, and the inevitable rats!'

Theodore Granger, who was opening the Monday morning's mail, threw a letter down on his table in disgust. Sandford, who was sitting on the other side of the table, looked up from the ledger that he had been examining.

'What is it, Vice-master?'

186

'Parents, Sandford. Worried parents, anxious for the safety of their precious sons! I thought we'd weathered this particular little storm. Evidently I was wrong.'

He snatched the discarded letter up from the table and looked at it again.

'This idiot writes to say that he'd like to withdraw his son for the term, 'in view of the violent death that we hear has taken place at the school'. What violent death? That tramp fellow had been poisoned, according to Manning. What was violent about that? When these boys write home, Sandford, they show infinitely more imagination than they ever do in their lessons.'

Granger returned to the rest of the morning's mail. There were seven more similar letters, asking, with varying levels of belligerency, what was being done to protect the boys from intruders. Two fathers threatened to remove their sons for good from the school at the end of the current term.

With an oath Granger gathered the letters up in a bundle and plumped them down on top of the open ledger that Sandford was consulting.

'Look at them, Sandford! Read them! Then tell me what to do. These people make me sick!'

Granger threw himself into his chair and

watched Sandford patiently reading the letters. Poor Sandford! He looked unwell, with blackish-yellow shadows beneath his eyes. It was an onset of an old complaint, he knew. Jaundice? No, it was something else, but it would leave Sandford weak and drained. Luckily, he had coped much better with the aftermath of the Forman business than had seemed possible.

'Well, Vice-master,' said Sandford at length, 'if I were faced with the problem presented by these letters, I should determine very quickly to scotch any unfounded rumours about what may have happened here.'

'And how would you do that?'

'I would have a letter printed and despatched to all the parents, giving an unsensational account of what took place, and saying that extra precautions were being taken to ensure the absolute safety of the boys.'

Sandford smiled suddenly, an engaging smile that lit up his usually guarded face.

'What those 'extra precautions' would be,' he added, 'you could determine at your leisure.'

'Excellent! You've confirmed for me what I'd already decided to do,' Granger replied. 'Thank you very much for your advice, Sandford.'

His colleague flushed red at the compliment. It was a custom of his to spend time with Granger, going through the account books and ledgers of the school, and keeping tally of some of the domestic expenses. It never occurred to him that he should be thanked for his pains.

'You are too good, Vice-master,' he muttered. 'Certainly these parents are being tiresome to a degree. I should think that at this strained time everybody should pull together to smooth the headmaster's path.'

Granger flushed with anger. He rose from the table in agitation, and crossed to the windows, from which he could see Dalton's creation, Foliott's Building, rising above the wall to his left.

'The headmaster's path? Smooth the headmaster's path? What about your own path, Sandford? What about mine? You don't seem to realize what you and I could do if we weren't constrained and shackled by Dalton's corrupting inertia!'

'Good heavens, Vice-master, what are you saying? Dr Dalton is one of England's foremost educational theorists — '

'Yes, yes, I acknowledge the great things he's done in the past, but what about the present? He just sits down there in his house, making the occasional stately sortie into the school to see that his museum-piece is properly dusted. Nobody but the good doctor is permitted to have ideas. We must all knuckle under to the great educational theorist, liar and hypocrite!'

Sandford sprang up from his chair, quivering with indignation.

'Sir! You forget yourself!'

'What? Do you think I should meekly submit to Dalton's veneer of pompous self-righteousness, knowing what I know!'

'Why, sir, what *do* you know?'

The question seemed to assuage Granger's mounting anger. He sat down at the table, and Sandford did the same. But Granger saw that it was too late for reservations.

'Sandford, I am more and more convinced that Dr Dalton is a whited sepulchre! Did you know that he is at this very moment in lone conference with Lady Jane Ashwood? Ever since Sir Walter Foliott's dinner she has called regularly at Headmaster's House. I believe he's drawing her into his toils. I don't know how he's doing it, but she'd better take care!'

'But surely, Vice-master, there's no need to read impropriety into Lady Jane's visit?'

'Sandford,' said Granger in low tones, 'your charitable nature does you credit, but the world is not as you would like it to be. I have a brother who practises medicine at a little place called Draycot St Peter in Oxfordshire. Very unfortunate for Dalton, because my brother wrote to tell me about our headmaster's clandestine visits to someone whom I'd best refer to as the Widowed Lady.'

'But surely — '

'Please, Sandford, credit my brother and me with some native common sense. I say 'visits', but I mean something more substantial than that. There are ways of finding out these things. And that's why at times I can scarcely bring myself to be civil to him. He is a moral fraud!'

'A fraud?'

'Yes! Do you remember him telling me that he was going to Oxford — to Corpus Christi College? Well, he wasn't. Fletcher found out the truth, and told me. Dalton lied. He went to Draycot St Peter to visit the Widow!'

Granger moved uneasily and glanced covertly at Sandford, who seemed now to be rooted in shock.

'Widow be damned!' he muttered. 'Poor old Fletcher knew all about it. That was clear enough from something he said to me at the Special Dessert. 'Damnable' he called it, and damnable it is!'

'Dr Dalton is a bachelor, as far as I'm

aware — ' Sandford began. Granger cut him short.

'Yes, he is, and as such is entitled to have lady friends. But this particular lady is kept hidden from sight, and lied about. Why does she not visit him here? I know for a fact that there are children . . . There, Sandford, I've said more than I should, and pushed this confidence to the limit.'

'Children? Do you intend to make these things public knowledge?'

'Not yet. Not unless I must. I may despise Dalton, but I have no remit to destroy his reputation. But I'll tell you this, Sandford. If he attempts to compromise Lady Jane Ashwood, then I will be implacable in exposing his vice!'

Talking so frankly to Sandford, a man whom he trusted implicitly, seemed to restore Granger to something approaching equanimity. He sat down at the table, and unsealed the last letter of the morning's post.

It was from an English doctor resident in Cannes, who informed him, with deep regret, that the Reverend Ambrose Gledhill, recuperating from typhoid, had quite suddenly died of a seizure.

9

The Man in the Night-gown

These men, thought Jackson, looking at the expectant faces of the masters assembled for the second time at his request in Dr Dalton's study, can sense that this is to be no ordinary meeting. They had all seen the arrival of the posse of police vehicles shortly after ten o'clock, and the dramatic sealing of the entrance to Foliott's Building.

Dr Dalton sat in the large winged armchair near the fireplace, with Granger near him. The others — Valentine, Caswell, Sandford and Fielding-Stenhouse — were positioned more or less in a line facing the desk where Jackson had established himself. A uniformed police constable sat at a small table near the window, a pencil poised over his open note-book.

On Jackson's left sat Sergeant Bottomley. And on his right? Jackson wondered what these masters would make of the fiercely intimidating man who had spent the last few minutes poring over a portfolio of documents without deigning to acknowledge the presence of anybody other than Jackson in the room.

Somebody outside the room quietly closed the door. It was time for Jackson to address his audience.

'Gentlemen,' he began, 'I have a great deal to say to you this afternoon, and I'm very much afraid that one or two of you may be upset before I've finished. When I first came here eleven days ago, you presented me with two mysteries, a dead man, and a missing man. As for the missing man — Mr Fletcher I mean — I believe that I know what happened to him, but I don't intend to talk about that side of the affair today.'

'One moment, Inspector,' said Granger. 'I fail to see how Fletcher's disappearance can be divorced from the murder. That unknown man was not only in Fletcher's room, but was actually clad in his night-gown and lying in his bed. There must be a connection.'

'Well, yes, Mr Granger,' said Jackson mildly. 'I never said there wasn't a connection. But the connection between the unknown man and Mr Fletcher is like that of two men in a railway accident. One man could be killed, and another man injured, but just because they were together in the same carriage doesn't mean that they necessarily knew each other.' He made certain that

194

Granger would hear the tone of hard finality in his voice as he concluded, 'But I don't propose to talk about that side of the affair today.'

Granger sat down again quietly on his chair near to the headmaster. Jackson turned over two pages of his note-book, and then looked slowly and deliberately at each member of staff in turn.

'I remember, gentlemen, that you all disclaimed any knowledge of the unknown man when I came to see you last. Some time has passed since then, and maybe one of you can now recollect having seen him somewhere before. Perhaps this photograph will assist you.'

He nodded to Sergeant Bottomley, who handed a photograph to Dr Dalton. The head uttered an exclamation of disgust and passed it to Granger before replying.

'No, Inspector,' said Dalton, 'I, for one, have never seen him before. And I must add that it is most distasteful to be asked to look at such a thing. That photographic portrait has clearly been taken after death.'

Jackson made no reply, but waited until they had all looked at the photograph, and it had been returned to Bottomley. No one, it seemed, had seen the man before.

Jackson leaned forward slightly in his chair,

consciously adopting a more official, public stance. When he spoke, it was with the measured formality of a policeman reading evidence in court.

'On the afternoon of Sunday, the eleventh of September, 1892, Dr Walter Manning, a physician, caused to be removed from these premises the body of a man who may have died under suspicious circumstances. The body was conveyed to Warwick, where an autopsy was performed. Tests applied to the contents of the stomach and to other organs showed that the deceased man had died from poisoning by aconitine, a vegetable alkaloid. The therapeutic dose of this substance is one three-hundredth of a grain. More than ten times this dosage was found in the body.'

He paused, and glanced at Fielding-Stenhouse, who had turned pale. Dr Dalton, he noticed, stirred in his seat, seemed about to say something, and then refrained from doing so.

'Dr Manning retrieved from under the bed upon which the dead man lay a wine glass, which was also submitted to forensic examination. Traces of aconitine were also found in this glass. The man, therefore, had drunk from the glass containing the poison, and so died.'

Jackson stopped, and sat back in his chair.

'I want you now, gentlemen, to listen to a report from the gentleman on my right, who is Dr Julian Richards MD, Forensic Police Specialist from Birmingham.'

Dr Richards was not given to preliminary courtesies. He spoke in a firm, high, testy voice. Jackson smiled to himself. Richards, he knew from experience, was a man who went in awe of nothing and nobody.

'This morning, as you may have noticed, my colleagues and I made a thorough inspection of the premises known as Foliott's Building, and the herb garden and glass-house adjoining. In the garden we found well-grown specimens of thorn-apple, henbane, deadly nightshade, monk's-hood, and foxglove.'

Dr Richards had a bristling moustache, which now moved sinisterly upwards to reveal a sort of snarling smile. His teeth were very white, and very regular.

'Now these plants are not just pretty flowers. They are not designed as ornaments of the boudoir! From the leaves and flowers of thorn-apple and henbane one may extract the alkaloid hyoscyamine, and the same substance may be got from deadly night-shade, or *Atropa belladonna* to give it its botanical name. The roots of monk's-hood yield aconitine. The leaves of foxglove yield

197

digitoxin. All these plants, therefore, could be used — and were used — to produce most deadly poisons.'

Fielding-Stenhouse cleared his throat nervously. If ever an innocent man looked guilty, thought Jackson, then it was this untidily dressed head of science.

'And now,' continued Dr Richards, 'we come to the glasshouse. My assistants and I had no difficulty gaining entry, as it was unlocked. We found growing inside it thriving specimens of the opium poppy and the yellow jasmine, which again yield lethal substances. That the authorities of a school could countenance this Garden of the Borgias to flourish openly where young boys could find these plants passes my comprehension.'

His voice grew louder and more scornful, as he added, 'Young boys will eat anything. Anything! They will chew privet leaves and grass stems, eat berries from hedges, put pieces of tree bark in their mouths — I once knew a boy who ate a worm for a wager. To let such poisonous plants as these grow openly where boys could find them was both reprehensible and irresponsible.'

No one said anything, but Dr Dalton blushed crimson. I don't suppose, Jackson thought, that he's ever been on the receiving end of a tongue-lashing.

'After inspecting the garden,' the testy voice continued, 'we entered the building and made a thorough examination of its contents. There was much clutter and untidiness, both dangerous faults where chemicals are being used. In a laboratory on the first floor we found a large press or cupboard, again, unlocked, containing among a medley of other things twenty-eight phials of chemical substances, each stopped with a cork and sealed with wax. These — '

'Twenty-eight?' Fielding-Stenhouse inter-rupted tremulously. 'There are thirty such phials in that cupboard. They contain the powdered specimens of the alkaloids and glycosides that I have extracted from my plants. Each phial is labelled with a number, and you will find a small book in the cupboard in which the contents are identified by a brief description following each number.'

'In that cupboard, sir,' retorted the implacable Dr Richards, 'there is a large card depicting the periodic table of the elements. It had been carelessly pushed against the shelves and the doors closed over it, presumably because it was hindering you from depositing some other item of clutter on an acceptable surface. I removed this card, and saw immediately that there was a gap in the rows of phials. Two phials, numbers eight and nine, were missing, but because of that card masking the contents of the shelves, I assume that you did not notice.'

Dr Richards gave vent to a mirthless laugh, which had more of the quality of a slap in the face for Fielding-Stenhouse.

'Those two phials may have been missing for weeks, or months, or years for all I know,' Richards continued. 'I need hardly tell you that, on consulting your note-book, we found that numbers eight and nine were phials of aconitine.'

Richards rummaged though the papers on the desk until he found a particular sheet, which he held up some distance from his eyes.

'The twenty-eight phials that we found contained refined specimens of hyoscyamine, atropine, hyoscine, colchicine, morphine, narcotine, gelsemine, digitoxin, digitalin, and strophanthin.'

Richards threw the paper down on the desk and fixed his gaze on the head of science.

'Mr Fielding-Stenhouse,' he asked, 'would you agree with me that the contents of those twenty-eight phials would be more than sufficient to kill every man, woman and child in this school?'

'Yes.'

Dr Richards seemed to have finished for

the moment. Jackson could sense that his own mellower tones came almost as a welcome relief.

'Yes, well, thank you very much, Dr Richards. Now, Dr Dalton, I have been told that you were obliged to pay a nocturnal visit to Mr Fielding-Stenhouse's laboratory on the night of the eighth of this month. Would you care to tell me what occurred?'

'Certainly, Inspector. I was working very late in my study that night. Some time towards half past two I looked out of the window, and saw a light glowing in Mr Fielding-Stenhouse's laboratory. I am always conscious of the great danger of fire from naked lamps and candles, and, unwilling to rouse a servant at that early hour, I went out myself to Foliott's Building. In the laboratory upstairs I found a candle burning. I blew it out and snuffed the wick, and then returned to my house. Next morning, I sent for Mr Fielding-Stenhouse and reprimanded him very severely. He, however, denied that he had left the candle burning.'

'Do you still deny it, Mr Fielding-Stenhouse?' asked Jackson.

'Yes, Inspector, I do. That gentleman there,' — he indicated the redoubtable Dr Richards — 'has accused me of carelessness, and I must plead guilty to that. But I have never left lamps and candles burning, and certainly on that day I had left Foliott's Building well before it was time to light the lamps.'

'Well,' said Jackson, 'we can leave the matter of the burning candle to a later time. Dr Richards, do you wish to say anything further?'

'Just this, Detective Inspector. My colleagues and I have removed all the phials of alkaloids and other lethal substances from the laboratory, and we have also uprooted and taken away all the plants from the garden. We have left untouched the less exotic acids and other chemicals in the laboratory. I think that's all. I shall go now, Inspector, and ask Mr Fielding-Stenhouse to accompany me. I wish to talk to him at some length, in private.'

With a curt nod, he gathered up his papers, and left the room, followed by the badly shaken head of science.

As soon as the two men had gone, Inspector Jackson addressed his listeners once again.

'Gentlemen, we have now explained to you that the man was poisoned with aconitine, obtained in some way from Mr Fielding-Stenhouse's laboratory. This poison is a white, soluble powder, and it had been put into a glass of spirits and given to the man to drink. I believe this murder to have been a very cleverly devised plan, calculated to cause the maximum amount of confusion. What I want to emphasize at this moment, gentlemen, is the unpleasant fact that, whoever murdered the man is a member of the staff of this school.'

No one spoke for a while, as the enormity of this suggestion took root in their minds. Then Dr Dalton stirred himself out of the daze in which he seemed to have been lost for the preceding half-hour.

'Inspector Jackson,' he said, 'we have been very grateful for your care and persistence in investigating this distressing affair. But I think that I speak for my colleagues as well as for myself when I say that we are rapidly tiring of these — these dramatic lectures with which you regale us. We would be more impressed if you found out who the wretched fellow was. Perhaps then you would be justified in seeking a connection between him and my staff.'

Inspector Jackson looked steadily at Dalton for a few moments before replying. He was thinking of John Hudson, hotelier, and the treacherous, suety Mr Pickavance. Then he spoke.

'He was Stephen Peter Ball, sir.'

The others were still looking at Jackson, and it was the sudden, uncharacteristic flicker of triumph which momentarily lit up the inspector's face that made them turn and look at Dalton. He remained seated in his armchair, but every trace of colour had drained from his face. His impressive figure seemed to shrink, as though wishing to hide from the solid, comfortable Warwickshire man who had uttered a name unknown to any of them.

'Stephen Peter Ball was second porter at Nelson College, Plymouth, from 1874 to 1880. He was a chronic alcoholic, and was dismissed for persistent drunkenness in the February of the latter year. The present headmaster of Nelson College, Dr Stone Maynard, has furnished me with a document, which I have here, to the effect that it was at your instigation that Ball was dismissed.'

Jackson picked up the photograph of the dead man and held it up for Dalton to see. The headmaster shielded his eyes and turned aside, but Jackson continued to hold the picture up. There was an awed silence in the room.

'Now I put it to you, sir, that you *must* have recognized this man. Why were you so overcome when you saw his dead body? According to Captain Valentine's testimony, you nearly fainted, and had to return to your house. Why did you say that you had never seen him before? Why did you pretend that you did not recognize his photograph?'

Dalton's reply, when it came, was merely a choked whisper.

'I have nothing to say.'

Inspector Jackson sighed. He turned slightly towards Sergeant Bottomley and gave him a barely perceptible nod.

'On the night of Saturday, the tenth of September, 1892,' said Bottomley, 'the staff of the school held a dinner, known as the Special Dessert, in Staff House. At approximately a quarter past nine that evening, Joseph Hodge, a groundsman or pasture-keeper, saw in the half light a man, whom he had never seen before, walking rather furtively and unsteadily up the path to the front of the headmaster's house. He noted the man's appearance well, observing that he was not a gentleman, and wondering why he would go to the front door rather than round into the stable yard.'

The sudden utterance of a different voice in the room came as a kind of shock. Dr Dalton removed his hand from his eyes and looked at Bottomley as though he had noticed him for the first time.

'On the sixteenth of this month,' Bottomley continued, 'I showed Hodge a photograph of Stephen Peter Ball. He positively recognized him, and asserted that he had been the man whom he had seen approaching the headmaster's house. Hodge had just decided to leave his work and question the man when the front door of the house was opened, and to his great surprise Hodge saw that the man now known to be Stephen Peter Ball was admitted to the house not by a servant, but by Dr Dalton himself. He saw him motion the man to enter, and then close the door.'

As suddenly as he had commenced speaking, Sergeant Bottomley stopped, and sat impassively, his arms folded. Again, the quiet tones of Inspector Jackson assumed control of the proceedings.

'Dr Dalton,' he said, 'by refusing to make any statement to me, you have obliged me to reveal certain facts in the presence of your colleagues. That, I am sure, has been very painful to you. Before I continue with what is my duty in this matter, I ask you again, is there anything that you think you should tell me?'

Hoarse and low, the voice came again from the armchair.

'I can say nothing.'

'Gentlemen,' the inspector continued, 'I am putting you on your honour not to repeat outside this room anything that you have heard this afternoon. I must also advise the that the whole of these proceedings is being recorded by the shorthand-writer.'

Jackson turned again to Dr Dalton.

'Dr Dalton, I am now suggesting to you that Stephen Peter Ball never forgave you for the part you played in his dismissal from Nelson College, and, as he sank lower and lower through his addiction to drink, he determined to apply to you, with threats, for money. For a long period of time you yielded to these threats, but when Ball became more demanding, you determined to bring the matter to an issue. You summoned Ball here on the night of the Special Dessert. While he was in your house — a man quite unknown to your colleagues — you plied him with drink, in which you could have placed some noxious substance, such as aconitine. Thus the terrible threat to your career and reputation could be silenced once and for all — '

'Stop!' The vehement voice of Granger startled them as it suddenly broke across Jackson's terrible narrative. 'All this is mere supposition! Are you suggesting that the headmaster wantonly took another human life simply because he did not like this man?'

'Oh, no, sir, I'm not suggesting that at all. The pr? ?ess that I have described is called ? l', and it is payment for keeping silent about what some people call a skeleton in the cupboard. Dr Dalton's skeleton is that for many years he has been secretly married to a lady who, had he not entered into matrimony with her, would have given birth to a child out of wedlock. That, Mr Granger, is the tragic reality underlying this case of murder by poisoning.'

'Married? Impossible! Dr Dalton is, and always has been, a bachelor.'

There was a genuine bewilderment in Granger's voice.

'No, sir. Dr Dalton is married to Lucy Eynesham, of Plymouth. Seven months after the marriage a son, Eric, was born to them. In order to preserve his professional reputation, Dr Dalton concealed this marriage, and ever since, Mrs Dalton has lived in secrecy under an assumed name. I have reason to believe that she is known as 'Mrs Dolling' — '

'Good God!' cried Granger. 'The Widow of Draycot!'

'Yes, sir, but not a widow! I suspected that you had found out about Dr Dalton's clandestine visits to this lady, but that you had not realized that she was, in fact, his wife. I am also convinced that Mr Fletcher knew this secret. It was an ideal subject for blackmail, and I very much fear that, in the pursuance of it, Stephen Peter Ball was done to death.'

While Jackson was speaking, Granger had knelt down near the shattered and humiliated form that still cringed in the big armchair. There was a touching contrition in Granger's voice as he said, 'Dalton, I had no idea . . . I did not think for one moment that you were married to that lady . . . I thought it was some vulgar liaison — '

Dr Dalton suddenly laughed.

'Liaison! Oh, Granger, you're such an impossible innocent! But I have nothing to say. Nothing! I will neither affirm nor deny what this man has said. Now, I beg you all, let me retire to another room.'

'At least,' said Granger, his voice betraying the shock that he felt, 'let me send for Leo Farmer.'

'Send for him by all means. Perhaps the time has come for legal support. Now, please, let me retire.'

Inspector Jackson stood up, and Sergeant Bottomley began to gather up the various documents that had been spread out on Dalton's desk. Dr Dalton walked slowly towards the door. He was just about to open it when Jackson said, in gentle, almost apologetic tones, 'Dr Dalton, for reasons that will now be very obvious to you, you must not leave the school premises. If you venture out of the buildings and into the grounds, you must not be offended if you are kept continually in sight by one of my officers.'

The headmaster nodded wearily, and left the room. He was a prisoner in his own house, and his own school.

★ ★ ★

Once again Jane Ashwood glanced along the polished table of Sir Walter Foliott's dining-room. Today, though, there were no silver appointments or costly crystal, no deep tinge of red from decanters of old port. It was not soft candle-light but the harsh glare of morning that glanced off the shining mahogany surface.

'I called this hurried meeting of the Court of Governors,' said Sir Walter, 'because we must make a decision immediately. There are seven of you, enough to constitute a quorum. You know why we are here. The other week I said that Kingsmere was like a close and trusting family, with Dalton as the father. It is a view that I may be called upon to revise.'

Jane wondered how her fellow-governors would react. Some, she knew, would have a lot to say. Others would say nothing. It had not been possible to get all twelve members of the Court together at short notice. It was the Friday following Jackson's dramatic exposé of Dalton's private sins.

Leo Farmer, the school's solicitor, would, as always, be shrewd and taciturn. Mr Leopold Cotton, MP, a man with an almost agonizing sense of public decency, would follow whoever took the most drastic course. Mr Tyson Roberts was a rich and opinionated bully, and Mr Joel Bradshaw, a quiet, nervous mine owner. It had been his exuberant wife, Jane reflected, who had asked Dalton about the merits of headmasterly marriage.

Across the table sat Lord Doncaster, a constitutionally silent man who always voted with the chairman, whatever the merits of the issue, and Mr Olave Pennington, a Foreign Office diplomat who was rumoured to have more influence on national events than was either decent or possible.

'It is vital, Sir Walter, that the school is not compromised in any way,' said Leopold Cotton, casting his eyes round the room in what seemed very like despair. 'Have you spoken to this policeman? They're saying that Dalton was quite intimate with the man who died in the school — '

'The man who was killed in the school,' Sir Walter corrected him. 'The man who was *murdered* in the school, to put it bluntly. Yes,

Cotton, I spoke at length yesterday to Inspector Jackson. He was very frank and very fair, but of course he told me only as much as he wanted me to know. Dalton did indeed know the dead man, and had once done him an injury. Yet Dalton denied twice that he knew the man. Things look very bad.'

Mr Tyson Roberts burst into indignant speech. His face reddened and his prominent eyes flashed with indignation.

'It's obvious that Dalton must go at once! We are faced with a definite possibility that he will be found guilty of murder! I hear that he actually cried out in guilt when he saw the man's dead body. Send him away! Let the vice-master assume the headship on a temporary basis.'

'Mr Tyson Roberts is right,' said the timid Mr Bradshaw. He was rewarded with an approving glance from the rich bully.

'Mr Farmer, you're the school's 'man of business'. What have you to say?'

'Sir Walter, I intend to make myself professionally useful to the headmaster and to Mr Granger, his deputy. I am therefore unable to join effectively in this discussion.'

Sir Walter sat back in his chair. Jane thought: he knows already what he's going to do. He's called this meeting through constitutional necessity. She knew that he would ask once more for comments before he gave his decision. When he did so, she was ready with her own response.

'Sir Walter,' she said, 'I, for one, do not believe the sinister charges that are being laid against Dr Dalton, and I venture to suggest that he is being hastily judged before he has even been formally accused of any crime.'

She saw Leo Farmer's nod of approval, which encouraged her to continue. She recalled her conversation with Dr Dalton on the night of Sir Walter's dinner.

'I am convinced that many parents would feel angered if we acted hastily and unjustly. Mr Tyson Roberts says that Dr Dalton cried out in guilt. I suggest that what he did was cry out in horror.'

The furious Tyson Roberts began to splutter with growing rage. His pale round eyes bulged in his crimson face.

'But *something* must be done! It's all very well, Lady Jane, being feminine and compassionate, and all that, but we're living in the real world! Ask Mr Leopold Cotton, MP. He'll tell you.'

Mr Cotton nodded agreement, and cast up his anguished eyes to Heaven.

'It's true, Lady Jane! Why, it seems that Dalton's been married all these years, and yet has hidden his wife away in the country!

213

Why? There's no smoke without fire. The man's no longer fit to be head of the school.'

'Married?'

'Yes, Lady Jane. At least, that's what I understand,' said Cotton mildly.

Sir Walter held up an admonitory hand. His eyes were fixed upon Jane, who had gone very pale. He hastily rearranged his ideas and then spoke.

'There's a great deal of truth in what Lady Jane Ashwood has just said. Dalton is in law innocent of any crime until he is first charged and then found guilty. At the same time, it would be foolishly irresponsible not to heed what Mr Tyson Roberts and Mr Cotton have said. So this is what I suggest.'

He paused for a moment and looked down the table. They all knew that Sir Walter's suggestions had the nature of commands.

'I suggest that Dr Dalton be publicly permitted to continue as Headmaster of Kingsmere, so that the monster of Rumour can be scotched before it has devoured the place and its inhabitants. The boys are already on the edge of a precipice. The disappearance of Dalton would push them into the abyss.'

'And Granger?' asked Leo Farmer. His calm voice was a welcome change from the impassioned tones of the other gentlemen governors.

'I will see Mr Theodore Granger myself today,' Sir Walter replied. 'He must be from this moment headmaster in all but name.'

There were murmurs of approval when Granger was mentioned, and Sir Walter's motion was carried without dissent. It was clear to all that he derived no particular pleasure from his success. He sighed and shook his head.

'It's a sad time, fellow-governors,' he said. 'A very different scene from when we last met in this very room! I've always been an optimist by nature, but in this matter of Dalton I very much fear the worst.'

10

The Pursuit of Letters

The 7.40 morning train from Warwick to London via Oxford and Reading clattered busily through the autumn countryside. Jackson and Bottomley had secured an empty third-class compartment.

'This, Sergeant,' said Jackson, consulting his watch, 'is by way of being a leisurely journey for both of us. It's only nine o'clock, so we've ample time to discuss the case.'

Sergeant Bottomley had been reading a crumpled pink sporting paper, which he carefully folded up and crammed into one of his overcoat pockets. He sighed.

'Are you quite sure we shouldn't change destinations, sir? You should let me go on to London to see Mrs Bell-Forest, while you tackle this Tommy Baxter. It's only a matter of swapping tickets.'

Jackson chuckled and shook his head.

'No, Sergeant Bottomley. I'll take care of Mrs Bell-Forest. It's the 'dreaming spires' of Oxford for you. And while you're there you can pay a call on Captain C.P. McKerrow.

Find out for certain what kind of debt it was that Mr Fletcher paid for Mr Harry Caswell.'

'Whatever it was, sir, it turned Mr Caswell into a staunch friend. It's Mr Fletcher's turn to be the debtor.'

Jackson laughed, and shook his head as though in disbelief.

'A staunch friend, Sergeant? He's certainly that, is our Mr Caswell. A staunch friend — and a prize ass!'

The train rattled through a short tunnel and emerged into a stretch of wooded countryside where the leaves were turning golden.

'Today, Sergeant,' said Jackson, 'we'll track down the writers of three of those letters. Tomorrow, if all goes well, we'll call on Dr D.K. Granger and Mrs Dolling, at Draycot St Peter. Mrs Dolling — '

'Alias Lucy Eynesham of Plymouth, who married Dr Dalton on the eighteenth of October, 1876 — '

'And had a son, Eric, born in May, 1877, and so now aged fifteen. Where is he now? And more to the point, why doesn't Dalton recognize his existence?'

'I don't know, sir. But regarding the matter in hand, I do know that Dr Dalton was the only person at that school who knew Stephen Peter Ball, and that Ball was murdered. I think Dalton gave him a poisoned drink, waited until he was dead, and then lugged him up the stairs into the staff quarters, taking the wine-glass with him.'

'And what then, Sergeant?'

'I reckon he dragged or carried the body along the passage, and barged into Mr Fletcher's room, thinking it would be empty. But it wasn't. So Dalton says to himself, 'If Fletcher sees me with this corpse, I'm a goner'. He ups with a walking-stick, or something else to hand, and clouts the old man over the head before he can see properly who it is that's come in. He drops the wine-glass on the floor, and beats a hasty retreat.'

Jackson was unconvinced. It sounded very plausible, but it was wrong. Wrong . . . Why should Dalton murder a man to conceal the fact that he's married? It wasn't a crime, to be married . . .

The small train drew fussily into Oxford Station, and Sergeant Bottomley got down on to the platform. Jackson could see him muttering his memorized directions: Hythe Bridge Street, George Street, turn right into Cornmarket . . . High Street . . . Merton Street . . . Corpus Christi.

Bottomley leaned on the sill of the carriage door and looked at Jackson, who had begun to settle down for the long haul to London. The sergeant frowned.

'But, of course, sir, it could be something else. So here's another little thought. Dr Edward Dalton seems to be something of a ladies' man. He's got a way with him, so they tell me. Kingsmere's a remote village deep in the countryside, and yet, within a mile of each other, and within the space of a few days, two people are done to death with a rare poison, aconitine. Alice Patching and Stephen Peter Ball. And it's quite obvious where the aconitine came from. Is that another reason why Dalton won't speak, sir? Alice Patching?'

★ ★ ★

The porter at the ancient Oxford college of Corpus Christi ushered Sergeant Bottomley out of the lodge and into the sunlit quadrangle. Like most visitors to the college, the sergeant was surprised to see the column with its sundial and crowning image of a pelican rising up just beyond the arched entrance from the gate-house.

'You'll find Mr Baxter a little difficult, Sergeant,' said the porter. 'You'll need to talk loud if you want to make yourself heard.'

He was a stooping, hatchet-faced man of fifty, with a serious expression and humorous eyes. The lapels of his well-worn frock coat were stuck full of pins, evidently used for some special porterly purpose.

'Difficult? A bit lacking, is he?'

The serious face lengthened into a frown, but the humorous eyes twinkled.

'He's — he's what we term an emeritus fellow, Mr Bottomley, which means he's retired. He lives here. This is his home. No, he's not lacking. He's very clever. But he's getting on. Forgetful. Difficult, if you see what I mean.'

'And where will I find this Mr Baxter? Always supposing that he's in.'

'He's in, all right. Go round to your left until you come to staircase five. You'll find him there. Go up the stairs.'

★   ★   ★

'Not a word, sir, I beg you: I'm awaiting my medicine!'

Mr Baxter was a large old man, rooted in a high-backed chair which seemed long ago to have moulded itself to fit his particular contours. Man and chair were essentially a single composition. The most striking feature of Mr Baxter was his vinous, fermented countenance, purple as the grape, and enlivened by bright, staring eyes. His voice was a lively, fat croak.

Bottomley had no option but to sit and wait for the medicine, whatever it was, to arrive, while his host sat in a sort of glazed and immovable trance. Scattered around Mr Baxter's great chair were numerous pieces of screwed-up paper, many covered in dust. Bottomley wondered whether the servants were forbidden to gather them up and dispose of them.

At last there came a knock on the door, followed by the entry of an elderly servant wearing a baize apron. Bottomley stared fascinated. Could there really be two of them? The newcomer was in every respect a facsimile of Mr Baxter. He had a bright puce face, and the same staring eyes, and when he spoke, it was with a similar strangled croak. He had brought Baxter his medicine.

'What've you brought me, Porson? It's not that bottled stuff, is it?'

'Certainly not, sir. It's a nice drop of beer, is this, with a good head on it. I'd never bring you no bottled stuff.'

Mr Baxter took the proffered medicine, and drained the tankard in a single gulp. He remained transfixed for several seconds, and then delivered himself of what had better be called a sigh of satisfaction. Porson retrieved the empty vessel, and withdrew. Bottomley heard him croaking to himself on the stairs: 'No; I'll never bring him no bottled stuff.'

While the old scholar refreshed himself, Bottomley looked in awe at what seemed to be a sea of books covering one wall of the room from floor to ceiling. One set, extending to over twenty bound volumes, caught his eye. Each volume was labelled *Baxter's Laws and Statutes of Edward III.* Could this wizened old soak have written all those books?

Bottomley jumped with fright when Baxter's newly oiled throat exploded into speech.

'So, sir,' said Baxter, 'you've come from Amyas Fletcher, have you? What's he done now? Run off with some filly? I have your note somewhere' — he glanced vaguely at the screwed-up pieces of paper lying around his feet.

'Well, Inspector Jackson, you don't look like an inspector, always assuming that inspectors have a special sort of look of their own. You look to me more like a groom, or one of those men you find at racecourses — what do you call them? They take bets and write your name in grubby little books. What do you call them?'

'Bookmakers, sir. But I'm not one of those. And I'm not Inspector Jackson, who happens

222

to be my guv'nor. My name's Bottomley. Detective Sergeant Bottomley.'

Mr Baxter sighed and shook his head. Too much for the poor old dosser, thought Bottomley. Too many questions and too much booze.

'So Fletcher's run off with a filly, hey?'

'Not exactly, sir, no. Not to my knowledge, sir. What he's done is disappeared, and there's a lot of folk, sir, me included, who want to find out where he's got to.'

Bottomley outlined to Mr Baxter the events that had occurred at Kingsmere School. After he had finished, the old don sat for a while in thought. Then he spoke.

'So, Fletcher's murdered this man in the night-gown, has he? Well, I'm a bit surprised to hear that. Thought he'd run off with some filly. He was very keen on the ladies, you know. But I didn't think he'd do a murder. I'm a bit surprised to hear that.'

Bottomley tried again, with some measure of success, to make Baxter realize the nature of his visit. He was able to bring the conversation round to the brief note that he had found in Fletcher's package: *'Dear Fletcher — No, he hasn't, and no, he didn't.'*

'Yes, I remember that. You know, Sergeant, Fletcher's a nosy, prying feller, and no secret's safe from him. He was always like that. Should have been a policeman!'

'And what did Mr Fletcher do, sir, to make you send him that reply?'

'Well, he sends me this note — it's on the floor here somewhere — asking if Dr Dalton, his headmaster, had visited Corpus on such and such a day, and whether he'd been here on other previous occasions. And I thought to myself, why do you want to know that, you old snooper? That's why I wrote him such a short note. None of his business!'

'So Dr Dalton has never been to this college?'

'Why should he? He's a very famous man, you know, and an Oxford man, too, but he wasn't a Corpus man. Anyway, he's never been here, you can take my word for it, and when you see Fletcher, tell him to stop being so damned nosy. If he goes on like that, Sergeant, he'll get his fingers burned!'

★ ★ ★

Captain McKerrow's house in the gloomy slate-grey suburb of St Ebbe's was a decidedly superior residence, with crisp lace curtains on the windows, and a polished brass plate beside the door, bearing the legend, 'Captain C.P. McKerrow.'

A bright little servant-girl showed Bottomley into an ornate and overheated sitting-room. There was a good deal of flashy gilt furniture, heavy drapes of some oriental material, and a florid marble grate, in which a heaped-up fire was burning.

In a few moments, Captain McKerrow, a stout well-fed man with a round, perspiring face, came into the room. He wore an elaborate smoking-jacket and a tasselled silk cap, neither of which looked amiss on him. Despite his name, his swarthy complexion was more suggestive of the Levant than of Scotland.

'I do declare, Sergeant Bottomley,' he said, 'this is indeed an honour! I assume that you have not come to, er — ?'

He paused delicately, his cold uneasy eyes fixed on Bottomley. His refined voice held a slight foreign intonation.

Bottomley smiled and shook his head.

'No thank you, Captain McKerrow,' he said, 'I'm not in need of an advance at the moment, but when I am, I'll know where to come. This is by way of being a social call, though I hope you'll be able to help me with a bit of information.'

McKerrow visibly relaxed.

'I'll be delighted to help you in any way I can, Sergeant. I've devoted my life to helping

225

those in need, those whose lives could be shattered for want of a few pounds at the right time. Many unkind things are said about people like me, but virtue is its own reward.'

Bottomley leaned forward in his chair and beamed at the moneylender.

'A very choice sentiment, sir,' he said. 'Now, I'd like you to give me some details about a little receipt of yours that's come my way, Captain. It was dated April the seventeenth, 1887, and acknowledged the payment of a sum of money by a man called Fletcher to terminate the account of another man called Caswell.'

'Caswell, Caswell?' muttered Captain McKerrow. 'Oh, yes! I remember.' He sighed. 'How sad it is when these young men gamble! Oh, why will they do it? I was so glad to help him. And then this other gentleman, this Mr Fletcher, called upon me that day, and gave me a draft upon Coutts's Bank for the full amount of the young man's debt.'

'The sum being — '

'Four hundred pounds exactly, Sergeant. I remitted the odd few shillings.'

McKerrow clasped a pair of beringed hands together in ecstasy.

'What a noble thing for this Mr Fletcher to do! How kind! But, of course, I would have allowed Mr Caswell as long as he liked to repay the loan. He could have taken fifty years had he so wished!'

'I'm sure he could, sir,' said Bottomley, 'you being such a kindly man. When I see him next, I'll tell him what you said. I'm sure he'll be very pleased. Good day, sir.'

★　★　★

Just after two o'clock that afternoon Jackson presented himself at the house of Mr and Mrs Bell-Forest in Exeter Place, a staid enclave of tall brick houses near Bedford Square.

Meeting this stern, fanatical woman in her rich but bleak residence was a depressing and in some way unsettling experience. Tall and impressive, clad in a black silk dress with jet adornments, she sat unmoving in a high-backed chair, holding his warrant-card, but making no offer of a seat.

'Your rank and occupation, Inspector Jackson, make me in duty bound to grant you this interview. Family honour, though, will oblige me to be prudent in my choice of words concerning my cousin. Mr Bell-Forest and I are both Pilgrims of Mount Sion, who have left behind the abominations of this world, setting our faces firmly against Sin, and looking upward to the Heavenly Jerusalem.'

227

Her voice held scorn, but no joy. Whatever the consolations of her sect, thought Jackson, they had dried up within her the springs of compassion.

'Again, after all these years, I am to be burdened with the transgressions of my cousin Lucy Eynesham. I was asked once before to reveal her shame, and refused to do so, lest our name was sullied. Now, I will make an end of it, whatever the outcome.'

'The reason I have come today, ma'am — '

The stern woman held up a hand as though to ward off an evil spirit.

'I do not ask why you want to know of her shame, Mr Jackson, nor do I wish to hear your reasons. When Mr Bell-Forest and I died unto Sin, we rose again unto Righteousness. My cousin, sir, died unto Righteousness. Verily, she hath her reward.'

'Will you tell me what it was that your cousin did to incur your displeasure?'

'I will, sir. I have said, I will make an end of it! But it is not a case of *my* displeasure, but the condemnation of Him whose righteous commandments are written openly in this Book.'

She struck rather than touched a large Bible which was lying on a table near her hand. The rings on her fingers clicked sharply against the brass clasps of the heavy book.

'My cousin entered into a relationship with a man, a relationship that led to Fornication. Who the man was I never knew, and have no desire to know.'

Mrs Bell-Forest drew her brows together in a frown that seemed to suggest the anger of a purpose frustrated. Her pale cheeks began to show some colour, driven there by indignation.

'I charged my cousin with the truth. I urged repentance. My cousin, far from donning sackcloth and ashes, rejoiced in her iniquity, and disappeared with this man. A giddy, vain fool! She cut herself off for ever from all decent society, and from the Household of Faith. She was a fallen, but unrepentant, Magdalen.'

'So you have had no communication with her since that time?'

Mrs Bell-Forest had given him a strange, speculative glance, almost a look of disbelief.

'Communication? My cousin is dead — dead unto Righteousness. To my husband and myself, it is as though she had never lived.'

★ ★ ★

Jackson and Bottomley walked along the wide and well-paved High Street of the elegant

229

Oxfordshire town of Draycot St Peter, which lay six winding miles by railway from Abingdon. It was a town of mellow red brick, and, for variety, some neat stuccoed houses with classical porticoes.

They passed the Town Hall, an exquisite building with a pitched and pedimented roof crowned with a white wooden octagon with a gilded weather-vane gleaming in the morning sun. A short walk brought them to Old Well Lane, where, in an ancient low-roofed house, lived Dr D.K. Granger, Theodore Granger's brother. The far end of the lane was closed by an elaborate but graceful set of wrought-iron gates, behind which rose a slender church tower, boasting a clock with four gilt, lozenge-shaped dials.

In response to a ring on the bell, the door was opened by an elderly maid, who ushered the two police officers into a room at the rear of the house. Seated on either side of a chess table in the window embrasure were two men, who had evidently been locked in deadly combat. An old man in clerical dress sat in a wing chair, staring intently at the board, while his companion, an elfish, restless-looking small man of middle years, gloatingly moved a piece, and cried out, 'Mate!'

'I don't know why I bother,' sighed the old

clergyman to no one in particular. 'Twice a week I go through this charade of playing the game, and watching this slayer of kings take my bishops captive!'

The puckish little doctor rubbed his hands together with evident satisfaction.

'Gentlemen,' he said, 'let me introduce our good vicar, Parson Betteridge, who believes that one day he will defeat me at this game, which is why he keeps coming back! But he fails to see more than ten jumps ahead, and so is doomed to failure! Betteridge, this is Detective Inspector Jackson, and his colleague Sergeant Bottomley.'

The old clergyman bowed, and moved towards the door.

'I wish you gentlemen a pleasant visit,' he said. 'If you have any time to spare when your business is done, the church here is well worth a visit.'

He looked at Jackson speculatively for a moment, and then left the room.

'Now, Inspector,' said Dr Granger, 'sit down there on the settee. Just move those magazines on to the floor. That's right. And you, Sergeant. This is a pleasant room, fifteenth century, with Stuart embellishments.'

Their host was silent for a while, dropping the chess pieces one by one into a neat box with a sliding lid. There was a pleased, cat-like smile on his face. Jackson suddenly realized that D.K. Granger MD was no longer in practice.

'So, you've come about all this skulduggery at Kingsmere, Inspector Jackson. Who put you on to me? It wasn't Theodore, surely? Maybe it was old Fletcher. From what I hear he's a man who likes to keep a finger in every pie! But there: you're not going to tell me!'

Best come straight to the point, thought Jackson. Otherwise he and I will engage in a fruitless battle of words. This man is a prattler.

'I'm here, Dr Granger, to ask you about Dr Edward Dalton's visits to this town. From what I gather, they are regarded as something of a scandal. Maybe you can enlighten me.'

Dr Granger's eyes gleamed with the fire of mischief. It was, Jackson thought, rather a smouldering fire. He had already decided that Granger was a gossip. Perhaps he was something more.

Dr Granger chuckled with glee.

'Dr Edward Dalton, Inspector, is regarded in society as an Elder in Israel. But from what I've observed over the last year, I think the great Idol of Education might have feet of clay!'

'What do you mean by that, sir?'

'I came to live here, Inspector, just over a year ago. I'd intended to practise part-time, but this town is well served by two doctors, so I retired completely. I've plenty of time to observe the world go by, you see. I'm not like Theodore — my brother, you know. He likes to be at the centre of things. I belong to the byways. As some poet or other said: 'I was the stricken deer that left the herd long since'.'

'And Dr Edward Dalton, sir, does he belong to the byways?'

Granger laughed.

'Very good, Inspector! I stand chastened. I know I'm a gossip, so I must stick to the point. Just beyond the church here, in St Peter's Lane, there lives a lady called Mrs Dolling. To all intents and purposes she's a very respectable and respected widow. But walls have ears, Inspector, and people talk. Servants, you know, and trades-people. I'm not the only gossip in Draycot.'

The doctor's eyes narrowed and the smile disappeared from his face. He leaned forward in his chair and lowered his voice.

'Dalton has been visiting our good widow for years. He stays regularly in her house. What's more, there are children, one as young as nine — '

'Children?'

'Yes, two sons. Eric is fifteen, and boards at

a school near Abingdon. The younger boy, Julian, is nine. You've only to look at both the boys to see the uncanny resemblance to Dalton. It's a family, Mr Jackson, a father, a mother, and two children, both, I venture to say, born out of wedlock.'

'And you acquainted your brother Mr Theodore Granger with these assumptions?'

'I did — oh, dear me, Inspector, I can hear disapproval creeping into your voice! But consider this: here is a man who has built up a family by means which he dare not acknowledge. He keeps them here in secret exile for the sake of his career. I don't say that he openly asserts that he is a bachelor, but he's very content to let folk assume that he is.'

The doctor's face suddenly showed what until that moment had been a latent angered resentment.

'My brother was Headmaster of Kingsmere in all but name when old Pierce-Littledale was alive. Everyone assumed that he would succeed the old man. But that self-opinionated canal-builder Walter Foliott thought differently, and brought Dalton there with a mighty flourish of trumpets.'

Dr Granger rose from his chair in agitation. His impish features worked with volatile anger.

'And a few years ago the same thing happened again! Dalton withdrew to his study, and left the whole school to my brother's care. He has received no thanks for his great labours, only condescending snubs from Dalton. So please, Mr Jackson, don't judge me too harshly. I've not gossiped about this to all and sundry, and certainly not to Parson Betteridge. But don't condemn me if I seem ruthless in exposing this self-seeking hypocrite to my brother. I have a moral right to do so. And Theodore has a right to be told.'

⋆　⋆　⋆

Mrs Dolling glanced briefly at Jackson's warrant card and then motioned him and Bottomley to sit down. She had received them in the light, airy drawing-room of her house in St Peter's Lane, a quiet little road lying behind the picturesque church.

'I received your letter some days ago, Mr Jackson. It's very thoughtful of you to pay me this visit. Dr Dalton has in fact written to me, telling me that there are currently difficulties at the school, but nothing that he could not overcome.'

Her voice was musical and low, but firmly and fluently articulated. She was more poised than he had imagined her to be, a fair-haired woman of upright carriage, handsome, and impeccably dressed. Somehow, she was different from what he had expected. Her face conveyed frankness and courage, but he could detect a hint of some carefully concealed sorrow lurking there.

Jackson chose his words carefully. It was clear that this woman had no idea that her husband was living in the shadow of the gallows. It was part of his grim duty to make her aware of that fact.

'Mrs Dolling,' he began, 'I very much fear that what I have to tell you will cause you great distress, but I feel that you should know the facts of the situation. I am not here to speak of your relationship with Dr Dalton, but let us say that I know you have an interest in his well-being.'

Jackson felt a sudden stab of compassion for Mrs Dolling. There was a quality of restfulness about her elegant house and its tasteful furnishings that reflected her own dignified demeanour. There were framed photographs on the mantelpiece, one of a dignified young man in a yachting cap, and two others of young boys, both looking uncomfortable in starched Eton collars. He felt that he was an intruder into an intimate family circle.

Mrs Dolling composed herself to listen. Jackson told her of the death of Stephen Peter Ball, of the evidence steadily accumulating against Dr Dalton, and of Dalton's refusal to make any statement of defence or explanation.

'I've told you all this, ma'am,' he concluded, 'because Dr Dalton refuses in any way to defend himself, and I can only assume that he's trying to shield you from any scandal. For that, of course, we can only respect him, but I am sure that you will realize that his behaviour makes him the prime suspect in this case of murder.'

Mrs Dolling had sat quietly during Jackson's account, and remained fully in command of herself, although she had turned pale. There was a tremor in her voice when she replied, but no sign of her giving way.

'Mr Jackson, I am greatly distressed by what you have told me. Dr Dalton has given me no hint of the monstrous accusations that have been made against him. They cannot, must not, be true!'

She rose from her seat and clasped her hands together in anguish.

'How I hate rumour and innuendo! Mr Jackson, whatever the outcome of your investigation, I am ready at any time of the day or night to come to Dr Dalton's assistance, should I be of any use. When you see him, tell him to speak the truth without fear. He must not imperil himself by foolishly shielding me from gossip.'

'I will do so, ma'am.'

Jackson hesitated for a moment and then said, 'I want you to understand, Mrs Dolling, that I have full knowledge of Dr Dalton's matrimonial affairs, including the circumstances of his son Eric's conception. It is not my wish to be indelicate.'

Mrs Dolling's eyes showed briefly what looked like puzzlement rather than surprise. Evidently she was a woman of considerable fortitude.

'Naturally, Mr Jackson, you will have made a thorough investigation of Dr Dalton's history. He and I would expect no less. Tell him what I have said. Let him speak out boldly the truth of the matter. If you knew Dr Dalton as well as I do, Inspector, you would know that he would never harm a single living thing.'

When the two detectives left Mrs Dolling's house they walked in silence out of St Peter's Lane and down a narrow grassed alley that took them through a wrought-iron gateway into the churchyard. Parson Betteridge emerged from the deep porch of the church and greeted them. Jackson wondered whether he had been deliberately waiting for them.

'Gentlemen,' he said, 'what a warm day it is! Why not sit down for a while?'

Betteridge indicated a long wooden bench against the north wall of the church.

'So you have been to call on Mrs Dolling? I hope things will turn out well for her. My friend Dr Granger has told me something of the disturbing events at the school where his brother is vice-master. Mrs Dolling and Dr Edward Dalton, the headmaster of that school, have been good friends for many years.'

It was a kindly way of putting it, Jackson thought. Evidently Parson Betteridge did not share his friend Granger's waspish spite.

'Poor Mrs Dolling! It was very sad! But there, the laws of Church and Crown must stand. Otherwise, I think, something might have come of it.'

'I beg your pardon, sir, I'm not quite sure what you mean.'

'Well, Mr Jackson, I'm referring to Mr Dolling. Still sound in wind and limb, you know, but a lunatic! She was only seventeen when she married him. Arthur Dolling, his name was. She has a photograph of him in her house in yachting rig. A very nice young man he looked. He was a marine engineer by profession.'

239

Bottomley uttered an inarticulate sound. Jackson's mind reeled. Some of the sure foundations of his detective edifice were beginning to shift.

'A lunatic?' he heard himself say in a high, dry voice.

'So tragic!' said the old parson, shaking his head. 'She came from Plymouth, you know. She and Mr Dolling married and set up house in a place called Mannamead, where she was born. Mr Dolling showed signs of madness almost immediately. He saw things, you know, and began to do himself injuries. Within the year he was judged insane, and confined to a lunatic asylum for life.'

'And when you said something might have come of it — '

'I mean that had the law permitted divorce in such circumstances, she might very well have married Dr Edward Dalton. There's a little boy, you know . . . But, of course, there's no prospect of marriage, with the husband still living.'

Sergeant Bottomley had sat apparently transfixed for the past few minutes. He suddenly burst into speech, causing the old clergyman to start in surprise.

'Reverend sir, I've always been under the impression that Dr Dalton was already married — married to a lady called Lucy Eynesham — '

'Ah! Lucy Eynesham! Yes, indeed, Mr Bottomley. Come, gentlemen: let me show you.'

Parson Betteridge led them round the tower of the church and along an overgrown path flanking the nave to the south, where there were a good number of sunken sandstone graveslabs of a century earlier. He suddenly stooped, and swept back the long grass from a more recent memorial in granite. Together, and in silence, they read the inscription.

Sacred to the Memory of
LUCY EYNESHAM DALTON
Died March 18th, 1880,
Aged 28 years.
Beloved Wife of Edward Dalton,
and Mother of Eric.
'So He giveth His beloved Sleep'

11

The Gate to Nowhere

'Stephen!'

The boy's whisper held an edge of fear. He seemed to deliver the word as though it was an incantation. *'Stephen!'*

Noel Valentine stopped and narrowed his eyes to peer through the heavy wreaths of glowing mist that hung about the trees, obscuring the morning sun. He had left the school buildings to stroll across the unkempt rear grounds of the school, and had come upon a pair of padlocked iron gates marooned in a circle of tufted grass, with no trace of flanking walls or paling. The gate to nowhere, he had thought, and then he had heard the strange whispered incantation from within the mist.

He quickly picked up one of a number of well-defined tracks leading to the Mere. Soon he discerned the figure of a youth sitting upright on a wooden bench within a few feet of the water's edge. He knew at once that it was Gerald Mostyn.

He allowed the boy to hear his approach.

Mostyn turned and stared at him for a moment apparently without recognizing him. Then he smiled a brief greeting and looked out again across the water, where swathes of sunlit mist moved about between the islets, as though with purposes of their own.

'Did you hear me talking just now?'

'Yes. I heard you whisper a name.'

Valentine walked nearer to the boy until the gently eddying water was lapping near his feet.

'I hear his voice sometimes,' said Mostyn. 'Stephen Dacre, his name is. He died out there on the water. It was four years ago. I hear his voice, and I imagine that he's telling me to join him out there.'

Mostyn's gaze remained fixed on a glowing halo of light far out on the water.

'These things are mere fancies, Mostyn,' said Valentine. 'The atmosphere today has combined with the late sad news of Mr Ambrose Gledhill's death to bring about this melancholy mood.'

Gerald Mostyn burst into tears. He covered his face with his hands and sobbed. Valentine said nothing. He knew quite well that his explanation of Mostyn's mood was mere anodyne. He had seen this kind of thing before.

'I've never seen Stephen,' said Mostyn at

243

length, when the sobbing had stopped. 'But I've seen Mr Gledhill twice since — since he died. I saw him in the head's garden yesterday. He was looking in at Dr Dalton's study window. And I saw him today, standing by the ruined boat-house over there.'

He waved a hand vaguely towards a sagging timber building a hundred yards off, which seemed to have been frozen in the act of falling into the Mere.

'Do you think there are such things as ghosts, Captain Valentine?'

'Well, there's a man called Sidgwick at Cambridge who seems almost persuaded that there might be such things. But then, he's a philosopher. I don't expect the Church would approve of the idea.'

'The Church?' For a moment the boy seemed bewildered, and then he lightly shrugged his shoulders. 'Oh, that.'

He appeared for the moment to have forgotten his intention to read for Orders.

'Courage, boy! These things are merely fancies, tricks that the brain can play upon you. Don't be afraid of them. They'll pass.'

Mostyn wiped his eyes on his sleeve. For a slightly autocratic youth it was a reassuringly boyish gesture. When next he spoke he remembered to call Valentine by the usual schoolboy's term of address. Valentine noted it. Mostyn was beginning to throw off the dangerous mood of melancholy.

'Sir,' he said, 'if ever I have anything special to talk about, will you listen to me?'

'I will, Mostyn. You can put your trust in me.'

The boy smiled, and took his leave of Valentine, who watched him striding back confidently to the school buildings. He was amused to see the rather ungainly figure of Sergeant Bottomley raise his battered bowler hat to the boy as he passed him on the rear terrace.

'Bottomley,' said Valentine, when the sergeant was within earshot, 'your Inspector Jackson's one of the most cunning men I've ever come across! That was a *lesson* he was teaching us last week in Dr Dalton's study. He was the Master, and we were his class of little boys!'

Sergeant Bottomley sat down on the bench and looked out across the water.

'Yes, sir,' he said. 'I expect it seemed like that. Mr Jackson's a thinking man, you see. So am I, for that matter.'

Captain Valentine took out his cigar case, opened it, and offered it to Bottomley. The sergeant regarded him gravely for a few moments, and then extracted a cigar. Valentine sat down on the bench beside him.

In terms of class and background the two men were poles apart, but they shared a common past.

'Sergeant,' said Valentine, drawing slowly on his cigar, 'do you remember Lance-Corporal Whelan?'

'Yes, sir.'

'That boy I was speaking to just now — the one you passed on your way here — he reminds me very much of Lance-Corporal Whelan.'

Sergeant Bottomley balanced his cigar on the edge of the bench and produced his battered hip-flask. He refreshed himself with a smooth swig of gin.

'Gerald Mostyn, his name is, sir, aged seventeen. Second son of Sir Hugo Mostyn, baronet. Sir Hugo is known to Mr Jackson and me. Gerald Mostyn is a hero to the other boys, if what some little lads were telling me is true.'

'You evidently have the knack of finding things out, Sergeant.'

'Well, yes, sir, but that's my job, finding things out — though the guv'nor and I sometimes find out things that make a mess of our theories!'

'And what do you do then?'

'We lick our wounds, sir, and start again! But here's something that'll interest you. Mr

Harry Caswell's been to see me. He told me that he used to have a set of six Indian loving-cups, but that when he rummaged through his cupboard yesterday he found that two of them were missing.'

'And do you draw any particular conclusion from that?'

'I do, sir. That school building back there is what I'd call a mesh of interconnections. There's a way in to Staff House from the boys' quarters on the third floor. Underneath the whole range of school buildings there's a massive common cellar, with little brick stairways leading up and down to all sorts of places.'

'So with respect to Mr Caswell — '

'With respect to Mr Caswell, sir, I think those cups could have been purloined from his set very easily, without anyone noticing. Mr Jackson and I know all about Mr Caswell — and about Mr Fletcher too, for that matter. But we're saying nothing about Mr Caswell at the moment.'

Sergeant Bottomley stood up. He dropped his cigar butt on the path and ground it into the shale with his heel. He glanced across the meadows at the school buildings, and his brows drew together in a frown.

'Yes, sir,' he added, 'I remember Lance-Corporal Whelan. He was only nineteen. He thought everybody was conspiring against him, and that voices were telling him to do wicked things. In the end he . . . Yes, sir. I remember poor young Whelan.'

It was while he watched Bottomley making his way back to the school across the unkempt lawns that Valentine suddenly recalled the cryptic words of Ambrose Gledhill's letter:

'*Watch out for young Gerald Mostyn. I've no doubt that he will make himself known to you.*'
Watch out!

'Captain Valentine wants to know all about Dr Dalton,' said Sergeant Bottomley.

Jackson frowned, and looked up from the papers that he was studying. He understood what lay behind his sergeant's remark.

'I know, Sergeant. My performance up there in the study last week looked like the climax of the investigation, and they're all expecting me to pull an unexpected rabbit out of the hat. I was too clever by half, lecturing these schoolmasters as though they were a class of children. And all the time *I* was the prize ninny!'

'Well, never mind, sir,' Bottomley mumbled.

'What do you mean, Sergeant, 'never mind'? I've been minding ever since we got back yesterday from Draycot. I should have checked. I should have checked all the names and dates beforehand, at Somerset House — '

'Well, never mind, sir,' Bottomley repeated. 'But you're right, we should have checked. Then we'd have known about poor Lucy Eynesham. I don't think the folk at Draycot tried to deceive us, or anything of that nature. They all assumed that we knew who Mrs Dolling was, including the lady herself.'

Bottomley had removed a bundle of papers from the inside pocket of his coat. They were secured by a piece of twine, which he laboriously unknotted before spreading the pieces of dog-eared paper on the table. He picked up one of his pieces of paper and read from it.

' 'Mary Catherine Dolling, aged thirty-nine. Born Mary Catherine West at Mannamead, Plymouth, 1853. Father, George Paul West, victualler at the Royal Marine Barracks. On the Rate Books of Draycot St Peter since 8 May, 1880.' '

Jackson uttered a little sigh of disgust. Complacency . . . Was he getting too old for the proper business of detection?

'Lucy Eynesham!' he said. 'That woman

Mrs Bell-Forest actually *told* me that Lucy Eynesham was dead, but, of course, I was too clever to take her plain meaning for what it was!'

He sat down again with a half-humorous sigh. Nothing was to be gained from this approach to things.

'So that's who Mrs Dolling was — another young lady from Plymouth, known to Dalton in his carefree bachelor days. At least, that's what the old parson told us when we questioned him further. And then another child, Julian, came along . . . It can be very convenient, Sergeant, to call yourself a widow when you've young children running about your house!'

Sergeant Bottomley lit a minute stub of a cigar, burnt his fingers with the match, and made a noise halfway between a cry of pain and a chesty cough. He drew delicately on the vestigial cigar.

'This makes things worse for Dr Dalton, sir,' he said. 'This is the kind of thing that Captain Valentine and the others are waiting to hear.'

'Yes, Sergeant, it makes things worse for Dalton. That's why he won't say anything to me, because, in addition to fathering one child out of wedlock, he had decided to do the same thing again, and this time he has not married the lady in question.'

'A bit of a scamp, then, sir.'

'Yes, Sergeant, as you so elegantly put it. A bit of a scamp. And possibly a dab hand with the aconitine. That's why I've applied for a search warrant. Forewarned is forearmed.'

'Sir,' said Bottomley, 'when we were down at Plymouth, I met an old retired police constable in the public bar of Hudson's Hotel, who remembered Lucy Eynesham and Dr Dalton, and how sweet she was on him. He told me to watch out for a broken-down old lag called Simon Stockdale, who occasionally drifted in and out of the area. He was a bosom friend of Stephen Peter Ball and, according to my old constable, Stockdale knew some vicious secret about Ball that he'd never reveal.'

Jackson thought for a moment, and then said, 'Find out what that secret was, Sergeant. Use the telegraph — no, you'd better go down in person. It'll have to be next week. We'll fix a day later on. I'm beginning to think that the real truth about this whole business may have died with Stephen Peter Ball. Maybe this Simon Stockdale can resurrect it.'

★ ★ ★

Early the same evening, Noel Valentine sat at the table in what had been Ambrose Gledhill's set. He had finished reading a number of pupils' essays, and there was time for some reflection. This, Valentine mused, had been the quiet retreat of an academic clergyman. What would he have made of the crossed foils that he had fixed above the mantelpiece?

Poor man, he would never see these rooms again. He was to be buried in the Protestant Cemetery at Cannes.

There came a low knock on the door, and Gerald Mostyn entered the room. It was clear from his expression that something was gravely amiss.

'Captain Valentine,' said Mostyn without preamble, 'I asked you this morning whether I could confide in you. You probably realized, sir, that I already had something weighing heavily on my mind. I don't know what to do . . . '

'Tell me about it, lad. Sit there, at the table.'

Mostyn sat uneasily with downcast eyes, his hands clasped tightly together.

'Sir, it was on a Thursday night, the eighth, I think it was. I couldn't sleep, so I got up, and slipped out of Upper School to walk about for a while. I know it's against Night

Rules, but that's what I did.'

'What time was it?'

'It was about half-past two in the morning. It was very quiet. I walked down the Great Corridor, where night-lamps were burning. I had got about halfway along when I heard a noise. It was someone coming in through the side door from the herb garden. I'd have been in trouble if anyone had caught me, so I slipped into a classroom to wait until whoever it was had passed.'

Mostyn looked at Valentine briefly, then dropped his eyes. He licked his lips nervously.

'From where I was standing, sir, I could see clearly across into that part of the hallway where the trophy cases are displayed. There's a large mahogany table beneath them and, as you may know, the hallway is always well lit at night by the big corona of oil-lamps hanging from the ceiling.'

Mostyn stopped speaking. He looked towards the door, as though regretting his visit. Then he seemed to summon his courage once more, and continued.

'Well, sir, the person who came along the corridor was Dr Dalton. He was fully dressed, and I saw that he was carrying two glass phials, one in each hand. He must have just taken them from the laboratory. I watched him from the classroom door. For some reason he paused by the trophies, and put the two phials down for a moment on the table. In the bright light cast by the reflectors on the corona, I saw quite clearly that the phials were those containing aconitine.'

Valentine's voice came gently to ask a question.

'How did you know that the phials contained aconitine?'

'Sir, Mr Fielding-Stenhouse labels those phials in a special way. They have large numerals drawn on them in Indian ink. I distinctly saw the numbers, 8 and 9, which I knew were the numbers on the two phials of aconitine. I didn't appreciate what it meant at the time, but now . . . '

His voice trailed away into silence.

Valentine's mind raced back to that same night, when he had woken from fitful sleep to witness the headmaster's visit to the laboratory. Dalton had blamed Fielding-Stenhouse for carelessness, but now Mostyn's words put a more sinister complexion on the incident.

'Mostyn,' said Valentine after a while, 'are you quite certain of what you saw?'

'Quite certain, sir,' the boy replied firmly.

'Now, you realize, don't you, that you must repeat this story to Inspector Jackson?'

'Yes, sir.'

'Then come with me now, and do so. He's still in the school, and it's vital that you repeat this account to him. This school, Mostyn, is enmeshed in a web of lies and deceit. It is your duty — and privilege — to help bring the truth to light!'

* * *

Deep down in Forman's heart the hatred of Dalton smouldered and festered. He had a whole year ahead of him, his final year, which would be rendered a torment for him by the knowledge of his lost power to rule others through fear.

And then, as though by a miracle, the means of achieving his revenge fell into his hands. It was a simple sheet of paper, containing words so potently damning that Forman had sprung new-armed from his lethargic depression and organized a secret meeting after school hours in his set in Upper School.

He had contrived to pack a motley assortment of boys into his two rooms, having lured them with the promise of a sensational revelation. A number of Gentlemen had agreed to come, but most of the audience were Scholars of fourteen or fifteen. Boys sat on every available piece of furniture, on the floor, and in the adjoining bedroom, listening to the vehement, passionate tones of that most dangerous of all animals, an untamed youth with a grievance.

'Friends!' Forman cried, 'listen to me in silence while I read you the contents of this letter.'

He held the document aloft, and most of the boys recognized immediately the spiky, old-fashioned handwriting of Amyas Fletcher. There was a little surge of excitement, followed by a deathly hush while Forman read the letter aloud.

'Dear Headmaster

'I should like to consult you, if I may, upon what I consider to be an extremely grave matter. Rectitude and decorum are all very well, and certainly advance a man in the world, but they count for little when they are merely a mask for private rottenness and moral cowardice. There is a wrong to be put right, and I think that you will do me the honour of heeding my advice. It is no great sin as the world goes, but the school must not be compromised.

Ever yours,
A. Fletcher.'

A rather disconcerting silence followed. Forman realized that he would have to explain.

'Don't you see what this means? Old Flodders had found out about Dalton's secret life. You've all heard the rumours about him. Flodders was going to confront him. But Dalton made damned sure that the old man didn't get the chance to cause trouble!'

'Why? Do you think Dalton murdered him?' asked a voice from somewhere inside the bedroom.

'It's obvious, isn't it? He poisoned the two of them — Flodders, and the Man in the Night-gown. This detective fellow Jackson never leaves him alone. *He* knows he did it.'

'What did he do with Flodders?' asked another.

'Well, I don't know! Maybe he's hidden him in the chapel vault. That's what Gerald Mostyn thinks.'

'Maybe he's buried somewhere in the grounds.'

'I say, Campbell, that's an idea!' someone said.

'There's all kinds of things he could have done with Fletcher's body,' said Forman. 'Jackson knows quite well that Dalton did it, and this letter is added proof.'

'Why does it say that murder is 'no great

sin as the world goes'?' asked another voice from the bedroom.

'It doesn't mean the murder, fathead, I don't think Dalton had done the murder when Flodders wrote this. It means the way he's kept a mistress all these years out in Oxfordshire somewhere. Flodders knew that if that came to light, the school would be compromised.'

'You can't have a mistress unless you're married,' someone said.

'Oh, stow it, Goggles, what do *you* know about it?' said somebody else.

'Where did the letter come from?'

'I don't know, and I don't care, either. It was lying on the floor in the passageway just outside this room, and I shall take great pleasure in giving it to Inspector Jackson, to help him complete the case. But first,' — he looked round at his audience — 'what are we going to do?'

Nobody replied, as it had not occurred to any of them that they could do anything. Then Forman told them his plan. It was a mean, petty idea, but many of the boys seemed struck by it.

'Friends,' said Forman, 'we have spent years obeying every command and whim of Dalton's, because we thought he was a gentleman. And what do we find? A hypocrite, a moral leper, and a double murderer! Have we no courage? Are we so downtrodden that we can make no protest about the disgrace and dishonour that Dalton has brought to us and our school?'

These were stirring words from a ruffian in the making, and there were various cries of 'We're with you, Forman', 'Hear, hear', and so on. Only one voice, that of a youth called Prosser, was heard to dissent.

'You're only doing this because Dalton thrashed you.'

Someone shouted, 'Oh, shut up, Nancy, and do as you're told!' Somebody else fell off his chair with a crash, everybody laughed, and the meeting broke up.

Nobody seemed curious any more about the provenance of the letter. It was the single letter that had been abstracted from the packet of documents when the unseen thief had rifled through the desk in Fletcher's den.

* * *

The following Monday morning's assembly adhered strictly to the school's age-long ritual. The boys remained seated at the long tables where they had breakfasted until an unseen voice outside the hall door called out: 'All rise!'

259

There was a brief echoing rumble, followed by total silence as the boys turned to face the dais. Then the staff entered, led by the vice-master. They walked gravely on to the dais, and took their places according to seniority behind the long high table, to right and left of the headmaster's great carved chair.

There was a brief pause, and then Dr Dalton appeared at the door, and walked in his stately fashion the length of the hall, until he had reached the dais. He raised his square academic cap to the assembled staff, who replied in kind, and then he took his place in their midst.

It was as he reached his chair that the hissing began. Hesitant at first, then louder and more sibilant. It was soon accompanied by a rhythmic stamping of feet. It had started among the Gentlemen's benches, but some of the Scholars, without even knowing why, began to join in. Louder and louder it became, and then it was interspersed with shouts of 'Flodders! Flodders!' Then one shrill voice called out, 'Murderer!' This was Forman's revenge.

Dr Dalton swayed, and hastily sat down, or rather fell into his chair, but the mob spirit was abroad, and the hissing and the cries of 'Murderer!' continued unchecked. Some of the very young boys, bewildered and frightened as they witnessed their secure world crashing about their ears, began to cry.

Mutiny! thought Valentine, and half rose from his seat. But it was the usually mild and self-effacing Sandford who sprang forward to the front of the dais, his whole body quivering with almost uncontrollable anger. In a voice that carried right across the pandemonium, he bellowed:

'Stop this at once! This is an outrage!'

As though by a miracle the noise ceased, and silence reigned once again. All eyes were fixed upon Sandford. If he dithers now, thought Valentine, then all's lost. He need not have worried. The crisis of authority facing them all seemed to have liberated some latent power in Sandford.

'All you *Gentlemen*' — he spat the word out with withering contempt — 'will return immediately to your sets, and remain there all day, until the perpetrator of this foul insult is found and removed. Leave now, in silence.'

The Gentlemen moved, shamefaced, towards the door, some actually on tip-toe. Sandford dismissed the remaining boys according to the hierarchies, until the hall had emptied. Without looking back at his colleagues for any kind of reassurance, Sandford strode out of the hall in the direction of the Upper School.

Dr Dalton sat where he had collapsed in his chair, his eyes gazing unseeingly at the table-top in front of him. He was overcome with an ungovernable shaking, which he did not seem to heed. Theodore Granger sprang back to life.

'Valentine, Caswell, help me to get him out of the hall. I don't think he can stand up.'

Together the three men hauled the headmaster to his feet and virtually dragged him the length of the hall, across the entrance lobby, and into the privacy of Staff House.

'Take him into the dining-room,' said Granger tersely, 'he can't manage the stairs in this condition.'

Through the mist of delirium, Dr Dalton heard Granger's words, and wondered if they were addressed to him. His life's work was in ruins. They all knew. Even the boys. They had called him murderer. It was all over . . .

Someone was forcing a burning liquid into his mouth. Brandy. How this liquid burns! Now a round, stern face was nearing his, and he heard a voice. It was Jackson, the detective.

'I have here a warrant to search your house.'

'Indeed? Quite so, thank you.' Sleep. Yes, he would sleep . . .

'Inspector Jackson,' said Granger coldly, 'if you must search Dr Dalton's house at this terrible time, then you had better do so. I will answer for Dr Dalton in the matter.'

Jackson seemed totally oblivious to the distaste that Granger made no attempt to conceal.

'Thank you, sir,' said Jackson. 'Yes, we'll do that right away.'

* * *

In the extensive cellarage under the school, lamps and candles shed their fitful glow. It was cool and damp, and there were glistening patches of saltpetre on the walls, but the paved flooring was well swept and clean.

'It was the right time, Sergeant,' Jackson said. 'That boy Mostyn's story needed immediate investigation. Dalton's collapse after that infernal row in the hall gave me the moment I was waiting for.'

'Mr Granger didn't like it, sir,' said Bottomley.

'Then Mr Granger must lump it, Sergeant, as the saying goes.'

Jackson and Bottomley were standing in the area under Staff House, where massive, square brick piers supported the floor above. An open archway to their right led directly into the cellars of Dr Dalton's house. Carrying lanterns, the two men passed under the arch, and looked about them.

The cellar was surprisingly small, and was filled almost entirely with well-stocked wine-racks. Part of the floor space was taken up by several mouldy-looking trunks. Jackson took several candle-ends from his pockets, lit them, and placed them on the edges of the racks.

They worked in silence for nearly half an hour, carefully removing every bottle from its place, and probing into the dark recesses of the racks. After a while, Inspector Jackson said, 'Come and look at this, Sergeant.' He had found a wine bottle lying near to one of the racks, and had placed it upright on a shelf.

'What do you think?'

Sergeant Bottomley picked the bottle up, sniffed at its neck, and shook it. It still held a small quantity of wine.

'Well, well, sir,' he said, 'maybe it's a little souvenir left by our friend from Plymouth.'

Jackson nodded in agreement, and without further words the two men resumed their search. A few minutes later Sergeant Bottomley said quietly, 'Here they are, sir.'

Jackson stopped what he was doing and joined Bottomley, who had been working in the corner near the door to the staircase. The sergeant had gingerly withdrawn two small, dusty phials from one of the recesses in the rack which he had been searching. They glinted in the light of his lantern, crusted at the neck with broken sealing-wax, and carrying gummed, blue-bordered labels, upon which had been painted the numerals '8' and '9' respectively. One phial was half full of a white powder. The other was virtually empty.

The two policemen sat down together on one of the trunks, each holding a phial.

'I didn't really think we'd find them, sir,' said Bottomley presently, 'despite what that boy said he saw.'

Inspector Jackson sighed, and shook his head. A half-smile played around his lips.

'All this business, Sergeant — the poisons taken from the laboratory, used to deadly purpose, then hidden here in the cellar — what is it supposed to say about us? Do these people really think we are so stupid?'

'If they do, sir, then it's lucky for us, I suppose. But it's a childish, amateur affair altogether, considering how much Latin and Greek they do here.'

Jackson seemed lost in thought for a moment. Then he seemed to make up his mind about something.

'I think the time's come, Sergeant, for me

to deal with Mr Harry Caswell. I'll arrange to take him for a little ride tomorrow.'

Sergeant Bottomley made no reply. They extinguished the candle-ends, and walked back into the main cellarage under the school. They mounted a steep flight of steps, opened a door, and emerged blinking into the sunny vestibule of Staff House.

12

Baiting the Traps

'Mr Caswell,' said Jackson, 'I've been told that you're free of teaching this morning. Would you care to ride out with me into the country?'

The invitation was so unexpected that Harry Caswell found himself lost for a reply. Inspector Jackson was sitting in a smart trap drawn up on the drive, holding the pony's reins slackly in one hand while the other rested on the brake.

'I hope you won't refuse, sir. I'm sure you'll find it very interesting.'

They were soon bowling along the narrow dusty road leading away from Kingsmere into what proved to be a remote tract of farming country. Caswell stole a glance at his companion and stirred uneasily.

'Inspector — '

'I know, sir! Familiar territory, I think?' Jackson smiled, and kept his eyes on the road. Eventually they turned into a track that brought them to an old farmhouse, half hidden behind tall yew hedges.

Jackson reined to a halt.

'Here we are, sir, at Maxley's Farm. Now, Mr Caswell, do you want to tell me all about it, or must I tell you myself?'

Caswell bit his lip with vexation. He looked so thoroughly crestfallen that Jackson felt compelled to laugh out loud.

'Come, sir,' he said, 'it's not as serious as you think! I've already paid a visit to Mr Maxley, and he and I have talked. He knows we're coming this morning.'

Jackson's words had an immediate effect on Caswell. He swung nimbly down from the trap.

'Very well, Mr Jackson. I see that the game's up. I'll tell you the whole story.'

He motioned Jackson to follow him along a path to the rear of the farmhouse, where there was a small orchard. Two elderly farmers were sitting in silent companionship on a rustic seat. They wore loose-fitting smocks, and sturdy boots, and their brows were shaded by rather battered, wide-brimmed hats. On a weather-stained old table in front of them reposed two empty pewter tankards and two long clay pipes.

One of the men had dozed off quietly, his chin sunk on his chest, so that only the wide-brimmed hat could be seen. His companion, though, was awake and alert, and evidently expected his visitors. He was a man of about sixty, with grisled hair and a face heavily tanned by long years of work out-of-doors.

'Good day to you, Mr Caswell,' said the elderly man, 'and to you, Inspector Jackson. You gentlemen will want to talk alone, I expect. There's a fire lit in the parlour if you'll go through to the house, and there's ale on the hearth.'

While Maxley was speaking, Jackson had been staring at the sleeping man in growing fascination. An old farmer, in hat and smock, and dangling from a cord around his neck, a pair of gold pince-nez . . .

As though interpreting Jackson's unspoken question, Maxley leaned forward and gently removed the old farmer's hat. Jackson looked closely at the sleeping man. The white hair was carefully combed and brushed in such a way as to hide, though only partly, a bruised and jagged scar above the ridge of the right eyebrow. Here, then, was the man who, until that moment, had been simply a name to him — the missing schoolmaster, Amyas Fletcher.

Jackson followed Caswell into the little parlour at the front of the house. Caswell poured them both a measure of ale from a pewter jug on the hearth. They sat opposite each other in high settles flanking the fire.

Caswell launched into his story.

'I've had Fletcher hidden away safely here ever since that frightful Sunday morning after the Special Dessert,' he said. 'But you know that already, don't you, Inspector?'

'I do, sir. I've known all the time.'

Caswell's eyebrows rose a little, but for a moment he said nothing, gazing at the fire. He seemed to be arranging his ideas. Finally, he spoke.

'It's a strange, desperate story I have to tell, Inspector, and it all began with a cry in the night.'

'A cry, sir?'

'Yes. It came around two o'clock in the morning, from Fletcher's set, which is next door to mine, as you know. I hurried in, and found that dead man, Stephen Peter Ball, sprawled on the bed. Fletcher himself was lying on the floor between the bed and the wall, with an ugly open wound on his forehead. I knelt down to examine him more closely, but before I could do anything he suddenly seized my hand, and cried: 'Harry, Harry, hide me, for God's sake! I am in mortal danger'. I told him that his attacker was dead, and that he had nothing else to fear. 'No, no!' he cried, 'you don't understand! That man was never any danger . . . he's just as much a victim as I am. Oh,

Harry, hide me, hide me!' '

Caswell cradled his pewter tankard between his hands and looked at the fire, reliving the scene. Eventually he continued his story.

'That was enough for me, Jackson. I picked him up bodily and hurried with him to my set, where I put him in my bed. I was able to bind and dress the wound in his forehead. After I got him here, I procured a doctor from a neighbouring village. I told this doctor that Fletcher had been attacked by a drunken lout — which was true, I suppose. The doctor never asked me any further questions, and I volunteered nothing.'

Jackson looked keenly at the young games master.

'Was it you who dressed Stephen Peter Ball in Mr Fletcher's night-gown?'

Caswell blushed, and nodded his head.

'Yes, it was. It was not a pleasant thing to do. Had I not been so angry, I doubt whether I could have done it. I was driven by a desire to distance my old friend from the ethos of that vulgar ruffian. I burnt most of the man's clothes in one of the kitchen stoves. I tied the suit into a bundle, and pushed it deep into the school midden.'

Caswell smiled ruefully, and put his empty tankard down on the hearth.

271

'I tried to create an impenetrable mystery for greater brains than mine to solve, while I gained time to bring Fletcher here to safety. One day, maybe, I'll tell you the great debt I owe to Amyas Fletcher, but now is not the time.'

'There'll be no need to tell me, sir. I know all about that debt, too.'

'Do you, by George? Is there anything you *don't* know about the matter, Inspector?'

'Well, sir, I'm not quite clear about how you spirited Mr Fletcher away from the school.'

'I'll tell you. Mr Maxley's son, Jem, is my sparring partner. When I offered to search the school, I sent a message to Jem via the school messenger. Jem and his father came out to the school in their cart. When the undertakers arrived to remove the body of Stephen Peter Ball later in the morning, I had the Maxleys smuggle Fletcher out of my room in a trunk.'

'And it was you, sir, who took Mr Fletcher's watch and pince-nez.'

'It was. I saw him peering short-sightedly at me while I was making my arrangements, so I went back to his set and fetched them. Nobody was watching me, you see! I was the chief searcher!'

Jackson laughed and shook his head.

'In that simple action, Mr Caswell, lay your

downfall! Once I knew that the watch and pince-nez had been there when the body was discovered, but missing later in the morning, I knew why they'd gone, and who'd taken them. I had you discreetly followed and observed, and my officers reported that you had Mr Fletcher hidden here at Maxley's Farm.'

Caswell sighed, and looked nervously at Jackson.

'What do you propose to do?' he asked.

'I rather think, sir, that I'm not going to do anything for the moment. I've a shrewd idea that Mr Fletcher's safer where he is. But I'm disturbed by what he said to you. What *was* this danger that he spoke of?'

'Mr Jackson, Fletcher's memory has gone — it's slipped away, for want of a better way of putting it. He seems only to remember things in patches, and there are great gaps in his recollection. When I ask him to tell me the nature of the danger from which I rescued him, he can't remember.'

'Do you sense that he's still afraid?'

'I do. I'm sure that he'd stumbled upon some deep and perilous mystery back at Kingsmere. That's why, Inspector, with your permission, I'll continue my guard over Fletcher. He can't recall any details, but of this he is certain: he is in mortal danger from someone, and while that fear remains, whatever it may or may not portend, here he stays, until he remembers everything, and says to me, 'Harry, it was so-and-so!' '

★ ★ ★

In his modest office behind the school hall, Theodore Granger listened to the measured and dispassionate tones of Leo Farmer, the school's 'man of business'.

'Now, you understand, Granger, that mine's not a criminal practice, but as to what will happen to Dalton, I can only reiterate what I have just said. That he has been morally delinquent has been proved beyond all shadow of doubt, and the Court of Governors have acted accordingly. If they hadn't done something positive, the parents would have been up in arms.'

Granger thought of the stricken headmaster, who had so dramatically collapsed in full view of the whole school at that hideous assembly. Dalton had been very lucky not to have succumbed to brain-fever. One thing was certain: his career was irretrievably ruined.

'As for the other matter,' the level voice continued, 'the alleged murder of this man from Plymouth, I can only say that things look very bad. Jackson, the policeman, came to talk to me yesterday, which was very civil of him. I found him a most agreeable and respectful person.'

He paused for a moment and looked shrewdly at Granger.

'I also found him to be a very clever person. As you know, he searched the cellars under Dalton's house and found physical evidence of an alleged misdemeanour with respect to the concealing of poisons. He further told me that he has a signed testimony from a boy in the school that can be turned into an affidavit, and used in evidence against Dalton.'

'I still feel that Jackson's missed something — '

'What can he have missed? He has Dalton's stubborn silence. He has the motive of blackmail. He has the undoubted truth that Dalton alone knew who that dead man was. And very soon now, I believe, Jackson will arrest him for murder.'

'I still find it impossible to believe,' said Granger slowly. 'I deplore and condemn his moral lapses, and his attempts to hide them from the light of day. But murder? No! I don't believe it. He will not confide in me, and I can't blame him for that. But I will now do all in my power to support him.'

Farmer moved impatiently. Granger's loyalty was all very well, but he seemed unwilling to face the brutal reality of the situation.

'Your attitude does you credit, Granger,' the lawyer replied. 'But don't you try fencing with Jackson! There are deep waters in this case, and I'm convinced that Jackson has not revealed all that he knows. Please remember, too, that you have the governors' mandate to act as head of this school. That, Granger, must be your first concern.'

That, thought Granger, was certainly true. He had always commanded respect, but now there was an indefinable deference in the boys' attitude towards him. Sandford's status, too, had changed dramatically since the day of the terrible assembly. The boys had witnessed his assumption of command at a moment of grave crisis, and his entrance into the classroom was now invariably greeted with deferential silence. That terrible assembly . . .

'I was no great success as vice-master the other day, Farmer, during that hideous assembly. We were paralysed, all of us! We simply sat there like waxworks in an exhibition when the vile hissing started.'

'How did you quell it?' asked Farmer.

'I didn't! It was a man called Sandford who did that, a man who, a few days earlier, had seemed unable to control a class of senior pupils!'

'Sandford? Isn't he that quiet, rather stiff fellow with the scarred forehead?'

'Yes. He was one of the few appointments that I made as acting Head before Dalton came.'

'Sandford,' the lawyer murmured. 'I suppose there could be two teachers of the same name . . . I used to wonder whether he was the Sandford I'd heard about from some friends of mine. If your Sandford had the courage to quell that boyish mutiny, then he's probably the same man. He'd been for a time at St John's Grammar School in Birmingham.'

'Yes, that's the man. He was there only a matter of months before I got him to come here. I think he taught in Scotland before that, and he'd been ill for a year or so before he went to St John's. So you know him, then, Farmer?'

'No, not personally. But I know *about* him. I'm surprised that *you* don't.'

Granger rose from his chair and moved restlessly towards the windows, as he tended to do when agitated. He stood for a moment looking out at Foliott's Building.

'You know, Farmer, I feel that I can't sustain any more shocks about this school and its staff. You seem very reticent about Sandford. Tell me about him. Tell me that he is a wanted murderer, a thief, an embezzler, an escaped felon — '

'Steady!' The lawyer's voice betrayed the amusement that he felt at Granger's typical outburst. 'I'll tell you none of those things, and as Sandford has clearly not thought fit to tell you anything, I shan't betray his secret.'

Leo Farmer rose to his feet, and moved towards the door. He had other work to do. He paused with his hand on the latch, and added, 'But I can calm your troubled breast by telling you this: if your Sandford is my Sandford, then he is one of the bravest and noblest men living in this brave and noble land of ours.'

★   ★   ★

Jane Ashwood stood in one of the tall window embrasures of the Great Gallery, listening to the surly, resentful thunder muttering over the wooded chase of Hervington Park. There had been the threat of a storm all morning, and by noon the sky had dimmed. It would rain soon. She longed to be at Kingsmere School, twelve miles to the north-east, listening to Edward Dalton give shape and purpose to her dreams.

Suddenly she saw a man on horseback turning off the road at the gates and into the park. Even as he did so the heavens seemed to open their flood-gates. She saw the heavy, sloping rain beating off the man's oil-skins. Nearly half an hour elapsed before Juckes came into the Gallery, carrying a salver.

'A letter, My Lady,' said Juckes in his soft West Indian tones. 'By messenger. From Dr Dalton.'

The envelope had been neatly slit open, as was the custom of the house. When she saw that her father's valet, rather than one of the household servants, had brought the letter to her, she knew that Lord Hervington would have seen it first. She motioned to Juckes to remain, and he retreated discreetly to the door. Jane sat down in the window-seat and removed the letter from its envelope.

Dear Lady Jane (Dalton had written)

As you are aware, Sir Walter Foliott has judged me unfit to govern the school. For the moment I am bound to accept his judgement. Since we spoke last I have suffered terrible indignities. You may have heard something about them.

Yes, she had heard. A recalcitrant youth out for blood had demeaned him before the whole school. And then a search of the school cellars had been instituted. There was talk of concealed poisons ... Sir Walter Foliott's cousin, the bird-like Miss Pringle, had called, to whisper the story to her with scarcely-concealed pleasure. Jane turned again to Dalton's letter.

I tell you solemnly that I am innocent of the death of Stephen Peter Ball. Come to me at the school and I will tell you the truth of my jealously guarded past. It is a tale of folly and human failure, but it will banish the foul rumours that are abroad. If you will hear it, you will, I hope, decline to sit in judgement upon me, as Foliott and the others have done. I am not permitted to leave the premises, or I would come to you myself ...

Jane found that her hands were trembling. Was it fear or anger that brought the welling tears to her eyes? The truth of his jealously guarded past ... What would that truth reveal?

There were a few more lines in Dalton's firm sloping handwriting, in which he talked wildly of justice and calumny. The letter ended:

In severe agony of mind, and drinking the bitter draught of humiliation, I dare to sign myself your devoted colleague and friend, Edward Dalton.

It was imperative to go to him. She despised the petty lies and tales that had been woven around him. Colleague? Yes, he was that, and more. Much more. Not to go to him now would be to demean herself in her own regard. With a sudden firm resolution Jane went to the long table, where her writing-case stood.

'Juckes,' she asked, rather imperiously, 'is that messenger still in the house?'

'He is, My Lady.'

'Then make sure he stays. I am about to send him back with a written reply to Dr Dalton.'

Convention could think what it liked. Dalton held the key to all her dreams. She would go to him that very evening.

★ ★ ★

Lord Hervington wrote laboriously with a lead pencil on a sketching-pad that Juckes had placed in his hand. When he had finished writing, he looked from the pad to his valet, who leaned down to read the shaky writing.

Has she really gone to see this fellow Dalton? He is a rogue and a seducer.

Juckes sighed, and considered for a moment before he replied. 'She has answered his summons, My Lord, because it assaults her heart and mind. That is what the man had designed it to do, and we cannot blame him. Like has called to like, and she has gone.'

Juckes finished talking, and sat upright in the window-seat beside the Marquess, who was seated in his invalid chair. The Great Gallery was lit only feebly by a few candles.

Lord Hervington made no attempt to struggle with words, but his eyes moistened, and he sighed. Tears began to course down his cheeks. Juckes produced a handkerchief, and very gently stemmed the flow. He placed a strong black hand briefly over the nerveless hand of his aristocratic master, and treated him to a wide and encouraging smile.

'The time has come, My Lord, for us to say certain things to Captain Noel Valentine. You and I seem to know where all this will end. Maybe an Angel of Grace has been sent to tell us. So let her go to Dalton, and let her take me as her servant. Then, My Lord, we shall see what we shall see.'

★ ★ ★

Jane had not been prepared for the chill gloom of Dalton's study when she arrived in her father's closed carriage at Kingsmere Abbey. She had been met at the school lodge by a porter, who had conducted her to the inner door of Dalton's residence. She had walked down the private staircase and entered the study.

Dalton sat unmoving at his desk, his brow resting on his hand. He glanced at her for a moment as though failing to recognize her, so deeply was he engrossed in his own thoughts. A feeble fire burnt in the grate, and there were a number of candles lit, but the atmosphere was arid and unwelcoming.

'You wrote to me — ' she began. Dalton suddenly sprang back to life. He rose from the desk, and beckoned towards the great winged chair near the fireplace.

'Lady Jane — forgive me, I was fast bound in melancholy thoughts. Please sit there, beside the fire. I am going to speak to you directly, and without preamble. My situation, and your presence here, both require it.'

Dalton resumed his place at the desk, and

shaded his eyes with his hand.

'Sixteen years ago, Lady Jane,' he said in a quiet voice, 'I married a young lady called Lucy Eynesham. Seven months later, she gave birth to our son, Eric.'

'Seven months?'

'Yes. To my eternal shame I hid my wife away in the country, providing her with a house in the small town of Draycot St Peter, in Oxfordshire. In mitigation I must add that Lucy agreed to this plan. My academic career would have been ruined had knowledge of my indiscretion become public.'

'So you are a married man?'

A coal fell from the grate into the hearth, and the candles flickered. Dalton was silent for a moment, though he shifted slightly in his chair. He had heard the slight tremor in Jane's voice.

'In the month of March, 1880,' Dalton replied at length, 'Lucy died. For the last twelve years I have been a widower. I have never claimed to be a bachelor, though most of my colleagues have assumed that I am. I have never enlightened them either way.'

'What happened to Eric? He will be a grown youth by now.'

'I could not bring up a little boy alone. I knew a lady called Mrs Dolling, who agreed to go to Draycot St Peter and look after my son, Eric. Mrs Dolling and I became close friends. In the fullness of time she bore me a son, whom we called Julian. So I have two boys, both thriving.'

'It would be an understatement, Dr Dalton,' said Jane tremulously, 'if I were to say that your conduct surprises me.'

She was satisfied to see Dalton blush crimson with shame. She continued in gentler tones.

'Why did you not marry Mrs Dolling? I assume that she was a widow when she entered your household.'

'She was not, Lady Jane! Chained by cruel laws to an imbecile husband, she was forbidden to marry a second time. But she had found some happiness, I believe, with me. Poor woman! Her health is precarious, and I very much fear that her time upon this earth is fast running out.'

Jane heard Dalton groan. He seemed to sink lower in his chair, a picture of hopelessness. When he spoke, his voice was uncharacteristically low and thin.

'Let me make an end of this confession. That man Stephen Peter Ball, of whom you have heard, knew of my marital indiscretions, and from time to time I gave him small sums of money to stop his mouth. In the end, he accosted me here, in the school — it was on the night of the Special Dessert — and I sent him about his business. Can you imagine my horror when, the very next morning, I saw him dead in Fletcher's bedroom? I told you about that at Sir Walter's dinner, but I could not reveal to you my numbing fear. I was afraid that I would be accused of killing him, and so I said nothing. I have still said nothing to Jackson, the policeman, but I have told you the truth here tonight.'

For the first time that evening Dalton turned his ravaged face to look at her directly. He seemed desperate with misery, but there was still some glimmer of the old fire in his eyes. She felt herself being drawn once more by the man's strange power.

'So, Lady Jane, you must make up your mind at once. You know what I am, and what I have been. My days as headmaster here are over, but that doesn't prevent my still working for another cause. Do you still wish me to help you build the Royal Alexandra School? Speak — do you believe what I have said? Or will you turn your back upon me with the others?'

'Dr Dalton,' said Jane, 'your relationships with your late wife and with Mrs Dolling are private to yourself, and you must wrestle with your own conscience where those matters are concerned. But as for the monstrous charge of murder levelled against you, I have never believed it. I treat it with the contempt it deserves. So when this affair is done, let us go forward as we have planned. I need you, both as my colleague and my guide.'

Jane was unaccountably shocked to see the tears well up in Dalton's eyes. It would not be safe to remain with him much longer. She turned towards the door.

'You are no paragon, God knows, Dr Dalton,' she said, 'and you have much of which to repent. But in the matter of this vile charge of murder, you have been cruelly wronged.'

★ ★ ★

Noel Valentine crossed the school terrace, and entered the pasture. He had walked only a few yards when he caught sight of Juckes. The valet was dressed in a suit of sombre black, relieved by his usual flowing white scarf. He was wearing a very smart and racy silk hat. Sitting on the rough grass in a semicircle were half-a-dozen boys of fourteen or so, listening with rapt attention to Juckes's lilting tones.

'And then, young gentlemen,' the valet was saying, 'the blow to my hopes fell like a thunderbolt from the heavens! My master sold me to the captain of a privateer for five pounds.'

There was a subdued murmur of protest from Juckes's audience.

'I say, what rotten luck!' somebody commiserated.

'It was, as you say, young sir, rotten luck.'

Juckes glanced up, saw Valentine, and treated him to a rather wicked smile. The boys saw him too, and scrambled to their feet.

'But, there, young gentlemen, your morning break has ended. If you really want to hear the conclusion of my tale, you must ask Captain Noel Valentine there, who is privy to all the secret passages of my life.'

'Juckes,' observed Valentine through his teeth as the group of lads dispersed, 'I have heard you described as a fibber, and now you have the nerve to involve me in your fairytales! Scoundrel! Do you realize that those boys will expect me to elaborate?'

Juckes removed his jaunty silk hat and examined the inner lining. He cleared his throat, and resumed his hat.

'Sir, forgive me. Boys have short memories. But if they do ask you, tell them that Juckes is a liar, and that you know nothing!'

'What are you doing here, anyway? I think I've seen you five times in the last day or two,

288

standing in the grounds like a piece of statuary.'

'Sir, I have taken to accompanying Lady Jane on her visits to see Dr Dalton. While she is closeted with him in his study, I take the liberty of walking in the grounds. The young gentlemen here are very amiable, and like to speak to me. I imagine that they've not seen a black man before. I tell them tales of my amazing youth — with slight embellishments. Then I go on my way, and think over old times.'

This fellow's concealing something beneath his wordy impudence, Valentine thought. He's putting himself in my way, and forcing me to speak to him.

'What old times in particular do you think about?'

'I think of the days, long ago, when My Lord Marquess was hale and hearty, and Lady Jane was a little girl of twelve. She liked to play in the meadow beyond the lodge and the old mill pond. And you, sir, were but a young man with your way to make in those days, and not above going out to find her, to play with her.'

Juckes moved slightly, and directed his gaze away across the pastures towards the distant Mere. Valentine suddenly lost sight of his surroundings. He remembered those precious years between leaving Charterhouse and joining the regiment. They had been a carefree time, during which he had made his first visits to Oxford, and forged links with young men there who were now fellows of his own college.

Always, though, he had cherished his visits to Hervington Park. Lord Hervington had always looked at him with a special, speculative expression which he had never understood. It had been both kindly and wistful, and was to be seen particularly when he had asked permission to seek out his young daughter in the meadows, to watch her climbing trees or rolling down grassy banks. 'Look, Valentine!' she would cry. 'Look at me!'

'What did you say?' Valentine forced his attention back to the present. Juckes was asking him a question.

'I was asking, sir, whether it was true that gentlemen teaching in the university are forbidden to marry? I have heard that such is the case.'

'Well, Juckes, it is not the case. There are many married Fellows in the colleges, though they are obliged to live outside. There's a whole suburb in Oxford full of houses built for married fellows to live in.'

'Thank you, sir, for telling me that. I'm

relieved to hear it.'

'And why is that, may I ask?'

Juckes withdrew his gaze from the Mere and treated Valentine to one of his quiet but expressive smiles.

'Why, sir, because I hear, too, that there are married headmasters!'

Valentine watched as Juckes swivelled skilfully on one heel until he was facing the blank windows of the headmaster's house. He suddenly felt a cold chill in the pit of his stomach. What was this fellow suggesting? For that matter, why did Jane need to make these visits to Dalton? She knew that he was in some way dangerously compromised. Was it loyalty? Or was it something else?

He nodded abruptly to Juckes and strode away. The valet lifted his hat in acknowledgement, but Valentine did not see the frown that creased the man's brow. It was a frown born of uncertainty.

'Valentine, look at me!' she would cry, in those far-off days. Had he stopped looking at Jane Ashwood in the right way? Had their verbal tussles and brittle friendship been little more than a gesture, a habit? What had Dalton been able to give her that brought her here to Kingsmere? He knew the answer to that question before he asked it. And the cold chill in the pit of the stomach? With a jolt that brought him to a standstill in the middle of the Great Corridor, Captain Noel Valentine realized that he was jealous.

13

The Faces and the Masks

Valentine walked down the Great Corridor and passed into the medieval undercroft where Fletcher had exercised his kindly rule. Since the terrible assembly the Children had been gathered up by the deputy master, and taken elsewhere.

His encounter with Juckes had left him ill at ease. Had he accepted too readily the outward attractions of Kingsmere School, without even attempting to probe beneath the surface? Caswell had once claimed that Sir Hugo Mostyn was 'simply hiding behind a mask'. One of these ostensibly civilized schoolmasters was hiding behind a mask of bland innocence, and it was a mask concealing a demon.

It looked as though Lord Hervington's valet had read the signs of underlying rottenness and decay more surely than he had. But Juckes was a man who liked to talk in riddles, perhaps because his station in life prevented him from speaking out. Valentine had never been at ease with that kind of subtlety. Curse Juckes! Why had he intruded himself into Kingsmere? He belonged firmly to the world of Hervington Park.

Valentine passed through the low door into Flodders' den. All was as he had last seen it, the untidy desk with its clutter of paper, the two armchairs, and the small table containing the tea-things. Beyond this table, in a dark corner of the little room, he saw that there was a miniature brown-stone sink, with a brass tap above it.

Idly, Valentine turned on the tap, and watched the ribbon of water streaming into the basin. Presently it seemed to leap from side to side of the mouth of the tap, then it hissed and sizzled, and stopped flowing. A subdued drum-roll from the pipes followed, which caused Valentine to glance up at the ceiling, noting how the supply-pipe curved along the cornice before disappearing through a hole into unknown realms above. He wondered . . . Flodders poked and pried. Had he hidden something away in the water-tank, something that was blocking the outlet to the tap?

At the end of the corridor beyond Fletcher's classroom Valentine found a narrow door that opened outwards to reveal a steep flight of stairs. In a few moments he was standing in a small musty attic, which contained little else than a few broken chairs and a water-tank, with a skylight above it.

Removing his coat and rolling up his sleeve, he gingerly plunged his arm into the cold depths of the tank. His fingers closed immediately on some kind of package. He withdrew it, and saw that it was covered in brown waxed paper. Various gurgles occurred as the system righted itself, and then there was silence.

Valentine sat down on one of the old chairs, dried the packet with his handkerchief, and carefully undid the string. Inside he found a letter in a handwriting that at first glance seemed vaguely familiar. There were also three folded sheets of paper tied with blue ribbon.

Valentine began to read the first letter, and immediately recognized the hand as that of Ambrose Gledhill. It was undated, and addressed to Amyas Fletcher.

My dear Fletcher
   I write this in haste, and in some perturbation, but there is every possibility that, considering the nature of my illness, I may not return alive from Cannes, and what I have to say is too terrible to leave unshared. I have known

and respected you for so long that I know you will take whatever action is necessary in the case of my demise. . . .

Valentine read on with growing horror.

There is a confidentiality about confession, but in this instance I do not scruple to breach that seal. Alice Patching . . . I urged her to tell me what man was responsible. She demurred. I insisted. The girl preserved two so-called 'love' letters. She fetched them at my behest, and I enclose them with this note as proof. If I should die at Cannes, then, Fletcher, I bequeath this painful affair to you . . .

Valentine now knew what demon it was that had lurked behind the mask.

* * *

'Jackson! Read this letter! The heartless villain! The damned, smiling devil . . . '

Valentine had blundered into the room behind the stairs where Jackson and Bottomley were poring over a set of documents. Jackson took one look at Valentine's ravaged face and sprang to his feet.

'Sit down, sir! You look quite sick! What's happened?'

Sergeant Bottomley rose from his chair and offered his battered flask to his former commanding officer, who drank liberally from its contents. He seemed to rally, and the pallor of sickness began to be replaced by a blush of smouldering anger.

'Sick? I've been a stupid, blind fool! Providence led me to the attic above Fletcher's den. In the water-cistern there I found that letter and those — those enclosures . . . Read them, both of you!'

It took Jackson and Bottomley ten minutes to read the documents. Bottomley finished first. He seemed to show no surprise, but he fixed a speculative eye on Valentine. Finally Jackson spoke.

'It's worse than we ever thought,' he said.

'It is, Inspector.' Valentine's voice had regained its firmness. 'What shall we do?'

'Do, sir? What *you* must do is leave the matter entirely in my hands. I wondered all along whether Mr Fletcher had secret knowledge of this type. Now, as you say, Providence has allowed you to discover it. Your task, sir, must be to keep your own counsel. Continue as though nothing untoward had happened.'

Valentine looked mutely at both men for a

moment, and then bowed his head.

When Jackson had seen Captain Valentine out of the room he shut the door and turned the key in the lock. He looked at Sergeant Bottomley, who had picked up one of the sheets of paper that had been enclosed with Gledhill's letter to Fletcher.

'A love letter, sir,' he muttered, turning red with anger. 'A love letter from a killer to his victim!'

Bottomley threw the paper down in disgust. He unscrewed the top of his silver flask and took a long, deliberate swig of gin.

'You suspected this, didn't you, Sergeant? This was *your* murder from the beginning, and now you have the answer.'

'Yes, sir, I wondered. 'Childish' was the word that sprang to mind. That girl Mary Wainwright, sir, was more than just poor Alice's friend. That's why she was so terrified. She'd kept secret company with him herself before ever he tangled with Alice Patching. I could see that in her eyes. She'd been content to dally with a gentleman and then retire gracefully when he gave the word.'

'You don't know that for a fact. That Mary Wainwright had kept company with him, I mean.'

The father of eight daughters looked briefly at his superior before saying, 'No, not for a fact. But I tell you, sir, I could read Mary Wainwright like a book. What I said is true enough.'

'What will Captain Valentine do?'

'Captain Valentine's a man who gives orders. Scholar he may be now, but he'll always be a soldier, and an officer. I think he'll hatch a plan of his own, sir. I know that stubborn, mute stare of his! You told him to keep out of it, but he never said he would.'

Jackson stood beside the table and looked round the drab little room. There was so much to do. Documents from the Home Office and from Somerset House had arrived that morning, and needed careful study. These letters found by Valentine had to be acted on, but was now the right time? Bottomley's murder was starting to interfere with *his* murder . . .

'Very well, Sergeant. Things are moving to a head. Now's the time to throw a cordon around Kingsmere School. I'll send a coded telegraph message to the superintendent. Discreet isolation should begin by dusk today. Then, at eight o'clock this evening, I'll interview Dr Dalton.'

Jackson briskly unlocked the door.

'As for Captain Valentine, Sergeant, we must keep him in our sight constantly. We have no power or right to restrain him, but we can at least control his ardour.'

* * *

The evening was close and still, but the sky was veiled in dark cloud, and the thunder still growled low and menacingly in the distance.

At one minute to eight, Inspector Jackson entered Headmaster's House through the inner door on the landing, and descended to the study. He knocked quietly on the door and without waiting to be bidden he went in.

Dr Dalton sat behind his desk, upon which a shaded oil-lamp provided the room's sole illumination. A book was open in front of him, and an untasted glass of port stood near his right hand. He glanced up as Jackson approached, revealing his haunted eyes and gaunt cheeks.

Suddenly Jackson was aware that they were not alone in the room. A movement from the big winged armchair near the fireplace showed him that there was a third person present.

'Detective Inspector Jackson,' said Dalton, 'allow me to introduce Lady Jane Ashwood. Lady Jane is one of the governors of this school.'

Jackson saw an elegant woman in a black

dress, who bowed slightly in his direction. There were books and papers at her feet, and what looked like a blueprint had been carefully laid over a stool near to her chair. Clearly she was there on business, but it seemed a curiously late hour for that. He suddenly sensed that he was an unwelcome intruder.

'Good evening, Lady Jane,' said Jackson. 'I have come this evening to see Dr Dalton on private business.'

He left his statement hanging in the air as a sort of question, and watched Dalton's eyes as they glanced keenly at Lady Jane. She half rose from her chair, but when Dalton raised a hand slightly from the desk she resumed her seat.

'Mr Jackson,' said Dalton, 'you have suddenly appeared here unbidden when I am engaged in an important consultation. It is my wish that Lady Jane Ashwood should remain. Please sit down, Mr Jackson, and say what you have to say.'

Jackson sat down opposite Dalton at the desk. He wished he could be away from this place, sitting at his own fireside. Some evenings Sarah Brown would come across from her croft beyond the orchard, her lantern winking among the trees. He would brew some tea in the blue china teapot, and

301

they would sit and talk, or listen to the silence.

But not this evening. Here, he was an intruder, tolerated, but feared and unwelcome. He would make one more attempt to secure privacy for this interview.

'Sir, what I have to say to you is intensely personal. Are you sure that you want a witness to our words together?'

A faint expression of questioning appeared in Dalton's ravaged face. His curiosity had been aroused, which would make it easier, thought Jackson, to say what he had come to say. He would not leave Dalton's study until he had the information he required.

'Inspector Jackson,' said Dalton, 'I am past caring for niceties of that nature, but I am proud to tell you that my life is an open book to that lady. Speak on!'

'Very well, sir. Let me then say this. You have stubbornly refused to say anything in your defence so far, and your silence has given rise to the most terrible suspicions. It is openly believed by many that you were responsible for the death of Stephen Peter Ball. You will appreciate that, if a jury were to find this proved, you would inevitably forfeit your life.'

Dalton uttered a long sigh, and stayed silent for a few moments, looking at Jackson.

Lady Jane sat quietly, shading her eyes with her hand.

When Dalton finally replied, his voice seemed to come from a far distance, so thin and feeble it seemed.

'What would you have me do?'

'Unburden yourself to me. If your life is an open book to Lady Jane Ashwood, then it must also be an open book to me. I must — and will — hear the truth from you. You are a man of great intelligence, and you must know by now that it is fruitless to conceal information from me. However closely you think you have guarded a secret, you may be sure that I will find it out.'

Dr Dalton inclined his head in acknowledgement of the truth of what Jackson had said. He reached for his glass of port, and took a cautious sip. His eyes never left Jackson's face.

'I want you to confide the truth to me,' Jackson continued, 'and to make that easier for you to do, I am going to offer you hope. I tell you solemnly that I now know for certain that you are wholly innocent of the death of Stephen Peter Ball.'

Dalton slowly drew himself upright in his chair, and his hitherto dull eyes seemed to light up with a sudden intensity. Jackson saw how he gave Lady Jane what amounted to a look of triumph.

'Innocent?' he said.

'Yes. I *know* this to be true. But I must hear from your own lips how you came to be involved with Ball. You must tell me fully and frankly. The time for prevarication is over.'

Jackson could see that Dalton was now fully alert, but still he hesitated. He would need to say more before he could unlock this man's tongue.

'Dr Dalton, I and my associates know all about your marriage to Lucy Eynesham. At first we thought that she was still alive, and that she was one and the same with Mrs Dolling. We know now that Lucy Eynesham died many years ago, and that Mrs Dolling is a lady who came to look after your son, Eric. We also know that you have another son, Julian, and that Mrs Dolling is his mother.'

Jackson noted that Lady Jane Ashwood remained still and silent. Dalton, then, had already confided these intimacies to her. Why?

Dr Dalton drank a little more wine. Although his hand trembled, he spoke now with greater firmness.

'I do not deny these things. Mr Jackson, I am like one who has crawled back from Hades, and no man could be more grateful than I am for the news that you have brought me. Yes, I am totally innocent of the death of Ball, and presently I will tell you everything about the connection between him and me.'

Dalton sat up straighter in his chair. He squared his shoulders, and placed the wineglass carefully down on the desk. Jackson felt a sudden grudging sympathy for this man, who sat amid the ruins of a life-long devotion to education, his career shattered, his only course of action a search for decent obscurity. Unless — ?

Another schoolmaster suddenly came into his mind, awful, ugly Mr Jardine, master of the parish school when he was a boy. He had lived and died in the village, survived by his wife, a woman who had been plagued all her life with a tubercular hip, and walked with a crutch. He wondered whether he had misjudged awful, ugly Mr Jardine.

'It was many years ago, Mr Jackson,' said Dalton, 'that I was instrumental in having Stephen Peter Ball dismissed as under-porter at Nelson College, in Plymouth. He was a drunken ruffian, slack and careless in his duties, and he had begun to exert a decidedly sinister influence on some of the boys. I never regretted my action, and while I naturally regret that the man is dead, I still do not think that I acted wrongly in ridding Nelson

305

College of his presence.'

'I suppose that Ball was not best pleased at being dismissed?'

'You may, I suppose, put it like that,' Dalton replied drily. 'Ball was of a vindictive and vengeful nature, and with the help of some disreputable associates he uncovered the shameful secret of Eric's conception, and began to write to me, asking for sums of money to ensure his silence. No doubt those sums seemed large to him, but they were trifling to me. His applications to me were sporadic, and, really, I regarded him as no more than a tiresome nuisance.'

Jackson saw an angry shadow pass across the headmaster's face.

'The matter became more serious, Mr Jackson, when, after Lucy's death, I became attached to Mrs Dolling. I had inherited a great deal of money from Lucy, and somehow Ball learnt of this. The demands now became more regular, and for greater sums. In the end, I determined to bring the matter to a head.'

'What did you do?'

'I summoned Ball here to the house — it was on the night of the Special Dessert — and in so many words I told him to go to the devil. He was virtually drunk when he came, and I certainly gave him no drink to exacerbate his condition, as you evidently thought I did.'

Dalton stopped speaking, and gazed into space. It seemed that he was never going to resume his tale.

'What happened next?' Jackson prompted.

'While the staff were celebrating the Special Dessert, I was engaging in a battle of wills and words with Ball, a battle which I won. Not one further penny would he get from me, and I told him that if he attempted to publish my secret, I would hand all his letters to the police. He knew he was defeated and, mumbling abuse, he reeled out of the study — through the hall door, not the private door into Staff House.

'I naturally assumed that he had left the house the way he had come, as I heard the clattering of his boots in the passage. How he got into Staff House is not clear to me. Whatever the truth of the matter, he somehow found his way into Fletcher's room.'

Dalton shuddered at some haunting recollection.

'I don't know what actually happened in Fletcher's room. But you can imagine my horror when, on the Sunday morning, I went in there, and saw Ball lying dead in the bed!'

'And that is the whole truth of the matter?'

'It is. I did not kill Ball, nor can I imagine who did. You will, perhaps, think me rather callous if I say that the matter no longer interests me. I have been through the Valley of the Shadow of Death, Mr Jackson, but the news that you have brought me this evening has led me into the sunny uplands of hope!'

He suddenly smiled, a brilliant, unforced smile, and a renewed bloom seemed to suffuse his drawn and sallow face.

Jackson rose from his chair, knowing that his work there was done, but as he walked towards the door Dalton called him back.

'Just one moment, please, Jackson. I realize that you are not able to say much at this juncture, but tell me this: if you see me as innocent, am I to assume that someone else is guilty?'

'Yes, sir, you may make that assumption. But I can say no more at this juncture, as there is still work to be done, and people to watch. I would ask you, sir, and you, Lady Jane, to keep your own counsel about this interview. Meanwhile, Dr Dalton, I tell you once again most solemnly that your innocence of the death of Stephen Peter Ball is known.'

★   ★   ★

'Come in!' cried Harry Caswell, in response to a low knock on his door. Noel Valentine came into the games master's set. He was carrying a bottle of wine by the neck. Caswell motioned to a seat near the fireplace, where a low fire was burning. The room was cheerfully lit by candles on the mantelpiece and a shaded oil-lamp on the table.

'Is anything wrong, Valentine? You look grim tonight. What's amiss?'

'Nothing that a little thought and initiative can't put right, Caswell. I thought you and I might share a bottle of wine. At least, the half of it that's left.'

'Wine, hey? What is it? Port?'

'Madeira.'

'Well, I'll not object to that. There are glasses over there on top of the cupboard.'

Valentine busied himself selecting two glasses from a collection on top of Caswell's cabinet of curios near the fireplace. Caswell lit a slim cigar and looked speculatively at his friend as he carefully poured out the wine.

'What's the matter? You look completely different tonight, somehow. What's on your mind?'

Valentine replied with another question.

'Do you know Lady Jane Ashwood? She's taken to coming here regularly to see Dalton, and she brings her father's valet, Juckes, with her. Although I can't be certain, I think Juckes is hinting at some kind of romance between Dalton and Jane.'

Caswell chuckled, and accepted the glass that Valentine offered him.

'Romance? And you're jealous, are you? 'Romance' and 'Dalton' are not two words I'd readily put together. Juckes . . . He's the black man, isn't he? A friend of your old army servant.'

'A friend of Bottomley's? Why do you say that?'

'Well, I saw the two of them deep in conversation the other day, and they certainly seemed to be on intimate terms. They stopped talking when I hove in sight. Bottomley gave me a little jerky bow, and the black man seemed to turn to stone in the twinkling of an eye. Maybe they were discussing Dalton's romance!'

Caswell laughed again, and began to cough on his cigar. The idea seemed to amuse him greatly.

'Look here, Caswell,' said Valentine, 'what do you think of Dalton? As a man, I mean. Do you believe — ?'

Caswell held up a hand as though to ward off the question.

'Whoa! Steady there, Valentine. It's not fair to ask me what I believe about Dr Dalton.

310

Not at the present time, anyway. You're new to this place, but I think you've learnt already that there's something lethal in the atmosphere of Kingsmere Abbey. The less we think about Dalton, or about anyone else here, the safer we will be. That's why I won't bring Fletcher back, and that's why Jackson colludes with me in the matter.'

Valentine thoughtfully sipped the dark Madeira wine.

'When I first came here, Caswell, I visited Dalton in his study, and asked him to explain his educational philosophy to me. It was an enthralling vision. I was so impressed that I practically reeled out of the study when he'd finished. I'm trying to banish my feelings of jealousy, you see! After what I heard, I have to admit that Lady Jane could not wish for a better mentor.'

Caswell stubbed his cigar out in a brass bowl. He leaned his chin on his cupped hands, and looked quizzically at Valentine for a moment. The lamp-light gave his face a puckish expression.

'Enthralled, were you?' he said. 'By Dalton's speech, I mean? I've heard that speech of Dalton's, too, and I got the impression that all the passion — all the rhetoric, if that's the right word — had long ago become a captive to the past. We've *all*

311

heard it, you know, and more to the point, Dalton has heard it too! He can turn the Vision off at will, and let it go back to where it belongs — in the past. I rather suspect, Valentine, that that particular Vision has become fossilized.'

Valentine dismissed Dalton from his mind. There was work still to be done. He glanced at Caswell's shelves which held the set of white ivory dice, and the pack of playing cards tied with string, the Indian brasses, and the plundered set of wooden loving-cups . . .

He collected Caswell's glass, and poured out the remaining Madeira wine.

'I've been out to see Fletcher again,' said Caswell. 'Physically, Fletcher's just about recovered from the whole business, but his memory of that fateful Sunday's quite gone. I don't think he'll ever remember what happened to him, or what it was that made him so fearful.'

I could tell you the answer to that, Valentine thought. But I won't.

'Caswell,' he asked, 'will you lend me one of those Indian loving-cups?'

Caswell stirred uneasily. He drank some wine, and sat in silence for a moment.

'Sergeant Bottomley thinks that two of those cups were stolen, and used to commit a murder,' said Caswell at length. 'I happen to believe what Bottomley suggested. Talking of the police, Inspector Jackson's still here on the school premises. He's usually gone back to Kingsmere by this time. Why do you want to borrow one of those wretched cups?'

'Do I have to tell you?'

'No, not if you don't want to. Help yourself. You can take the whole damned lot if you like. Somehow, they no longer appeal to my collector's instinct.'

Noel Valentine smiled and shook his head. He opened the cupboard and carefully removed one of the pear-wood cups. They had finished the wine, and he picked up the empty bottle.

'I must go now, Caswell,' he said. 'I've arranged for Gerald Mostyn to come up to my set at nine o'clock. I'd better get back there before he arrives. There's stirring work afoot. One day soon, I'll tell you the whole story.'

'But not now?'

'Not now. You see, the story's not yet finished.'

14

When Hell's Gate Opened

It was just on nine o'clock when a tap on Valentine's door heralded the arrival of Gerald Mostyn. He looked nervous and anxious, but Valentine could sense his youthful eagerness and curiosity.

He motioned to Mostyn to sit down near the table. He himself chose to occupy a chair near to the door of the bedroom. The room was lit by a single shaded oil-lamp placed on top of what had been Gledhill's desk.

'Mostyn,' Valentine began, 'you know that you are intimately bound up in this business of the death of the man in Mr Fletcher's room. Acting on the account you gave of that fateful night when you could not sleep, Inspector Jackson searched the cellars of the headmaster's house, and found concealed there two phials of aconitine.'

Valentine watched the very boyish expression of triumph suffuse Mostyn's face. It lasted only a moment, and then was replaced with a kind of diffident concern.

'So Dr Dalton will be accused of murder?'

Valentine stared at Mostyn for a few seconds in silence, as though the boy had said something particularly stupid.

'What murder? There was no murder.'

'But — the man — the man they found dead in Mr Fletcher's room . . . ' Gerald's stammered words seemed to be those of someone personally affronted.

'He was not murdered, Mostyn. He died by accident.'

Before the astonished boy could make any comment, Valentine hurried on with his explanation.

'Listen, Mostyn. I'll try to piece the story together from the scraps of information I've been told, and from my own deductions. That man — his name was Stephen Peter Ball — came to the school early on the day of the Special Dessert to demand money from Dr Dalton. He knew all about the doctor's moral lapses, and had been receiving sums of money from him for a number of years.'

'So that was it!'

Mostyn looked thoughtfully at Valentine. It seemed that he had made some kind of mental list of problems, and had just placed a tick against one of them.

'Yes, Mostyn, that was it. Well, I think Dr Dalton had made up his mind that this man's habit of demanding money with menaces had to stop. I expect there was a row of some sort, and Ball stormed out of the study.'

'And what did he do then, sir?'

'I think he found his way to the doctor's wine cellar, where, I expect, he refreshed himself with further drink — '

'I see,' said Mostyn in a low voice. 'And then he must have stumbled into the main cellars and climbed up the stairs into Staff House. And that's why he was found in Flodders' room.'

'Exactly. That's what I think happened. He blundered up to the first floor, and saw the gleam of lamp-light under Mr Fletcher's door. He burst furiously into the room. Mr Fletcher never retired till very late, and was probably still fully dressed. He may have been sitting in a chair, reading. Before he could say a word, the drunken man struck him down.'

'But what happened to Mr Fletcher?'

'It doesn't matter what happened to him. It's of no concern to the matter in hand. I am talking about Stephen Peter Ball. He was an inebriate, a drunkard. Seeing the untouched glass of gin and bitters on the bedside table, he seized it, and drank it down in one gulp. And so he died. It was simply an accident, and Dr Dalton has been cruelly wronged.'

'But . . . but why should he die from

drinking a glass of gin?'

Valentine felt a rising anger about to break out. He made a strong effort to contain it.

'You know quite well why, Mostyn. He died because the gin was intended as a night-cap for Mr Fletcher, and earlier in the evening, while we were all at the Special Dessert, *you had mixed a lethal dose of aconitine in it.* You had intended to kill Mr Fletcher, but instead, you caused the death of Stephen Peter Ball — by accident . . . '

Valentine continued to speak in low, confiding tones, contriving to keep his voice rigorously free of any condemnatory tone.

'I really must congratulate you, Mostyn. You have been very, very clever. A brilliant scholar, you are also a brilliant plotter. It was hardly your fault that Stephen Peter Ball should have spoiled one portion of your handiwork.'

The boy's handsome face relaxed into a delighted smile, and at the same time a light was kindled in his eyes, bright, dancing, unhinged . . . It reminded Valentine of the face of Corporal Whelan, a brave soldier, but one who saw visions and heard voices, as this boy Mostyn had done.

'You are very kind, sir,' said Mostyn quietly. 'It has been a pleasant intellectual amusement, planning things, and watching those pygmy detectives rooting round for simple answers! Most people, you know, are either pygmies or bullies. One acts up to them, lets them think what they want to think, and see what they want to see.'

'Bullies, yes,' Valentine said thoughtfully, matching his tone to Gerald's. 'Like that fellow Forman. Brutes with stunted minds.'

'Forman!' Gerard uttered the name with withering scorn. 'I've saved many a poor little fellow from his clutches in my time here. He backs off if he sees me approaching. They know, all of them, that it's better not to trifle with me.'

Outside, the rain began to lash at the windows, and there was a noise of thunder, as yet far off, but presaging a restless night. In the corridor, and on the staircase beyond, the oil-lamps flared and flickered, but not a soul was to be seen. Although it was only half past nine, the Combination Room on the floor below was unlit and deserted. The man and the boy, sharing their secret knowledge, continued to be held in their cocoon of dim lamp-light.

'Forman is to be expelled,' said Valentine, 'for orchestrating that disgusting riot in hall.'

Gerald smiled, and relaxed in his chair.

'I engineered that, you know!'

'Yes, I rather thought you might have done!'

'I had a letter,' continued the boy, 'which I found in the desk in Flodders' den. I dropped it where Forman could find it, and he fell for it! He didn't know what it really meant, but he used it to rouse the mob against Dalton. I knew he'd get expelled for that.'

'Wasn't it rather hard on Dr Dalton, though?'

Mostyn's face flushed with anger.

'Dalton! I have lived in the shadow cast by that pompous ogre for years! Do you think I cared whether he hanged or not? They're all the same, these tyrants. Rectitude, masking the morality of the gutter. Power! He and his like seek power over other people. And it's done by lecturing, and hectoring, and beating.'

Valentine's determination to see this battle through suddenly wavered. What was he to do with this appalling, confiding, insanely reasonable boy?

'Listen, Captain Valentine,' Mostyn continued, 'I am seventeen years old. For all of those seventeen years I have been dominated and bullied by two men, Dalton at school, and Papa at home. Papa was always a brute, and his friends were brutes. Hard-drinking, coarse squires, ignorant, illiterate, seeing and

319

caring for nothing beyond their dogs and guns. And my precious half-brother Hugo is just the same. I hate them both. I hate them, and one day I mean to be rid of them.'

'And what of your mother? You have never mentioned her to me.'

The boy's angry face softened into a tender smile.

'The only happiness I ever knew at home was when Mama was with us. She was his second wife, you know, and as good as she was beautiful. But he was too coarse and depraved to see this, and so he put her aside, and now she lives abroad. One day, I shall pay him out for that, too!'

Gerald suddenly stirred himself, as though he were about to get up. Valentine gently restrained him.

'Before you go, Mostyn, let us discuss the intriguing question at the root of this matter. Why should you have wanted to poison Mr Fletcher? Everybody here liked him, and by no stretch of the imagination could *he* have been called a bully.'

The boy sat back, and leaned his elbows on the arms of his chair, joining his fingertips together. He was obviously on careful guard, but his natural curiosity was aroused.

'Well, Mostyn, I'll answer my own question. To use his own words, Mr Fletcher 'poked and pried', and one day he found out something that was not, shall we say, to your advantage.'

Mostyn did not move, but his brow became marred with a frown of vexation.

'Yes,' Valentine continued, 'I can see that you're rather bothered about that. When you searched through Mr Fletcher's desk in the den that day, you found only some letters, which were meaningless to you, and one letter — the one you gave to Forman — that Mr Fletcher had intended to send to Dr Dalton.'

Valentine leaned forward in his chair and fixed his glittering black eyes on Mostyn's face.

'The stupid Forman thought that letter referred to Dr Dalton. But you are not stupid, Mostyn, and you know as well as I do that the letter was about *you*! It accuses *you* — not Dr Dalton — of using a cloak of decorum and rectitude to mask private rottenness and moral cowardice.'

Mostyn's lower lip had begun to tremble, and it was clear to Valentine that the boy was being assailed by a psychic wave of fear. Mostyn would now be incapable of breaking away from Valentine until he knew all.

Valentine's voice sank to a kind of compelling whisper. Somewhere from the dark recesses of his mind he recalled the smell of blood and sand, and the excitement of the fray. With a tremor of shock he realized why these warlike images were coming into his mind. One wrong move, one word out of place, and this contest with the murderous boy could end in death.

'And what *was* that rottenness, so wicked and vile that old Mr Fletcher was to be silenced to keep it from the light? It was the seduction of a young girl. Oh, yes, Mostyn, you may well give a start of surprise, but I tell you it is as though I can read your mind as you sit there!'

Gerald Mostyn shrank back against the wall, his face as pale as ashes.

'You crept out of the school to visit a young girl in the village, and declared that you loved her. Her name was Alice Patching. She fell pregnant through your villainy and told you of her plight. You used all your charm to persuade her that you would marry her. Poor girl! She believed that you, the son of an ancient and distinguished gentle family, would be prepared to marry a daughter of lowly country folk. And so you determined that she must die . . .

Gerald had turned white, and his wild eyes were turned in fear to look at Valentine as though he were an avenging spirit. When he spoke, it was in little more than a whisper, and such was the state of his mind that he made no attempt to deny the terrible accusation.

'You devil! Magician! How can you know all this?'

Without deigning to reply to his question, Valentine continued his relentless reconstruction of events. As he spoke, he felt all his former regard for the boy slipping away, to be replaced by a bitter sense of betrayal. The handsome face and the brilliant blue eyes, the academic prowess — they were a mere husk, a shell concealing a rotten kernel. The boy's mouth was beginning to form into a weak, self-satisfied twisted sneer which for a moment gave him the appearance of a satyr.

'Mr Fielding-Stenhouse was culpably careless about his poisonous substances. You knew that in the big cupboard in the upstairs laboratory there were two phials of aconitine, one nearly full, the other nearly empty. That was the one you took. And then you made preparations to use its contents on that unfortunate girl.'

Gerald Mostyn made a sound of protest, but no words came. He seemed to be mesmerized by Valentine's narrative.

'Now here, Mostyn, is something that you didn't know for certain, but which you clearly guessed must have happened — something to do with conscience, a concept apparently alien to you! One Sunday in early August, Alice Patching went to church. Mr Gledhill was taking the services that day. He preached a sermon which moved that girl to see him privately, and to make her confession. In that confession, she mentioned you by name.'

Was that a noise in the next room? Valentine paused to listen. Mostyn remained frozen in terror in his chair. Valentine continued.

'Mr Gledhill returned to school, and was immediately overcome by the preliminary stages of typhoid fever. He was very ill until near the end of the month, but immediately after his recovery and before his departure for Cannes he summoned you to his presence, and told you of Alice's accusations. So he, too, would have to be put to silence . . . '

Mostyn's voice came now small and low, a kind of tremulous whisper.

'How could that be? Mr Gledhill died abroad.'

Valentine laughed, and Mostyn flinched as though he had been physically threatened.

'Do you think I am as stupid as you are? I'll tell you how you did it, you creeping seducer. You crept down here to this set when Mr Gledhill was out, and found that he had prepared a chest of medicines to take with him to Cannes. So you introduced a quantity of your aconitine in one or two of the bottles of medicines in that cabinet, and left, as you had come, unseen. On the next day, Mr Gledhill left for Cannes, and in the fullness of time, during a successful recovery, he drank some of the medicine that you had poisoned, and so he died. He died! You had murdered him.'

Gerald uttered a little inarticulate sound, but no words came.

The thunder was more insistent now, and the rain flung itself angrily against the window-panes. Neither boy nor man heard these sounds, so intent were they on the matter in hand.

'But I have moved ahead in my story of your crimes. I have described your second murder. What about the first? What about Alice Patching, the seventeen-year-old girl whom you had made pregnant? You crept out of the school one night in August, and met her secretly in her father's barn. A love-tryst! And so you swore eternal love, and told her to drink a pledge of everlasting fealty!'

With a sudden movement Valentine crashed down the empty Madeira bottle and the death-drenched carved pear-wood cup on the table in front of the terrified youth.

'There, Mostyn, are the instruments of your Devil's Communion! And so you let her drink from the poisoned cup, and sat there, and watched her die . . . '

'You saw me! You were there!'

Mostyn's high voice failed him, and his eyes suddenly swivelled away to the left, and seemed to fix their gaze on a darkened corner of the room. His lips moved, but no words now came. He uttered a strangled sob. Valentine suddenly felt that they had been joined in the room by the spirits of Ambrose Gledhill and Alice Patching. Perhaps Mostyn could see them over there by the door.

'And so we come to Mr Fletcher. On the second day of term I saw Fletcher talking to you privately. He knew that you had seduced that girl, and thought that she had committed suicide in consequence. But he was a mentor of youth, and was still prepared to help you. But your virtuous reputation was more precious to you than the lives of others, and so in your guilty terror you plotted the old man's death.'

Gerald's white lips trembled in a whimper of terror, but Valentine, more and more in the grip of some primitive desire for victory, gave him no chance to speak.

'I tell you, Mostyn, I know everything! I know how you crept up to Foliott's Building

326

on the night of Thursday, the eighth of September to get some fresh poison, because the first phial — the one you used to murder Alice Patching and Mr Gledhill — was virtually empty. Fool! You left a candle burning, which brought Dr Dalton out to investigate. And when you saw him in the corridor, you decided to throw suspicion upon him — upon *him*, a man to whose greatness you could not hope to aspire in a million years!'

By some superhuman effort Mostyn had dragged himself to his feet. He began very slowly to edge his way towards the fireplace. Valentine paid no attention.

'And so you hugged yourself in self-congratulation, and waited your chance, which came on the night of the Special Dessert. While we were in the drawing-room, you creeping Judas, you sneaked into Mr Fletcher's room and put the poison in his gin and bitters.'

Mostyn had reached the fireplace, and cowered fascinated against the wall. His bright blue eyes looked in what seemed to be permanent terror at the enraged Valentine.

'How unfortunate for you, Mostyn, that Mr Fletcher chose not to drink his gin and bitters that night! How unfortunate for Stephen Peter Ball that soon afterwards he blundered into that room, struck Mr Fletcher down, and drank the poison.'

Valentine suddenly lunged nearer to Mostyn, who put his hands before his face as though to ward off a blow. But none came. Instead, the man's voice reached a peak of violent wrath.

'Miserable, useless wretch! Sneaking into the head's cellar and hiding your poison bottles where Inspector Jackson would find them! And did you think for one moment that such a man as Jackson would be taken in? Did you dare try to match your puny intellect with his? Thief, liar, murderer — '

Suddenly the youth was galvanized into action.

'You're just the same as the others! A sneering bully! You call me a liar? Then what are *you*, swearing to be my confidant? Well, Captain Noel Valentine, so be it! Do you think I care what happens to a pack of teachers? Yes, I removed Gledhill, and would have done the same to Fletcher had he not escaped my clutches. And as for that girl, do you really think that that sort of people matter? She had amused me after I'd done with her pretty friend the dairy-maid, but she began to whine for things above her station, and so I silenced her. But as for you — '

The look of terror turned to an almost

inhuman mask of baffled hatred.

'How could you know all that you've told me?' he snarled. 'You're more than human . . . and you will betray me, too. So I must silence you as well!'

With a single sweep of his arm Mostyn pulled down one of the fencing-foils from above the fireplace and lunged at his tormentor. Valentine laughed. A single deft blow to Mostyn's forearm sent the foil flying harmlessly across the room. Valentine relaxed — and in that moment of inattention Mostyn's lithe hands fastened themselves around his throat.

Within seconds, the great soldier had collapsed to the floor, his lungs bursting for want of air, his sight dimming, so that he could scarcely see the convulsed, slavering face of the insane boy inches away from him. He had misjudged the manic strength and cunning of a crazed and murderous youth.

The door of the service-room burst open and the burly figure of Sergeant Bottomley plunged into the room.

Gerald Mostyn shrieked. It was a sound that Valentine was never to forget. As he staggered to his feet, clutching his bruised throat, the boy rushed to the outer door and flung it open. The solid form of Inspector Jackson blocked his path. Sandford and

Caswell had appeared further along the corridor.

With the litheness of youth Mostyn evaded Jackson's grasp and flung himself down the staircase, the rattle of his boots mingling with his almost involuntary shrieks, that grew fainter as he descended.

★ ★ ★

Mostyn evaded his pursuers by means of a way he knew through the cellars. He emerged from the school into the dark stableyard at the rear of Headmaster's House. He scarcely noticed the waves of cold, penetrating rain that beat against him, driven by a stormy wind from the north, but the voice of the thunder flightened him. He felt his way cautiously across the yard, and crept along the alley skirting the headmaster's lawn. Lamps burned dimly in the front rooms of the house, but there seemed to be no one about.

He edged warily towards the pasture-keeper's cottage, beyond which stretched the woods and open fields. That way freedom lay. He bent against the wind, and blinked to free his eyes from the stinging rain. For a moment he turned round, and glanced at the long, irregular bulk of the school stretching away to his right. There were lights everywhere, and — what was that noise?

'There he is!'

Seemingly from nowhere men with flickering torches appeared from beyond Foliott's Building, and above the wail of the wind he heard the thud of running feet. He turned, and began to sprint across the sodden grass of the pasture. He could hear his breath rasping in his throat, and the voices of his pursuers far off. Young, agile, and unencumbered, he would soon out-distance them.

He gained a small copse of trees and sank exhausted into the wet grass. Almost immediately he heard the tread of feet arriving within inches of where he lay. He held his breath and listened.

'Caswell's out there in the pasture somewhere,' said a voice that he recognised as Sandford's. 'But there are too many boys broken loose. There must be a dozen or so out in the park, and I just hope none of them crosses Mostyn's path.'

'He'll not get far, sir.' (That was Jackson, the detective). 'He'll try to cut across the fields north of Kingsmere, I think, but we've men posted everywhere tonight. We'll get him.'

He heard both men hurry away into the rain-sodden darkness. He waited for a moment and then got to his feet.

A sudden sheet of lightning revealed for a split second the pallid, churning foliage of the trees, the meadow, and the far-off Mere, before all was plunged again into Stygian blackness. Blinded, and then stunned by the ear-splitting crash of the thunder which followed, he stumbled, and in that instant he heard a new sound behind him the quick, light running of a young boy and, eerily distorted by the rain, a shrill voice calling, 'Mostyn, Mostyn!'

Mostyn heard himself scream, and as the lightning flickered again, there came with it once more the thin, sobbing cry: 'Mostyn, Mostyn!'

'No, Stephen, no!'

Stephen Dacre had come for him. If only there was light! Curse this pall of night and rain! Mostyn's over-riding fear lent him winged feet. He could hear himself panting as he ran in terror through the darkness. Fainter, now, came the younger, sobbing voice, 'Mostyn, Mostyn! Don't!'

The fleeing boy reached the edge of the Mere. He stopped. Suddenly the thin, frightened voice came again from near at hand, sobbing out his name as though it were a question.

'Mostyn?'

'No, Stephen, no!'

Mostyn launched himself from the brink into the dark, disturbed waters of the Mere. His arms flailing with fear, he swam desperately away from the shore. All that mattered now was to get away from the dripping, wailing spirit of Stephen Dacre . . . Frantically he swam through the cold, black water, until his clothes became heavy upon him, and a vicious cramp seized his threshing legs . . .

Next day, two policemen rowed out with grappling-hooks to free the body from the clinging reeds.

15

Echoes of All the Sorrows

Sir Hugo Mostyn sat in an upright chair near the windows of the masters' library in Staff House, where the sunlight emphasized the pallor of his haughty features, and revealed the red-rimmed eyes of a man who had just suffered the loss of his son.

The door opened quietly and Harry Caswell came into the room. He bowed gravely to the baronet and without speaking sat at a table nearby. Sir Hugo returned his bow with a slight inclination of his head.

'I have asked you to come and see me, Mr Caswell,' he said, 'because you are my kind of man. I feel that I can speak openly of family matters to someone such as yourself. Do you, perhaps, understand what I mean?'

'Yes, sir, I do.'

'Would you be good enough, then, to tell me what happened to my boy? I would appreciate the unvarnished truth, if you please. Inspector Jackson has told me that Gerald was guilty of the murder of the girl Alice Patching. Nothing that you may tell me,

Mr Caswell, can match the horror of that.'

Very tactfully, but truthfully, Caswell told him all that he knew of the events of the previous night. Sir Hugo listened silently until Caswell spoke of Gerald Mostyn's final terrified cry before he had plunged into the black waters of the Mere.

'Stephen?' he said. 'Surely that was the name of the boy Gerald attempted to save from drowning some years ago? Why should he think of him at that moment?'

'Some minutes before Gerald went into the water, Sir Hugo, a young boy called James Wilkin, one of a good number who had left the school buildings when the alarm was raised, ran after him, begging him to stop — '

'James?'

'Yes, sir. That is Wilkin's Christian name. I heard him cry out, 'Don't, Mostyn, don't', but the more he cried, the faster Gerald ran. 'No, Stephen, no!' he was crying.'

'Why did this boy in particular run after my son?'

'Apparently Gerald had been very good to him in the past, saving him from the tender mercies of a number of bullies and cads. Gerald was appalled by bullying of any kind. Wilkin had no idea what Gerald had done, but he was determined to stop him from harming himself. Alas! Your son, hearing the

335

boy calling him, seemed to think it was the phantom of the dead boy, Stephen Dacre, and it was this that drove him to plunge into the Mere.'

'But, even if Gerald thought it was a phantom, why should he have feared the spirit of a boy whose life he had tried to save?'

'When I talked to this boy Wilkin later, Sir Hugo, he told me something that all the boys knew, but that none dared speak about. The dead boy, Stephen Dacre, had caught your son Gerald purloining things from another boy's set.'

'Purloining? Stealing, Mr Caswell. Let's call a spade a spade.'

'Yes, sir. Your son Gerald pleaded with Stephen Dacre not to tell. Dacre yielded to his entreaties, and the two boys seemed to have become friends.'

Caswell removed his eyes from the baronet's face and looked down at the polished table at which he sat.

'But when that boat capsized on the Mere, and Stephen Dacre drowned, all the boys knew that Gerald had killed him. He held him down on the bed of the lake until he drowned.'

'He murdered him?'

'Yes, sir. It seems that boys know about this kind of thing.'

There was a long silence before Sir Hugo spoke again.

'Mr Caswell,' he said at last, 'I have been twice married. My first wife died of fever when my elder son Hugo was one year old. Soon after her death I married Lady Elizabeth de Wells, daughter of the Marquess of Welcombe, and within a year she gave birth to Gerald, my second son. He was a lovely child, and a cause of great delight to us both. But my wife proved to be a whited sepulchre, secretly associated with vices which even I would blush to mention. It was she, I believe, who schooled Gerald in the ways of cunning and deceit, and covertly refined his antipathy towards me. There was madness in her mother's family, Mr Caswell, and it had surfaced in her. What has happened here confirms in my mind what I have always feared: that my wife's insanity was inherited by her son. When Gerald did those things, I firmly believe that he was mad.'

'Is Lady Mostyn still living?'

'She is — if you can call it living. Two years ago, my wife finally lost all grip upon reality, and had to be confined. She languished for a while in an unspeakable asylum near Greenwich, and then, through the offices of friends abroad, I had her moved to the Hospital of the Jacobite Sisters near Lisbon. I shall, of course, visit her to tell her of Gerald's death. She will not recognize me, or understand a word of what I shall say.'

There was another short silence, and then Caswell said, 'I am very sorry for you, Sir Hugo. Thank you for telling me so much of your private griefs. Think now, sir, of your son Hugo, and place your faith in him.'

The baronet looked speculatively at Caswell for a moment and said, 'Yes, you are our kind of man. If ever you want to sit a horse or fire a gun, come over to us at Shenstone Old Place. You'll be able to help Hugo and me to lay the ghosts of madness and deceit.'

★   ★   ★

Inspector Jackson re-read the fatal letter that Valentine had found in the water-tank, where Fletcher had prudently hidden it away from prying eyes and thieving hands.

I write this in haste, Gledhill had written, and in some perturbation, but there is every possibility that, considering the nature of my illness, I may not return alive from Cannes, and what I have to say is too terrible to leave unshared. I have known and respected you for so long that I know you will take whatever action is necessary in the case of my demise.

During the late interregnum at Kingsmere I took a Sunday duty there. I cannot at the moment recollect which Sunday it was. I took an old sermon with me, in which I warned against the perils of fornication. When the service ended I was approached by a young woman who had been greatly agitated during my sermon. She told me that she wished to make a confession, and to seek ghostly counsel.

Now as you know, there is a confidentiality about confession, but in this instance I do not scruple to breach that seal. Here, then, are the facts of this girl's confession. Her name is Alice Patching, and she is seventeen years old. She is pregnant, and acknowledged tearfully that she was in a state of sin. I urged her to tell me what man was responsible. She demurred. I insisted. Finally, she told me that her seducer was Gerald Mostyn. Yes! One of our most brilliant boys has followed inevitably in the footsteps of his dissolute father.

What is to be done? I have told Mostyn of Alice Patching's accusation, *which of course he denies. What I have not told him is that the girl preserved two so-called 'love' letters that Mostyn sent to her. She fetched them at my behest, and I enclose them with this note as proof.*

If I return safe and well by Christmas, then I shall manage the affair myself. Discretion is paramount in this business. If I should die at Cannes, then, Fletcher, I bequeath this painful affair to you.

Jackson stopped reading, and looked wrathfully at Noel Valentine, who was sitting opposite him. The soldier-scholar had stayed mute and chastened all the time that Jackson was reading. They were both in the little room behind the stairs. Jackson threw the letter down angrily on the table and burst into speech.

'And so, Captain Valentine, having quite rightly brought that letter to me, you then embarked on a secret plan of your own! Did you imagine that you were Gledhill's executor? Did you think that I was incapable of dealing with the matter? Your irregular conduct drove that demented youth to his death.'

Valentine was silent for a moment. He clearly acknowledged Jackson's right to be angry.

'Mr Jackson,' said Valentine at last, 'I am convinced that it was Providence who led me to that letter. Gledhill had warned me about Mostyn in a note that he left me — 'watch out,' he said. I believe that Mostyn saw the note lying in Gledhill's set before ever I arrived here. It was sealed in an envelope, and Mostyn was too cunning a boy to interfere with it. But he badly wanted to know what Gledhill had written in that note. He virtually asked me outright about it.'

Jackson listened in silence, but his air of implacable hostility communicated itself almost palpably to Valentine.

'And then, Jackson, I discovered that letter hidden in the cistern, and saw how easy it would be to convince the boy that I knew everything about his wicked conduct. And what I didn't know first hand, I could piece out through intelligent common sense.'

'Your conduct, sir,' said Jackson, 'was outrageous! You, of all people, should have understood the nature of authority and the due exercise of command. *I* was the commanding officer in this situation. I *told* you to stay your hand!'

Valentine blushed. He was not used to receiving orders from others.

'You're right in principle, Jackson, and I plead guilty. But what else was I to do? By

341

then I *knew* that Mostyn had poisoned that girl, a fact quite unknown to Gledhill and Fletcher. I *knew* because Bottomley had virtually told me how it was done. I *knew* that Gledhill himself had paid the price of his scruples with his life. I knew that Fletcher had escaped only because that man Ball had died in his place. I nearly died myself, too confident of my own prowess . . . I have no regrets.'

Jackson sprang up angrily from the table. Really, this man was incorrigible!

'No regrets? I suppose you can afford that luxury, sir, but I cannot. I am a Crown Officer of the Law. Upon my word, Captain Valentine, I *knew* that you would not let well alone! Bottomley knew it, too! I had to dragoon Mr Caswell and Mr Sandford into helping me. Those two made sure that the floor was deserted, while Bottomley and I concealed ourselves about Mr Gledhill's set.

'There we waited, Bottomley and I, while you drove that boy to a confession. We waited until you were in grave physical danger from Mostyn before bursting in. We were *forced* to wait, against our professional judgement, because we both knew that you were going to succeed. And so we connived at the illegal interrogation of a suspect, and a minor, we became parties to a conspiracy to abstract an illegal confession by deceit — '

'And what would have been the alternative, Jackson? What would have happened to Mostyn?'

Jackson was silent for a while. He had made his point. The Law was not to be tampered with, or treated as some kind of military game. Now it was time to let the matter drop.

'Mostyn, sir, would have been confined to the state asylum for criminal lunatics at Broadmoor. And there he would have stayed.'

'He could have lived for another fifty years in that place.'

'Yes.'

Jackson resumed his seat at the table. Valentine sighed. Jackson wondered whether it was with relief.

'Bottomley and I knew a young soldier who was like Mostyn,' said Valentine. 'His name was Lance-Corporal Whelan. He heard voices and saw frightful visions.'

'What happened to him?'

'He drowned, like Mostyn. He jumped from the deck of the steamer bringing us back to England two days out of Alexandria. His mates told me that he'd been hearing voices again, urging him to jump. He flung himself from the stern, and was lost beneath the screw.'

It was Jackson's turn to sigh. This pleasant rural school for gentlemen's sons seemed to hold echoes of all the sorrows of the world. Valentine heard the sigh, and was encouraged to talk more about the school's tragedy.

'Whelan proved himself to be a dauntless hero at Tel-el-Kebir, but this boy Mostyn was a monster raging unchecked. He drowned that poor young fellow Dacre when he was only fourteen. Maybe other boys would have died . . . Maybe some did — from apparent accident or disease — and no one knows about it. I tell you, Jackson, I am not prostrate with grief over this business. I admired and trusted that boy, and he hideously abused my trust.'

Valentine rose from his chair, and made as though to quit the room. Jackson stretched out a restraining arm.

'Sir,' he said, 'I have said my piece, as I was bound to do. You and I started out as allies in this investigation. Let us now, at least, part as friends.'

The two men shook hands. Valentine, with a smile, and something approaching a bow, left Jackson alone in the little room behind the stairs.

Jackson still saw in his mind's eye the keen,

honest face of the soldier-scholar, and the alert yet curiously innocent expression of his dark eyes. He knew him for what he was, a guileless man, the bravest of the brave, a man of great learning, and at the same time a man of intense simplicity of heart.

* * *

'Caswell, are you looking after Fletcher's welfare or keeping him prisoner?'

Theodore Granger addressed the games master with characteristic directness. He had erupted into Caswell's set towards eight o'clock on the evening following Mostyn's death.

'Prisoner? What on earth do you mean, Vice-master?'

'Well, it looks like that, doesn't it? Inspector Jackson has told me the whole astounding tale, in the account of which I detected your apparent abduction of Fletcher. It's obvious to me that the danger he feared was some kind of foul assault by that frightful boy.'

'I'm inclined to agree with you, sir — '

'In that case, why are you still holding Fletcher incommunicado? I want him back!'

Caswell laughed good-humouredly. Granger's ways were not Dalton's: he was more volatile and impulsive, a man who liked to rule from the ground floor rather than from the aloofness of a distant study.

'Sit down, sir, if you can spare a moment. For goodness' sake, rest awhile! Now: why do you want Fletcher back?'

'Because he's an influence for stability. If the boys see him back safe in his kingdom at the end of the corridor, they'll settle down again. These are crucial times, Caswell, and stability is becoming vital.'

'Are things so very bad, sir?'

'Bad enough. There are still too many parents wanting to remove their boys. Sandford and I have written sheaves of placatory letters, and I've enlisted the help of some of our more influential alumni — people like Lord Frederick Guelph, General Pearson — oh, you know the people I mean.'

The restless vice-master rose to his feet and shook out the skirts of his black frock coat. He eyed Caswell with a lightly guarded oblique smile.

'Jackson told me this morning that another horde of policemen is about to descend on the school. I didn't ask why, and he didn't offer to tell me. But never mind about Jackson, Caswell! Just remember what I said: I want Fletcher back!'

Caswell's reply was both decided and immediate.

'You shall have him, sir!'

★   ★   ★

Halfway through the following Thursday morning, a morning on which all lessons seemed to have been abandoned, Valentine, Sandford, and a number of other colleagues positioned themselves at the long windows of the Combination Room, which overlooked the winding carriage drive leading up to the school. The grounds on either side of the drive were thronged with boys, and other boys could be seen sitting in the lower branches of the elm trees. It was a bright, sunny morning, dry, with a light breeze.

Sandford consulted his watch. 'It won't be long now,' he said.

He was right. Even behind the closed windows, they could hear the sudden murmur from below, followed by shouting and cheering. In the distance, directly ahead of them, and so foreshortened to their view, an elegant open carriage came into sight. At the same time, the noise rushed up to a crescendo of wild cheering.

'Granger's going out on the steps to greet him,' said Sandford. 'The boys will like that.'

'Very crafty of Granger,' Valentine remarked.

The carriage now came near enough for the masters to see it fully. On the box sat Caswell, and behind him, as sole occupant, was the smiling figure of Amyas Fletcher. He had put aside his usual rusty black and had dressed with great formality for the occasion. The sun glanced off the high silk hat that he wore as the carriage manoeuvred the gentle curve of the drive. He wore white suede gloves, and his hands rested on a silver-topped ebony cane.

So many boys now left the verge that Caswell was obliged to rein in the horse for fear of hitting them. As the carriage stopped, the vigorous old voice boomed out, 'Ah, you rogues, you rogues! Let me pass, will you?'

The carriage passed on, and the watchers saw their old colleague raise his silk hat in acknowledgement of the boys' cheering. Then the carriage disappeared from view.

Old Flodders had returned, bringing a much-needed sense of unity to the damaged school. But his memory of those crucial days at the heart of Mostyn's murderous tale was gone for ever.

★　★　★

'A shocking, unbelievable story, Headmaster. I am truly thankful that it's all over, and that such great anxiety has been lifted from you.'

Sir Walter Foliott spoke in his usual measured, slightly aloof tones. He wore his outdoor clothes, as though he had just called in on a passing whim. He sat with his hands resting on a stout walking-stick.

Dalton leaned forward across his desk and handed Sir Walter a sealed envelope.

'In that envelope, Sir Walter, you will find my resignation as Headmaster of Kingsmere, which I should wish to take effect immediately.'

The chairman's sigh of relief was so undisguised that Dalton smiled in spite of himself. When Sir Walter spoke, it was embarrassingly obvious that his words had been rehearsed for the occasion.

'I am empowered by the Court of Governors to convey to you their deep thanks for the invaluable contribution which you have made to the development of the school in so many ways. A written testimonial to that effect will be forwarded to you in the near future.'

'Please convey my thanks to the Court of Governors for their kindness,' said Dalton drily.

Sir Walter visibly relaxed, and his tone

became more informal.

'It was I who brought you here, Dalton, and I still don't regret my choice. Now, what I want to ask you today is this: what shall we do about finding a successor? Should we go outside — which would be the usual and safe thing to do — or is there anyone here who could do the task with . . . with flair, for want of a better word?'

'Well,' said Dalton, 'you would be accounted wise if you went outside, as you know. But, you'll appreciate, Sir Walter, that whoever succeeds me at this juncture needs to know what this school's problems have been over the last month, and in my view, needs to have shared the general doubt and suffering. Granted that, there is only one man amply qualified to take over here, and that is Mr Theodore Granger, my Vice-master.'

'Very interesting! Do you know, Dalton, that's exactly what we thought in the governing body. Granger's fifty-two, with the energy of a man of thirty, and in talking to him — which I have done — I received the impression of a man with many ideas, a man with plans as yet unfulfilled. Yes, what you have said confirms our own view of the need at this time for continuity.'

Dr Dalton sat back in his chair with a little sigh of satisfaction. He was immensely relieved. Granger would preserve what he had created, at the same time moving the school forward into the future.

'But tell me, Dalton: I gather that Granger and you have been at daggers drawn for quite some time now. How is it, then, that you are so ready to prefer him in this way?'

Dalton made a movement of impatience. Even to ask such a question seemed to cast doubt on his professionalism.

'Well, really, Sir Walter, I hope that a mere clash of personality would not prevent me from doing what is best for the school! Yes, we have not been the best of friends, but there have been faults on both sides, as we both now readily acknowledge. He has been a tower of strength to me during this terrible time, and I tell you that no one is better fitted to assume the headship than he is.'

Sir Walter rose.

'In that case, Dalton,' he said, 'I should like to go and offer Granger the headship here and now.'

★ ★ ★

Sandford was taking books from the shelves in his sitting-room and placing them in neat piles on the table when Theodore Granger strode into his set.

'Sandford — ' he began, and then stopped. He saw that the door of the small service-room was ajar, and that a large trunk with its lid thrown open had been dragged out on to the floor.

'What are you doing, Sandford?'

The scarred English master blushed with embarrassment.

'Mr Granger,' he said, avoiding the vice-master's eyes, 'I need hardly tell you that my time here has not been the success that you and I had hoped. Now that you are to be headmaster, I think it would be invidious for me to remain. In the task facing you, sir, you will have no use for failures.'

'I see. When you speak of failure, I take it that you are referring to that disgraceful riot in your classroom the other day?'

'That, sir, among other things. I knew you would never forget it. Only the intervention of yourself and Dr Dalton averted a frightful catastrophe.'

Granger sat down absently at the table. His brows were knit in a frown.

'It seems as good a time as any, Sandford, to look at another of your shortcomings. It seems that you have decided to leave us. If you ask me for a reference, I will be obliged to mention your arrant insubordination, both here and elsewhere.'

Sandford paled visibly. He stood near the window, still holding a book in his hand.

'What do you mean?' he faltered.

'I am referring to your outrageous behaviour in hall when the boys began chanting and stamping that morning. By what authority you assumed command of the school, ignoring both myself and the headmaster, I do not know. That we were not able to move in the matter is neither here nor there.'

Granger seemed to be working himself up into a passion. He pointed an accusing finger at Sandford, and when he spoke again there was an unpleasant mocking sneer in his voice.

'And now you are making these appalling incidents an excuse for deserting us at our most need! We are not good enough for you, are we? I know that you've glanced longingly in the direction of Rugby, comparing their ways with ours, and finding us wanting!'

Sandford, almost beside himself with shame and anger, finally found his voice.

'This is too bad, sir. You say I have glanced towards Rugby. Well, so I have. Perhaps it's time you realized that I am not the only sinner here. This school is an antiquated backwater! It's little more than a country grammar school with a laboratory attached! I

353

have spent hours with you, writing impassioned letters to former pupils — and all to shore up a rotten fabric on the verge of collapse!'

'Sandford — '

'No, sir! I *will* speak! Why do we not have houses? Where are the house-masters? Do you think that this . . . this tragedy that has overwhelmed us would have happened if the boys had been properly grouped and looked after, as they are at Rugby, or Eton, or any other decent public school? And in heaven's name, when are we going to look beyond Warwickshire? There's an Empire out there, you know — *did* you know?'

Sandford was panting with the exertion of his impassioned speech.

'How dare you!' Granger cried. 'I might have expected this! Your insubordination knows no bounds. It never did. Look what you did at Everett's Academy, near Edinburgh — ah! That's hit the mark, has it not? Leo Farmer hinted something about it, and I made it my business to find out the truth. A great fire broke out there, and thirty boys were trapped. Your headmaster told you quite clearly that nothing could be done.'

'But — '

'Silence! You, of course, knew better than your headmaster. In you dashed, and somehow or other, you brought all those boys to safety. Disgraceful! And you were so severely burned and scarred that you lay in hospital for eighteen months. How dare you do these things without permission?'

Granger suddenly burst out laughing. He clapped the bewildered Sandford heartily on the shoulder.

'Sandford,' he said, 'when I saw that you were packing up to leave, I knew that I'd have to force you to reveal your true feelings about this place through ridicule, and I succeeded. For years I have been unable to employ your particular talents to best advantage. Things will be different in future.'

'Then you really want me to stay? After the unforgivable things I've just said?'

'I do. As for your strictures on the school, Sandford, I agree with every one of them! I have already made it clear to Sir Walter Foliott that things will change very radically now that I am in control here. I intend to see that we are in effect refounded as a modern public school with a sense of mission and purpose, to carry us triumphantly into the twentieth century.'

Granger looked appraisingly and steadily at Sandford.

'In order to do all this, I'll need the unflagging support of someone of like mind, someone who copes triumphantly with difficulties and emergencies. Sandford, I came here today not to descant upon your supposed failings, but to ask you to be my Vice-master.'

★ ★ ★

Dr Dalton walked with his measured tread from Staff House to the school's telegraph office. He had chosen lesson-time for his errand. He had not yet sufficiently recovered from his ordeal to face the enquiring looks, half pitying, half embarrassed, of the boys.

When he opened the door he was surprised to see not the school's telegraphist but a uniformed policeman, a heavy, bearded man with a slight squint, sitting at the telegraph instrument. The man looked up enquiringly.

'I should be obliged if you would send this message for me,' said Dalton, handing him a slip of paper.

The policeman placed it on the frame in front of him, and stretched out his hand to the key. Then he stopped.

'I'm sorry, sir, but this message, I see, is for Draycot St Peter. I'm afraid the wires are down on the line for Draycot, so I can't send this message for you.'

'How very annoying. I shall write a short letter, and you can put it into the post bag.'

There was a supply of stationery in the telegraph-room. It took Dalton only five minutes or so to write his note and seal it in an envelope.

'There you are, Constable.'

'Thank you, sir.'

The constable watched Dalton leave the room. Then he opened a drawer, put the letter into it, closed it, and locked it with a key. He put the key back into his pocket.

16

A Noxious Thing

Inspector Jackson looked out of the living-room window across the weedy cottage garden towards the Wheatsheaf inn. He could see the glow of lamps in the back bar, and from time to time the sound of conversation drifted to him on the evening breeze.

Jackson took out his watch and opened the cover. Half past nine. Bottomley would be back soon, if the train had come in on time. He put a cast-iron kettle on the fire, and sat down at the table, where a glass-shaded oil-lamp burned smokily. He looked at the various papers that he had spread out on the table, where they lay in the pool of yellow light from the oil-lamp.

'Signed deposition of Anthony Jamieson, physician . . . Signed deposition of Elizabeth Warner, nurse . . . Deposition of Emily Thomas, nurse, unlettered, with her sign-manual affixed . . . '

There were other documents. Two pages of minute, neat writing, typical of Mr Angel at Warwick Mortuary. A long letter from the

Chief Constable of Oxfordshire, impressively composed on a typewriter, asking that Inspector J.W. Cartwright should be afforded every facility, et cetera.

The kettle boiled stridently, and Jackson brewed some tea. Within moments a heavy knock at the door signalled the return of Sergeant Bottomley.

Jackson poured out two cups of strong tea. Bottomley added to his own cup a generous shot of gin from his battered hip-flask, and sat down near the fire.

'Well? And how did things go at Plymouth?'

'Things went very well, sir. That retired constable I told you about took me down to an ale-house at the docks. He'd found Simon Stockdale, the old lag he'd mentioned to me who'd known Stephen Peter Ball. He was holed up in a back room there.'

Bottomley gulped down some of his gin-enhanced tea, and then resumed his story.

'He was far gone with consumption, and couldn't be moved. He knew he wouldn't live long, and wanted to clear the slate. So we bought him some rum, and he began to talk. He'd known Stephen Peter Ball for years. They'd cracked many a crib together in happier days.'

'You've a very poetic way with you at times, Sergeant,' said Jackson drily. 'Happier days, indeed! Were there just the two of you? You and this constable?'

'No, sir. A serving officer, Detective Inspector Poole, came along with us. And a police surgeon. Well, sir, Simon Stockdale's mind was already decayed with drink and disease, so it wasn't difficult to get him to talk about Stephen Peter Ball. It was Ball who'd used Stockdale to procure the arsenic. He'd promised him five pounds if he'd do it.'

'Five pounds! The price of a human life! How did this Stockdale get the arsenic? The usual way, I suppose?'

'Yes, sir. There should be a law against it, but there isn't. Arsenical Flypapers, six to the box, to be had from any chandler. He'd steeped them in boiling water, and then put the liquor in a bottle. I expect it was administered in soup. Or coffee, maybe.'

'And you've got all this in writing? With names and signatures?'

For reply, Bottomley levered a bulky packet of papers from the inside pocket of his overcoat and handed it to Jackson.

'Everything there's properly signed and witnessed. Stockdale dictated a confession of sorts, and signed it, with me as witness. There's a deposition from Inspector Poole, and a signed letter from the police surgeon. None of us did any prompting. All the names and places came from Stockdale himself.'

Jackson indicated the papers arrayed on the table.

'Well done, Sergeant. We've not been idle this end, either. The body was exhumed in total secrecy yesterday evening. Mr Angel was there from Warwick. He detected the presence of arsenic, which is what we'd expected. I've got written depositions from an old doctor, and from two nurses who were present at the death. It's all there. And now your papers from Plymouth complete the business.'

Jackson got up and looked out through the uncurtained window. Fine vertical rain had begun to fall, its drops caught like fireflies in the lamplight from the inn.

'I knew all along it was going to end like this, Sergeant. *Your* murder and *my* murder. Alice Patching, Ambrose Gledhill, Stephen Peter Ball — and what was that young boy's name? Stephen Dacre. Two Stephens! A lively dance they all led us, Sergeant, and so did Gerald Mostyn. And where has it all come to in the end?'

Sergeant Bottomley finished his tea, but made no reply. It was not a question that needed an answer.

'I'm glad you were able to come here today, Lady Jane. After my insistence on your staying the other night when Jackson came, I thought you'd fight shy of coming again!'

It was a bright and sunny Wednesday morning, 19 October, and the tall clock in Dalton's hall had chimed eleven as Jane entered the study.

Jane Ashwood smiled, and sat down in the winged chair near the fireplace.

'Dr Dalton, I was proud to brave that detective's disapproval, because I felt instinctively that you were a deeply wronged man. And by staying with you, I was able to hear him declare your innocence!'

Dalton shot her an appraising glance.

'Well, Lady Jane, I'll admit to you that I was on the edge of the pit of despair that night. By staying with me, you became a witness to a resurrection! That is a bond between us that I hope will never be broken. But come, let's get down to business.'

He picked up a letter from his cluttered desk, where Jane's blueprints lay open, together with her precious note-book, its pages now marked with dog-eared slips of paper.

'I wrote to Miss Dorothea Beale at

Cheltenham, outlining your plans for the Royal Alexandra School for Girls. Miss Beale, as I think you know, is Principal of Cheltenham Ladies' College.'

'And she had expressed an interest?'

'More than an interest, I think. Projects of this sort, if well thought out, and properly funded, fill her with enthusiasm. At the moment she's busy planning a college for women at Oxford. St Hilda's, she's going to call it. There would be real possibilities of links there.'

Jane Ashwood felt a growing excitement. Dalton had access to people like Miss Beale, and the means of presenting her as a serious exponent of girls' education.

'Miss Beale mentions three outstanding women who she thinks would make excellent foundation staff for your school. She'd also like you to visit her at Cheltenham Ladies' College. That, I may say, is a great honour, and I'd strongly recommend you to accept Miss Beale's invitation. This, I truly believe, is the beginning of the great adventure.'

Dalton rose from his desk, and moved towards the door to the private staircase that would take him up to Staff House. He was not wearing academic dress, and the absence of the flowing black gown seemed to make him look younger. He smiled, and indicated

Miss Beale's letter.

'Please read what Miss Beale has written, Lady Jane. I'm obliged to attend a little reception for Theodore Granger, which should detain me for half an hour. After that, perhaps we can discuss the possibility of a visit to the prospective site of the Royal Alexandra School? After today, as you appreciate, I'll have all the time in the world to devote to your project!'

★　★　★

'Gentlemen,' said Theodore Granger, 'I'm relieved to see that my address to you this morning has been well received. I tried to keep it as brief as decently possible! Dr Dalton has very kindly told me to consider my Headship of Kingsmere Abbey as starting from today. That's why I'm talking to you like this now. Very soon we'll dispense with words and translate our ideas into deeds.'

There was a murmur of agreement and the beginning of applause, which soon turned to vigorous clapping. Granger paused and looked appreciatively at the crowd of masters occupying the Combination Room. He turned to Sandford, who was standing at his side.

'Did you wish to add anything, Vice-master?'

Sandford flushed with pleasure. It was the first time the formal title had been applied to him. He glanced gratefully at Granger before replying.

'Only this, sir. We all have much to celebrate today. I suggest that we make our usual assault on the decanters, and get on with it!'

There was a gale of laughter followed by the noise of animated conversation and the tinkle of glasses. If not quite the Special Dessert, it was a fair imitation.

Granger made his way across the room to where his predecessor, Dr Dalton, stood in one of the window-bays that looked out on to the front grounds. One hand rested carelessly on the window-sill near him. The other was thrust rather awkwardly into one of his waistcoat pockets. Dalton looked much better, Granger thought. Perhaps he had misjudged his powers of resilience.

'I hear that Amyas Fletcher has taken himself off to Plymouth,' said Dalton. 'I gather he's staying at Hudson's Hotel for a week or so.'

'Yes, he's in need of some kind of convalescence after his ordeal. At the end of this academic year I'll ask him to retire.'

'You'd be considered wise, I think, Granger. He's a dear old man, but I think the time's come for him to rest. Fielding-Stenhouse, now . . . '

'He's already been poached, I'm afraid!' said Granger, laughing. 'That appalling scientist from Birmingham has offered him a research post in his forensic institute! Some folk fall on their feet in spite of themselves!'

Dalton smiled. Fielding-Stenhouse had been his own first appointment to the staff of Kingsmere Abbey.

'Well,' Dalton said, 'he's a very clever man. Let's wish him well. It's a time for partings.'

'Talking of partings, what will you do, now, Dalton?' Granger asked.

'Quite frankly, Granger, I mean to leave the school as soon as possible. You may have realized that I have become fired with interest in this project of Lady Jane Ashwood's to found a sister school to Kingsmere. I intend to become her adviser, or enabler, if that's not too arrogant a term to use. But first I will have to spend what I fear will be a very sad time for me at Draycot St Peter. My — Mrs Dolling, you know, is far from well. Her heart is fatally weakened, and I very much fear that she will not live long. So I must go to her as soon as possible.'

Granger spoke quietly and sincerely.

'I'm truly sorry to hear of this fresh trouble. You have certainly had more than your share of misfortunes.'

'It's very irksome. I have written twice to her, but have received no reply. I tried to have a message conveyed through the telegraph, but I was told that the wires are down along the railway track. That's why I must go personally, and very soon. I think that — But hello, what's happening now?'

The murmur of conversation had suddenly ceased.

Granger looked up and saw that Inspector Jackson and Sergeant Bottomley had come into the room. They were accompanied by an immaculately uniformed police officer with a bristling grey moustache, and a helmeted police constable. The masters stood silently, many still holding glasses of wine. They had turned in puzzlement to look at the phalanx of stern-faced policemen.

Jackson walked the length of the Combination room and placed his hand on Dr Dalton's arm.

'Inspector Cartwright,' Jackson said, 'this is the man.'

The uniformed inspector turned to Dr Dalton, and said, 'You are Edward Alberic Dalton. I have here a warrant for your arrest.'

'Upon what charge?' The voice held disbelief.

'That you did, in or about the month of March, 1880, at Draycot St Peter, in the County of Oxford, administer to your wife, Lucy Eynesham Dalton, a noxious thing, namely, arsenic. And did murder her.'

The staff watched in stunned silence as Inspector Cartwright swiftly secured his prisoner's wrists in front of him. There came a metallic click, and then Dalton, his ankles chained by the constable, shambled fettered from the room.

⋆　⋆　⋆

After Dalton's dramatic arrest, Theodore Granger had abruptly left the Combination Room, and most of the staff had instinctively followed their new leader. Only Sandford and Caswell remained. They stood at one of the long windows, looking down in silence at the carriage-drive below.

A horse-drawn police van came in sight from the left and then disappeared from view on its way along to the school's main entrance. Soon they heard the sound of confused foot-steps, and then the harsh crash of an iron-bound door closing. The van came back into their line of view, rumbling slowly along the straight carriage-drive, a uniformed policeman on the box.

Inspector Jackson came into the room, and joined them at the window.

Suddenly, the van stopped, and the constable driving it jumped down from his seat and ran round to the back. He fumbled at some kind of lock, and the door of the van was thrown open. Inspector Cartwright almost fell out on to the path, followed by two constables. They turned, and looked up at the figures they could see standing at the windows.

'What is it? What has happened?' asked Sandford.

'Well, of course, sir,' said Jackson, 'he's poisoned himself.'

'Poisoned himself?' cried Caswell. 'But how — ?'

Jackson was still looking out of the window at the scene below. He made a signal with his hand to Bottomley, who had joined Cartwright and the others on the path, and the waiting police returned to the van. In a moment it resumed its melancholy journey. They saw Bottomley turn and re-enter the school. Jackson sat down at one of the tables.

'It wasn't my case at this stage, Mr Caswell — not this part of it, at any rate. That's why I came back up here. Etiquette, you see. No, it was Inspector Cartwright's affair. Very quick with the handcuffs, he was, and the leg-irons too. But if it'd been my case at that stage, I'd have searched him first.'

'Dalton kept fumbling in his waistcoat pocket,' said Caswell. 'I expect he'd concealed the poison there.'

'Yes, sir. He had to have it somewhere about him. Cyanide, I suppose it was. So when he knew the game was up he contrived to swallow it, and cheat the gallows.'

The door opened and Sergeant Bottomley came into the room. He glanced briefly at the two masters and then addressed his superior officer.

'Sir, it was cyanide, sealed in a small glass ampoule. Mr Cartwright fastened his hands in front of him, so he was able to manoeuvre his fingers into his waistcoat pocket. It was in his mouth and crushed in seconds.'

'Cyanide . . . What's Inspector Cartwright going to do now?'

'Our people are taking him back to Warwick. They'll leave Dalton's body at the mortuary. They'll let the coroner know. And Mr Angel. Very busy he's been this last week.'

'He has, Sergeant. But now, by God's grace, I hope Mr Angel can take a rest.'

Harry Caswell ventured a remark.

'Dalton must have felt that something like

this was going to happen, and kept a phial of poison in his pocket for that very purpose. To commit suicide, I mean.'

Sergeant Bottomley turned red in the face and made an inarticulate sound. Very slowly, an amused smile began to invade Inspector Jackson's face. He looked first at Bottomley, who shook his head, and then at Caswell. A staunch friend — and a prize ass! Could an educated man be so obtuse?

'Oh, Mr Caswell, sir,' he said, 'I don't want to be disrespectful, but dear me, what an innocent you are! Of course he kept a phial of poison in his pocket! I knew it was there, or as good as knew, as they say. But it wasn't intended for him.'

'Not intended for him? Then who *was* it intended for?'

'Mr Caswell, sir, he was going to use it to get rid of Mrs Dolling.'

★ ★ ★

Jackson knocked on the door of Granger's office near the exit to Foliott's Building, and entered the sparsely furnished room. Granger seemed stunned, and it was obvious that he had been merely sitting at his desk, bemused, and oblivious to his surroundings. As he looked up, Jackson saw how his eyes seemed to focus as he recalled himself to the present.

'Sergeant Bottomley came in here some minutes ago,' Granger said without preamble, 'and told me that Dalton was dead. Jackson, I feel almost paralysed with shock! Murdered his wife? However did you batten on to that?'

'Sir, it was that cry he uttered when he saw the dead body of Stephen Peter Ball.'

'Surely that was a sign of innocence? He had not caused Ball's death, but he knew that investigation of it would reveal his own shameful secret. That was why he cried out, Inspector. It was the horrified cry of a man innocent of Ball's death, but fearful of the inevitable exposure of his moral delinquencies that would inevitably follow the discovery of that man's dead body.'

Inspector Jackson smiled, and said, 'Mr Granger, in police investigation, it's vital not to believe everything that people tell you. It was *Dalton himself*, and no one else, who spread abroad this nonsense of being blackmailed for his moral failings. It was a lie, plain and simple. Dr Dalton was afraid that if we identified the dead man, we'd find out what he was really being blackmailed for — the cruel murder of his wife by arsenical poisoning.'

'I'm beginning to realize many things, Jackson . . . He was terrified! That's what lay behind his stubbornness in saying nothing to you about Ball. Terror . . . '

'Exactly, sir. And that's why he collapsed in the hall when your boys kicked up that unholy row. That collapse, sir was in response to the word 'murderer'. He was convinced that the boys had found out about Lucy Eynesham.'

'Wasn't it brave of him, though, to dismiss Ball and his threats in the way he did?'

'Oh, yes, sir. He was brave enough, as desperate men often are. But for all that, he was rotten to the core! I have a copy of Lucy Eynesham's will, drawn up a year after her marriage to Dalton, and sent to me from Somerset House. In it she left to him, absolutely, money, property and land to the value of £90,000. That, sir, is a very good motive for murder.'

Granger clenched his fists in what was scarcely controlled anger.

'I *knew* he was a scoundrel, Jackson, and then I persuaded myself that he was a wronged innocent! But I was the innocent! I should have trusted my own judgement.'

'Yes, sir. And if I may say so without offence, you should trust your own judgement more in future.'

Jackson's face assumed a stern, almost frightening expression. Granger caught the chilling tone of low menace in his voice as he added, 'Your predecessor, Edward Dalton, was decisive, talented and two-faced. He was a ruthless, cruel killer, and that's why, despite the intrusion of the Mostyn affair, which was really Sergeant Bottomley's case, I hunted him down to the end.'

Sandford came in to the room, carrying a sheaf of papers and a pewter ink-well. The new vice-master had assumed a mantle of quiet authority that seemed to have banished his former diffidence.

'Mr Jackson,' said Sandford, 'I want to thank you for laying bare all the rottenness and secret decadence of Kingsmere Abbey School. I resisted you when you first came. I now offer you my sincere apology for that.'

'You've always been devoted to this place, haven't you, Mr Sandford?'

'I have, Inspector. I expect, though, that you've conceived a hearty dislike of the school since you came here. I could quite understand that.'

'You know, Mr Sandford, that's only partly true. This school has harboured so much virtue and so much vice — so much good order and evil confusion, the noblest ideals and the basest behaviour — well, I'm beginning to feel just a little fondness for it after all!'

Sandford seemed very pleased. 'I managed to waylay your sergeant on the way here,' he said, 'and made my peace with him too. I told him that I'd been far too haughty to admit to the vileness that can take up residence in any closed society. He shook my hand. I thought he was a remarkably astute and kindly person.'

'He is, sir: he's a treasure beyond price. And talking of Bottomley, he seems to have disappeared somewhere in the building. I must go and find him, and carry him back with me to Warwick.'

'I believe Mr Bottomley's gone to seek out Captain Valentine,' said Sandford. 'When I left him, he was joined by that black servant of Lady Jane's. I heard him tell your sergeant that Captain Valentine was walking in the pasture.'

Jackson shook hands with both men.

'Goodbye, Headmaster,' he said. 'Let me wish you every success for the future of Kingsmere Abbey School. Goodbye, Vice-master. Perhaps we'll meet again, some day, in the back bar of the Wheatsheaf.'

'The Wheatsheaf?' Sandford's tone of refined horror had returned.

Granger laughed as Jackson added, 'One of the duties of vice-master, Mr Sandford, is to drink a pint of best ale several times a year with Mr Holland, the landlord. If you don't believe me, sir, ask Mr Granger there! Now, if you'll excuse me, I'll see if I can find what Sergeant Bottomley's getting up to. Goodbye, gentlemen.'

★   ★   ★

Lady Jane Ashwood realized that something was gravely wrong when nearly an hour passed, and Dr Dalton did not return. She rose and left the study, lingering uncertainly for a few moments in the sunny deserted hall of Headmaster's House.

As she stood there undecided, the front door of the house opened, and a big, shambling man in a yellow overcoat stepped over the threshold. He removed a rather battered bowler hat, and offered Jane a clumsy bow. He opened the door opposite the study, and peered into the room beyond.

'Lady Jane Ashwood,' said the man in the yellow overcoat, 'would you care to step into this room for a while? I'd like to talk to you about Dr Edward Dalton.'

He showed her some sort of official card, at which she merely glanced. She had already realized that he was a policeman.

'Lady Jane,' said Sergeant Bottomley without preamble, 'a little while ago, Dr

Dalton was arrested for the murder of his wife, Lucy Eynesham Dalton, in the month of March, 1880. While in police custody, and before he could be removed from the school precincts, he swallowed posion.'

Jane stared at Bottomley in a kind of trance. This man had the rough accents of the countryman but there was an odd tenderness behind his words which she knew had been conjured up for her sake. What he had told her was the brutal truth.

Dalton, she remembered only too well, had told her about Lucy Eynesham on the night when she had answered his dramatic summons. Lucy had borne him a son, Eric, and had died . . . Now, this man with the kindly grey eyes sitting opposite her in the bleak, featureless parlour of Dalton's house, had told her that the young mother had been murdered.

'And Dr Dalton has poisoned himself?'

'He is dead, Lady Jane. Dead.'

So much, then, for her school in the air. The tall, red-brick teaching blocks, the great assembly hall, the octagonal non-denominational chapel, the acres of games courts and playing-fields — the whole airy fabric of the Royal Alexandra School for Girls crumbled and collapsed.

She sat in cold desolation, blinded by tears

of humiliation. She felt stunned, sickened and defeated. That man had been using her for his own ends. He was cruel and heartless, a poisoner, the kind of man that her father called 'gallows-fodder'. And yet . . .

She saw that the big rough man in the yellow overcoat was watching her silently. His attitude of expectancy forced her to speak.

'But he was so sincere! He was caught up in the whole project! Of course, you won't know what I mean . . . It was a project to build a great new school. A school for girls. Even a villain couldn't have assumed a mask as effectively as that. I don't understand . . . '

'You'd be surprised how complicated human beings are, ma'am,' said Herbert Bottomley. 'I expect he was sincere at the beginning of his career, but he knew that ideas cost money. So he married poor Lucy Eynesham, a wealthy young lady of twenty-four, and then poisoned her for her fortune.'

'Poisoned her . . . Is that true?'

'Yes, ma'am. He poisoned her with arsenic. Very cruel and painful. He inherited ninety thousand pounds from poor Lucy. After that, he was content with Mrs Dolling for a good many years. You'll have heard about Mrs Dolling, I dare say? But she had no money, ma'am, and then you came along, with a new idea and a fortune behind it . . . That's part of the way that Dr Dalton looked at you.'

Jane remembered Dalton's keen glances across the smoking candles at Sir Walter Foliott's dinner. She had been wearing the Versailles Cascade. She had wondered at the time whether she, or the necklace, had been the object of his admiration. Perhaps his glances had been more subtle than that . . .

'And so, ma'am, Dr Dalton realized that the time had come to poison Mrs Dolling as well. Cyanide — that's what he was going to use. You can't pass that off as natural causes, so I think he'd have made it look like suicide.'

Bottomley looked speculatively at Lady Jane before adding, 'Mrs Dolling is a very nice lady, who will now be in great distress. She'd benefit from a visit, ma'am, if you could bring yourself to make it.'

Jane Ashwood got up from her chair. She wondered if she looked as ghastly as she felt. She would let the idea of a visit take root in her mind, but now it was time to return to Hervington Park, time to hide her shame and humiliation from the light of day. The carriage, she knew, would have been brought round to the front of the Headmaster's House in readiness for her departure.

She was suddenly stopped with her hand on the door by a further observation from

Herbert Bottomley. There was a tone of respectful but purposeful mockery in his voice that held her fascinated.

'I hear that you were going to help Dr Dalton with one of his new ideas, ma'am. I'm told that you were going to be his assistant. But all that's over and done with now, I'm afraid.'

Jane suddenly felt a stimulating indignation urging her back to life.

'*Assistant?* You impertinent man, what do you mean by that? *He* was going to help *me*! His idea? Do you think that women are incapable of conceiving original ideas?'

Bottomley shuffled awkwardly for a moment, dropped his battered brown bowler hat that he had been clutching, retrieved it, and knuckled his forehead.

'Well then, ma'am, that's all right then,' he said. 'So it was *your* idea all along, was it? Well, now you'll have to put it into practice without Dr Dalton's help. Or anybody else's help, for that matter, unless you ask them for it. Asking your pardon, My Lady, and meaning no offence.'

Jane Ashwood smiled. This man's quiet, gentle mockery had restored her self-worth. Strange, that a man of the lower ranks could tease her like that, without any hint of unwelcome familiarity. The pain of betrayal remained, but Dalton's hypnotic spell was broken.

'What's your name, Officer?' she asked. 'I couldn't read it when you showed me your special card.'

'Bottomley, ma'am. Detective Sergeant Bottomley. Warwickshire Constabulary.'

'Ah! Valentine's right-hand man in the army! I've heard about you. Well, Mr Bottomley, I'll take your advice. If I want help, I'll ask for it. Meanwhile, I'll do the thing myself!'

★　★　★

Jane pushed open the door of Dalton's study. She had no wish to re-enter it. It had never held any sense of personal identity, as though Dalton had only ever been passing through, and had laid down no roots. It was in this hateful place that her hopes had been raised, only to be dashed to pieces. But she had to retrieve her papers, and the precious note-book.

As she entered the room she drew in her breath sharply. A figure in academic dress sat at the desk, poring over her plans, and apparently making notes on her blueprint. She sighed with grateful relief when she saw that it was Noel Valentine. He stood up,

381

crossed the room, and took both her hands in his.

'My dear Jane,' he said, 'you *must* continue this project! And I want you to know straight away that I place myself at your service. Cicero and Livy can look after themselves. In fact, they can go hang if you like.'

She began to gather her things together — her note-book with Dalton's many paper place-markers, the precious letter from Dorothea Beale. She looked with open affection at her old friend. He was a true convert to her idea, a man of trust and honour.

'Look at these pencilled notes, Valentine, these sheets of observations by that man! Can you believe it? And all of it is valueless, all part of his vile charade!'

'Charade? No, Jane, I don't think that's true. You must steel yourself to value what he has written, because I'm convinced that his interest in your school was genuine enough.'

'Even if he could glimpse the potential for wealth and influence behind it?'

'Yes. People, you know, are very complex things . . . '

She winced. That was exactly what the rough-edged Sergeant Bottomley had said to her. She looked once more at Noel Valentine.

'And Oxford?' she asked. 'Can that go hang, as well?'

'Certainly. And so can Kingsmere Abbey, if you wish. When I say I place myself at your service, I mean it. I really do, Jane.'

Valentine removed his academic gown and placed it over a chair. Jane Ashwood began to roll up her blueprint. She saw that in one vacant patch of paper Noel Valentine had sketched the floor-plan of an extra building. 'Principal's House', it said, and a small arrow pointed to an oblong extension marked 'Nursery'.

Jane Ashwood blushed, and then laughed out loud. Valentine smiled, and gently took the bundle of plans and papers from her. Somehow the act underlined his assertion that he would become her helper, if she asked him.

She glanced once more round the soulless room, then walked out into the hall. Valentine's arms were full, so she opened the front door for them. At the end of the path her father's carriage was waiting, the coachman sitting in readiness on the box. Juckes, his face almost supernaturally expressionless, bustled forward to let the steps down. She saw him dart a look in Valentine's direction before dropping his eyes to the ground.

Jane stopped abruptly on the path. So that was it! That villain Juckes, hovering on the path. Sergeant Bottomley, Valentine's old army servant, guiding her into Dalton's parlour. Valentine, conveniently stationed in the study. These three men had colluded to bring her back from despair.

'Valentine,' she said, as she resumed her walk down the path, 'I detect the whiff of conspiracy in all this! You, and the frightful Juckes, and that hulking great Sergeant!'

'Conspiracy! And do you mind? Always supposing that you're right?'

'As a matter of fact, Captain Valentine,' said Lady Jane Ashwood, entering the carriage, 'I don't mind in the least!'

THE END

Other titles in the
Ulverscroft Large Print Series:

THE FROZEN CEILING

Rona Randall

When Tessa Pickard found the note amongst her father's possessions, instinct told her that THIS had been responsible for his suicide, not the professional disgrace which had ruined his career as a mountaineer and instructor. The note was cryptic, anonymous, and bore a Norwegian postmark. Tessa promptly set out for Norway, determined to trace the anonymous letter-writer, but unprepared for the drama she was to uncover — or that compelling Max Hyerdal, whom she met on board a Norwegian ship, was to change her whole life.